# ZOONOTIC

## J.P. Banks

**MJ Bankowski**

Cover photograph credit: Copyright 2021 Matthew J. Bankowski

Hardback ISBN: 979-8-9908611-0-7
Paperback ISBN: 979-8-9908611-2-1
Ebook - Kindle ISBN: 979-8-9908611-1-4

Printed in the United States of America

*I am forever grateful for their love and support:*
*My parents - Mattthew and Martha*
*My wife - Denise*
*My daughter - Heather*

*"We must build  dikes of courage to hold back the flood of fear."*

DR. MARTIN LUTHER KING, JR.

# CONTENTS

# MAIN CHARACTERS

CENTERS FOR DISEASE CONTROL AND PREVENTION (CDC)
CHELA MILLIREM, MD, PhD: CDC Field Investigator, Infectious Disease and Epidemiology

CENTRAL INTELLIGENCE AGENCY (CIA)
ART LIFEHOLD (Alias TOD FIREHALL, alias EDITH FLORAL): CIA Case Officer
LEONID WASCOTT (Alias DELO WAINSCOTT): CIA Case Officer

DRUG ENFORCEMENT ADMINISTRATION (DEA)
MOJOS MARINERS: DEA Field Agent

FEDERAL BUREAU OF INVESTIGATION (FBI)
JOCK LAWINS: FBI Special Agent
MARGIE STARTERS, PhD: FBI Agent and profiling psychologist
CORPALIA BITOK: FBI informant

MEDICAL PERSONNEL AND INVESTIGATORS
ALISHA VYCORS, DChMS: Chief, Division of Medical Services, Koror, Palau
ELISE SWINDON, MD, PhD: Infectious Disease Physician and Associate Medical Investigator, Co-owner, Watkins & Swindon Medical Diagnostics (WSMD), LLC, New Orleans, LA
IAN CLEAT, MD: Infectious disease physician, Tulane Medical Center (TMC), New Orleans, LA
JILIN SLOCUM, MD: Infectious disease physician, TMC, New Orleans, LA
MELVIN CATECHIN, MD: Medical Examiner, New Orleans, LA

DANA MERRILY, MD: Pathologist, WSMD, New Orleans, LA

RHONE ECKMAN, PhD, D(ABMM): Ochsner Medical Center (OMC), Medical Laboratory Director, Clinical Pathology, Infectious Disease Diagnostics

ROOSA WILLING, RN, DNP: Nurse Practitioner, TMC, New Orleans, LA

TOMBAK WATKINS, PhD, D(ABMM): Medical Laboratory Director - Clinical Pathology, Medical Microbiologist - Infectious Disease Diagnostics - Molecular Microbiology and Public Health; Chief Medical Investigator, Co-owner, and CEO, WSMD, New Orleans, LA

YAHARA HEARNE, DO, PhD: Infectious disease physician, OMC, New Orleans, LA


MILITARY, WHITEHOUSE, AND U.S. CONGRESS

AARON LEGRAND: U.S. President, Commander-in-Chief

GOREN POTTAGE: Pentagon–Four-Star General, JCS CSO (Chief of Space Operations)

ROBIN ROSINOL: General, USNORTHCOM, NORAD, Department of Defense (DoD)


NATIONAL INSTITUTE OF HEALTH (NIH)

NATIONAL INSTITUTE OF ALLERGY AND INFECTIOUS DISEASE (NIAID)

DARNELL DHYANA, MD: Physician and NIAID Director, Vaccine Research Center, Emerging Virus Center

EWAN SMITHCRAFT, PhD: NIAID Director, Division of Microbiology and Infectious Disease

KAAREN ZAMA PENRITH, MD, PhD: Physician and NIAID research fellow


NATIONAL SECURITY AGENCY (NSA)

ZEP MATRIOSHKA: NSA Special Agent


DRUG TRADE and CARTELS

RAFAEL NACKET: New Orleans drug lord

MOOL CEROS: Costa Rica drug lord, Jingoes New Reactional Cartel (JNRC)
MARIETLA CORRION: JNRC falcon, Costa Rica

NEW ORLEANS POLICE DEPARTMENT (NOPD)
SHAKY OTTAVINO: NOPD homicide detective, New Orleans, LA

NEW ORLEANS VOODOO-HOODOO
MAIA REVALUE: Voodoo Queen, New Orleans, LA

NEWS MEDIA
SHEPARD ALTHORN: Editor-in-Chief, New Orleans Tribune
LARES TURNCOCK: Newspaper journalist, New Orleans Tribune
JENNA SAMPS: TV meteorologist, FOX 8, New Orleans, LA

PUBLIC HEALTH LABORATORY (PHL)
SATCHEL WHINNIER, PhD, D (ABMM): PHL Director, New Orleans, LA

ROANS MEDICAL SUPPLY, LLC (RMS)
JETHRO ROANS: Chief Executive Officer (CEO), RMS, New Orleans, LA

ROSTER PHARMACEUTICALS, INC. (RPI)
ARON MILLSTONE, PharmD: Executive Vice-President — Research and Development (R&D), RPI, Alajuela, Costa Rica
CHARRO BELONS, MD, PhD (Alias CARLO BRETONS, alias CESAR HOLBORN): R&D research fellow, RPI, Alajuela, Costa Rica
GREGOR OSSEO: CEO, RPI, New Orleans, LA
JOHN ROSTER, MD, PharmD: Owner, RPI, New Orleans, LA
KUNA MERMAN, PhD: R&D Clinical Research Scientist, RPI, Alajuela, Costa Rica
LEN RACHILLAS, MD, PhD: R&D Division Chief, RPI, Alajuela, Costa Rica
LILLE GARTER, DVM: Veterinarian, R&D, Vivarium Manager, RPI, Alajuela, Costa Rica

TEDY EVANS, MD, PhD: Senior Scientist, R&D, RPI, Alajuela, Costa Rica

U.S. DEPARTMENT OF HOMELAND SECURITY (DHS)
SLOGGER MORTLAKE: DHS Regional Director, New Orleans, LA

U.S. MARSHALS SERVICE–EASTERN DISTRICT OF LOUISIANA
ELIZA SPARKLY: U.S. Marshal, New Orleans, LA

# PREFACE

The year was 1953 when James Watson and Francis Crick discovered the structure of DNA. This solitary finding changed the world forever. Why? Although no simple answer exists, the exploration of DNA in humans and animals has led to significant scientific advancement, rapidly evolving.

DNA serves as life's blueprint. How does this happen? Essentially, DNA is like a code, full of instructions and details about how cells and even viruses should function and what determines individual characteristics. The genetic map applies to both small viruses and the largest creatures to roam the planet.

What happened to this life-changing discovery over the past 70 years? From 1953 to today, the development of advanced technological tools and research methods has revolutionized the "DNA world". In parallel, computers were the activation energy molding the digital age. This digital explosion has exponentially propelled DNA into every part of our life.

Scientists now can program DNA, to detect diseases in individuals and to search for cures. We have reached an age of personalized medicine, where scientists can genetically tailor each person to the best treatment option for them. Advanced tools such as CRISPR, whole genome sequencing, metagenomic analysis, MALDI-TOF-MS, cytochrome P450 profiling and other state-of-the-art analytical methods are now available. (Refer to the Glossary.)

The unfolding story in this novel explores the use of innovative technology and how it changes the relationship between DNA and us. Are there any unknown DNA forms lurking? Now, we possess advanced tools to uncover unimaginable answers. We are no longer bound by the limits of the past, and this book captures our current situation and the potential to discover new and emerging disease agents.

# PROLOGUE

Sunday, April 21, 7:23 A.M.

Chicago, O'Hare International Airport

Dr. Tombak Watkins was sitting contently at a table in front of an airport restaurant, sipping his coffee and caressing his cellphone. He wondered what was new and exciting in the morning news. The early morning was always when they released the best juicy news.

While trying to read his cellphone, early risers and colleagues returning from a medical meeting interrupted Dr. Watkins to grab breakfast. Some greeted Dr. Watkins with a simple "good morning". Others merely gave a nod and a quick smile. Luckily, their morning routines were more consumed with breakfast and being on time for their flight, so he could continue his perusal of the news.

Suddenly interrupted, his cellphone rang. It was his associate, Dr. Elise Swindon, an attractive, dedicated, and aggressive 42-year-old infectious disease physician. She called to inform Dr. Watkins about a mysterious pneumonia outbreak in New Orleans. This type of community pneumonia is more common in the winter months. Since this deadly series occurred in his hometown of the "Big Easy", Dr. Watkins was especially concerned. The cause is most likely of an infectious nature and worth investigating.

Dr. Tombak Watkins is a medical infectious disease investigator, tall and slender with a finely manicured, barely visible beard. He has a reputation for presenting himself with a "Sherlock Holmes" type of persona in investigating complex cases. He is a board-certified PhD microbiologist educated in molecular infectious disease medicine at the University of Michigan Medical Center. His many outstanding accomplishments in medical microbiology and public health have earned him international recognition and value in his field. Dr. Watkins is one of the foremost experts in molecular infectious disease diagnostics.

Dr. Swindon is his medical associate, but more precisely, a beloved partner in their joint venture, Watkins & Swindon Medical Diagnostics, LLC. Extremely intelligent and highly perceptive, she has a rare character, which is often displayed in the molecular microbiology laboratory. Socially, she exhibits an unorthodox character, which is typically scandalous and a fury at parties. However, what made her so successful in her field was her keen perception of human nature and her uncanny ability to solve challenging cases. She dedicates herself intensely to Dr. Watkins, not only out of affection but also because she respects his wealth of knowledge in molecular infectious disease medical diagnostics.

Dr. Swindon received her training at the Northwestern University Medical Center in Chicago as an infectious disease physician. She believes that one can control all infectious agents if they truly understand the nature of the agent, but not always eradicate them.

Dr. Swindon has often spoken the words,

"We have vast knowledge and control of so much life forms today. So, it's a matter of dedicating the time and energy to find the ideal control for existing or emerging infectious agents. I believe we can control even the most complex infectious agents. It is within our grasp using the vast array of modern medical diagnostic tools at our disposal."

Dr. Watkins belief is that you can reduce your chances of infection or even death from an infectious agent if you gain control of both the agent and its environment. Dr. Swindon and Dr. Watkins make the perfect partners in their mission to tackle deadly microbes.

Dr. Watkins would often declare,

"It is logical to assume that if an infectious agent continues to kill its host, both the agent and the host will eventually fade into extinction. A delicate balance often exists between the agent and host, which eventually evolves into a compromise that allows both to sustain life, but at a cost to the host. It is simpler, if the agent infects only one host, then an effective vaccine will probably eradicate the agent. This assumes that the agent does not have a hidden reservoir in another animal host. For example, we have evidence of the smallpox virus, which was eliminated from the world population in 1979. Today, many parts of the world have more control over tuberculosis (TB) and someday may even eradicate it."

"If you can prevent or even stop the proliferation of these deadly microbes by effective detection, intervention, and control, you will at least sustain human life as we know it."

Dr. Swindon has an impressive history of successfully translating complex microbial genetic information into molecular-based testing for detecting infectious disease agents. This type of approach (i.e., infectious disease diagnostics) provides the initial agent detection necessary for lifesaving solutions in most outbreaks. Many of her publications include high-value targets, such as tuberculosis, HIV, and other deadly infectious agents.

Dr. Swindon and Dr. Watkins have always taken a dispassionate 'lesson's learned' approach to all their infectious disease investigations. Even today, this has provided valuable insights into the control of existing (e.g., Ebola) and unknown, emerging, deadly disease-causing agents.

Dr. Watkins pondered this case with grave concern because he feared, if left uncontrolled, it could speed up into an unimaginable number of deaths. Today, there already exists a dramatic uprising in illness, stress, infectious disease, and death occurring as the result of uncontrolled human malady. His gut feeling about this case was disturbing. It will differ from all the previous cases, and no doubt be quite challenging. The root cause, which was yet to be discovered, controlled, or even treated, could lead to many more deaths before controlled.

Public health authorities have recruited Dr. Watkins frequently, including CDC, to consult on investigations involving infectious disease agents causing illness and death. Their lab has gained wide recognition as a leader for newly discovered and emerging infectious disease agents.

Dr. Watkins believes the current case descriptions match the signs and symptoms of pneumonia, but such sudden death with our state-of-the-art medical intervention protocols was quite perplexing. He expressed a major concern over the meningoencephalitis (i.e., brain and spinal cord infection) mentioned in two patients described by Dr. Swindon. This is indeed a very bizarre finding and, undoubtedly, further supports the possibility of an underlying deadly infectious agent being the culprit.

An overhead airport announcement suddenly interrupted his thoughts.

"Delta flight 352, now boarding for New Orleans at gate 14."

He forcefully grabbed his briefcase next to his seat, stood up, and dashed towards the gate. Dr. Watkins thought to himself,

"Going home, but what will I find?" And is it possibly too late?

# CHAPTER 1 - VALUABLE INSIGHT

Sunday, April 21, 7:06 P.M.

Louis Armstrong International Airport, New Orleans

Dr. Watkins had just finished a three-day medical conference at the Chicago Hilton with his distinguished professional colleagues. He was in flight and returning home from Chicago to the Louis Armstrong International Airport in New Orleans. It was a very pleasant flight with the approaching dusk, but his intuition sensed something was very wrong.

When the flight attendant announced, she awakened him from his comfortable sleep.

"We will be landing shortly, so please ensure that you fully fasten your seatbelts and store your belongings in the overhead or under your seat."

While trying to listen to the overhead announcement, Dr. Watkins sensed something strange in the atmosphere. The plane approached the landing, with the sun's appearance quite dramatic. The sunset's colors were the brightest he'd ever seen on any of his flights. Above the clouds, the sun blazed in a gigantic ball of fire.

Suddenly, as the plane pierced the clouds, a scary blackout enveloped the entire plane. In total darkness, the plane tumbled ferociously upon its descent. You could hear fellow passengers shouting and gasping from every direction. It lasted for only about 20 seconds, but it seemed like a lifetime. Finally, the plane escaped the cloud cover and stabilized. Thankfully, the reestablished serenity eased his fear of dying in a fiery crash.

Dr. Watkins thought to himself,

"What the hell happened? I have witnessed nothing like this on any flight!"

The rest of the passengers must have agreed with his thoughts because an intense pandemonium irrupted before landing. Loud voices, shouting, and crying filled the cabin, with passengers expressing both relief and trauma.

Following a safe landing, which elicited an explosive applause from the terror-stricken cabin passengers, the pilot abruptly announced,

"I apologize for the slight bumpiness upon landing. It was just a little cloud cover antics. We are now approaching the Louis Armstrong International Airport, and I want to be the first to welcome you to New Orleans or to wherever your destination may take you."

Dr. Watkins thought to himself,

Today was tough, but tomorrow will be tougher. He also wondered about the underlying cause of the highly unusual blackout on the plane.

On that note of imposed self-assurance, Dr. Watkins headed for baggage claim. He quickly retrieved his priority luggage and walked out of baggage claim, hailing a taxi to go home.

Sunday, April 21, 10:06 P.M.

Dr. Tombak Watkins residence

St. Charles Avenue and Tulane University of Louisiana neighborhood

New Orleans

The taxi ride home was relaxing, even after such a chaotic air flight. Tombak tipped the driver and walked to the front of his home. Fumbling with his keys, he finally opened the door. His faithful companion, Corona, a miniature husky, immediately greeted him. Corona was so excited to see him. She danced playfully around and placed her front paws on his legs to express her affection.

"I missed you too, girl!" Tombak said in a soft, affectionate voice.

He entered the living room, strategically positioning his suitcase beside the desk, then collapsed into an armchair. He settled in, vodka martini in hand, when a forceful knock interrupted. Taking a quick sip, he carefully put the drink down on the end table and walked towards the door.

"Who is it?"

He wasn't expecting anyone. Corona was whimpering softly. Tombak placed his forefinger on his mouth, signaling Corona to be quiet, and waved his finger in the air. Corona, being a very obedient companion, immediately lurched onto her dog bed and hid under the cozy cover.

He cautiously looked through the peephole and noticed two individuals in dark business attire. A man and woman stood in the dim light on the porch.

Tombak once again spoke, now in a loud, stern tone of voice,

"Hello. Who are you? What is it you desire now?

The man replied in a commanding voice,

"If you are Dr. Tombak Watkins, we have an urgent matter to discuss with you."

Again, Dr. Watkins asked,

"Who are you?"

The man replied, while begrudgingly displaying his credentials in the peephole.

"FBI. Open the door, doctor, we need to talk."

Dr. Watkins opened the door, staring at the two agents with an unwavering face. Corona promptly reached his side but concealed herself when the intruders appeared.

"Please assure me you have a valid reason for being here late, not just to frighten my dog."

Without answering or hesitation, the man introduced himself as FBI Special Agent Jock Lawins, and the agent displayed his credentials in clear sight. The other agent announced herself as Dr. Margie Starters, an FBI agent and profiling psychologist.

"May we enter, doctor?" said Special Agent Lawins.

"Yes, of course." stated Dr. Watkins with a puzzling facial expression.

Special Agent Lawins replied,

"We understand you are aware of the recent mysterious pneumonia deaths in New Orleans. We have already spoken to your associate, Dr. Swindon, about the matter."

In a confused glare, Dr. Watkins responded,

"Dr. Swindon did not mention that the FBI would contact me. I was only aware of the cases in the past few hours. Special Agent Lawins, what do you want from me?"

Special Agent Lawins replied in a stern, authoritative voice,

"This cluster of deaths described by Dr. Swindon appears to have the hallmark of a terrorist. This warrants involving the FBI and possibly other government agencies. We need to make sure you understand what we are saying to you."

Surprised and somewhat confused by Special Agent Lawins statement, Dr. Watkins replied,

"I believe I understand what you are telling me, but from my experience, I think an infectious agent is more likely to be involved. Therefore, they brought me into the case."

Special Agent Lawins boldly replied,

"Believe what you want, Dr. Watkins, but understand this is an FBI case. Do not interfere with our investigation. This may be a matter of national security and outside your purview."

Dismayed by the agent's answer and perplexed, Dr. Watkins respectfully nodded and escorted the two agents to the front entryway.

Special Agent Lawins turned to Dr. Watkins, saying,

"Thank you for your time, doctor. Have a pleasant night."

Dr. Watkins closed the front door and locked it securely. He immediately picked up his cellphone and contacted Dr. Swindon,

"Hi Elise. Late as it may be, I had a late-night visit from a couple of FBI agents."

"They mentioned they already spoke to you about the case we just discussed. What did they say to you? You did not mention the involvement of the FBI."

Dr. Swindon replied with a deep, concerning voice,

"FBI? Any agency, especially the FBI, did not contact me about this case. You know I would call you immediately if any federal, state, or even local agency contacted me, especially the FBI."

Dr. Watkins replied.

"I know you would, but I had to ask because Special Agent Lawins mentioned contacting you. I figured they had another source notifying them of our involvement, but who? What is going on with this case? Special Agent Lawins suggested it could be connected to a terrorist."

Dr. Swindon replied,

"I'm unsure, but I suspect it's more complex than we can imagine. Security concerns and interagency politics would be my take on the visit. Rest and meet me in the lab at 7 A.M. tomorrow to make sense of what all this hoopla means, from what we know so far?"

"Agree. See you at 7 A.M."

Dr. Watkins found it difficult to sleep that night. Sleep eluded Dr. Watkins that night as he obsessed over uncovering the truth as quickly as possible. It was already 4:10 A.M. on the clock by his bed. Restless from insomnia, he walked over to the window and gazed into the street. Staring out the bedroom window, he noticed a parked car across the street with a flickering light inside. He gently separated the window sheers and noticed a dark figure inside the car on the driver's side that appeared to be talking on a cellphone. In alarming disbelief, he mumbled to himself,

"Am I being watched? Who and why, if that's the case? Someone must be surveilling me."

That was it for a restful night. Turning on the light, he arose from the bed and begun with his morning routine before leaving for his meeting scheduled with Dr. Swindon.

Monday, April 22, 6:43 A.M.
Watkins & Swindon Medical Diagnostics, LLC (WSMD)
Mandeville, Louisiana

Traffic was moving at a slow pace on Interstate 10 that morning. The car parked in front of his house last night ended up following him to the lab, but at a barely noticeable distance. He arrived at the lab on time and headed to his office.

Dr. Swindon was already in her office and contemplating a lively discussion with Dr. Watkins. They both proclaimed a hardy, "Good morning" as they approached each other.

Dr. Watkins started the discussion with a thoughtful but concerned look on his face.

"Why are the FBI and possibly other governmental agencies so interested in trying to dissuade us from investigating this case? I don't respond to intimidation, as you know. I believe they might have even placed me under surveillance. Last night, I noticed a car parked outside my house, and now I see the same car parked across the street from our lab. Look!"

Dr. Swindon peered out the window and became noticeably concerned,

"I don't know for sure, but I have my suspicion. The case I spoke of is unlikely to be the work of terrorists, as the FBI agents say. It is likely that the deaths are related to an outbreak of some kind, potentially an infectious agent. The FBI or another agency may hide information from us. Obviously, they don't want us to discover more details, so they don't want us involved. It is very possible that national security concerns are at stake here. I agree with you. DHS, NSA, or some other federal agency or agencies may also become involved or even are involved now?"

Dr. Watkins agreed.

"We will investigate this case. Let's review the evidence and see where it leads."

Dr. Swindon continued with the debriefing.

"I know that the Public Health Laboratory (PHL) in New Orleans and the CDC are already involved. Our PHL director, Dr.

Satchel Whinnier, called me yesterday, just before I contacted you. He's asking if we'd consult on this case, like we have with many others in the past with the PHL."

"Dr. Whinnier mentioned that the exact number of individuals that may have been involved is unknown, but the actual number of related deaths is approaching ten. Both male and female victims are involved: most middle-aged adults. There appears to be a casual association with last weekend's French Quarter Festival, according to the PHL epidemiologist on the case. It could potentially lead to hundreds of additional cases."

"The signs and symptoms have an insidious onset: all those stricken have developed pneumonia, including a couple of cases with an unusual co-morbidity of meningoencephalitis (i.e., brain and spinal cord infection) as well. Broad-spectrum antibiotics and antivirals do not seem to alter the course of the disease. I am not aware of any other information."

Dr. Watkins replied.

"We must jump on this now! Why do you think the FBI believes a terrorist is involved?"

Dr. Swindon's eyes narrowed to a barely visible slit, accompanied by a very inquisitive facial expression,

"I would suspect the FBI is focusing on an individual(s) using a poison, toxin, or some type of infectious agent that would have the potential for lethal coverage. The insidious onset leading to a death among all individuals is an enormous flag for a terrorist profile. However, it makes little sense because, so few people were involved. Not a single child case, despite many children attending the event. Unless, of course, this is a budding terrorist or militia group testing the effectiveness of a response to a chemical or biological agent? A 'litmus test' of sorts. Not sure, but this is an extraordinary case. Exciting! Don't you think Tombak?"

Dr. Watkins sternly replied,

"Exciting, no doubt, but quite reprehensible. It's time to work on finding the source."

# CHAPTER 2 - THE EVIDENCE

Monday, April 22, 10:15 A.M.
New Orleans Coroner's Office
3001 Earhart Boulevard

It was midmorning when Dr. Watkins and Dr. Swindon arrived at the office of Dr. Melvin Catechin, New Orleans Medical Examiner (ME). Dr. Catechin is a 50-year-old pathologist, ordinarily striking and exuberant in appearance, but today he was noticeably older, exhausted, and disheveled looking.

"Dr. Watkins, to what do I owe the pleasure?" asked Dr. Catechin.

"Pleasure to see you, Dr. Catechin. The New Orleans PHL Director has invited us to consult in the investigation of the recent cluster of deaths that is plaguing our fine city."

Dr. Catechin replied,

"Dr. Whinnier had already informed me of your involvement in the case. Excellent timing. I was just about to review some preliminary autopsy findings, and I will appreciate your expertise."

"Note that I haven't performed autopsies on all bodies, but a common thread seems to emerge. The cause of death in all cases is pneumonia followed by severe septic shock, leading to cardiac arrest. A bacterial pathogen in the bloodstream (i.e., sepsis) is the most common cause of underlying septic shock. However, the blood cultures taken before death have, so far, shown 'no growth at 48 hours' in all cases. What are your thoughts on negative cultures?"

Dr. Watkins remarked,

"Baffling, I completely agree." However, I believe bacteria may still be responsible for the sepsis. It may be too early with the blood culture result; we need to wait for the result in five days. This alleged microbe may be challenging or even impossible to culture. Recall the difficulty the CDC had in culturing the bacterium responsible for Legionnaire's disease in 1976. Researchers could only grow the Legionella pneumoniae bacterium after detoxifying the culture media with charcoal. After many weeks, the researchers identified the responsible agent."

"Since time is always at a premium, nowadays, regardless of the type of causative agent, molecular testing is the most accurate, rapid, and state-of-the-art identification possible."

"A blood specimen collected before death would be ideal for molecular testing. The specimen should detect any microbial DNA. This method detects microbes, unlike the sometimes-lengthy process of conventional culture. 'Dead or alive, DNA doesn't lie', as the saying goes."

"Molecular testing is extremely sensitive and may not initially confirm the causative agent of disease. However, it should give us a list of possible microbial suspects. This approach will then allow us to reveal commonality among the agents identified from each victim's blood, hopefully finding the same causative agent in all specimens. We will also test for poison and toxin using other testing."

Dr. Catechin agreed and continued with describing the preliminary autopsy findings.

"A strange discovery in these cases was the small amount of dust in the victim's lungs. Although there wasn't sufficient particulate matter to cause suffocation or affect the COD, it could be a significant clue in unraveling the case. I haven't come across this type of finding in any of the hundreds of autopsies I've done. Why the dust?"

"I sent a sample of the particulate matter to the Forensic Lab for further analysis."

"In two patients, the medical chart also showed a diagnosis of meningoencephalitis along with pneumonia. This is unusual for a suspected bacterial sepsis. Especially when the Gram stain of the cerebrospinal fluid (CSF) does not show any organisms. You would expect to see bacteria in the CSF with so many white blood cells seen."

"Another unexpected finding was the cell type in the CSF. It showed a viral infection, which is consistent with meningoencephalitis. Why? If anything, this testing should support a bacterial infection like the blood test results. Are we discussing a coinfection of bacteria and a virus in these patients?"

"The lab CSF report also made note of the presence of 'tiny spheres, most closely resembling dead or degrading white blood cells' in the final report."

"Based upon these results, I ordered a Gram stain on the negative blood cultures. Still no sign of bacteria, but the report mentioned the same 'tiny spheres'. Hmm...., I don't know what this finding could mean. Is it a 'red herring', or a byproduct of the 'inflammatory storm' during sepsis? The Gram stain result could indicate extensive cellular destruction or even dead microbes of some sort appearing as tiny spheres or cellular debris. As you know all too well, it's a 'deadly hailstorm' when it comes to sepsis caused by one's own defense mediated by our own immune system."

"Let me add more confusion to the suspected bacterial sepsis with septic shock for the two meningoencephalitis patients. The test results from the CSF hematology and CSF chemistry reports indicate meningoencephalitis. Once more, these results indicate a viral infection."

"The CSF bacterial cultures also revealed 'no growth at 48 hours' in both cases. This is not surprising, since we know that bacterial culture media cannot be used to culture viruses. They require living cells for culture. It is surprising that there are no cultured bacteria in the blood and CSF."

"I should mention that we chose not to order a viral

culture because of the high likelihood of non-recovery, as clear from many human viral pathogens. Therefore, molecular testing of the CSF is paramount for support of either a bacterial or viral infection. Once again, many microbes defy cultivation."

"We need confirmation on whether a chemical or biological agent is involved." Does this fall into the category of toxin or poison? Could it possibly be an infectious agent? Until now, have we never encountered this entity? Let's include the CSF specimens in the molecular testing at your lab, Dr. Watkins, along with the other specimen testing. Molecular testing is our best approach for identifying the culprit. First, we must eliminate the possibility of poison or toxin."

Dr. Swindon interjected,

"It's unlikely that this picture shows a terrorist's act, rather an accidental spread of an infectious agent. If it is terrorist related, it is not a very effective agent or delivery method, with only close to ten people dying out of potentially hundreds. However, there could be more cases as we speak."

Dr. Catechin then bellowed in a loud voice,

"Why would you even claim these deaths result from a terrorist attack?" This is a preposterous supposition!"

Allow me to explain, said Dr. Watkins.

"I received an unannounced visit last night from two FBI agents. They proclaimed that this cluster of deaths was likely the work of a terrorist according to their profiling efforts. They also made it clear it was their case and implied that we should not obstruct the investigation. To that point, they did not want us involved in the case, and they were giving us ample warning. I also believe they placed me under a 24-hour surveillance."

"Very interesting." Replied Dr. Catechin with a worrisome glare,

"I apologize, but we need to continue our discussion later. Let me retrieve the specimens for you now because I have more autopsies waiting for me."

Dr. Catechin immediately arose from behind his desk and headed for the office door. Peering out the door, he instructed the secretary to alert the lab staff about the specimen retrieval and packaging for the visitors.

The doctors sensed Dr. Catechin's lack of transparency regarding FBI or other agency involvement. He especially seemed quite concerned about the FBI's alleged warning.

The specimens were hand-delivered to them in a carefully packaged box marked, 'Biohazardous–Infectious Agents'.

Thanking the Medical Examiner for his time, both doctors departed from Dr. Catechin's office and headed back to their molecular laboratory.

"What was that all about?" Dr. Watkins proclaimed to Dr. Swindon.

Monday, April 22, 1:32 P.M.

Watkins & Swindon Medical Diagnostics, LLC (WSMD)

Mandeville, Louisiana

On their return to the lab, they again noticed the same car tailing them. Determined, Dr. Watkins sought to uncover the identity of the person in the tailing car. Upon arriving at the lot, he parked the car in his usual reserved parking spot, opened the door and hurried towards the unknown vehicle. At that exact moment, the tailing car in a parking space distant from Dr. Watkin's spot quickly backed out, squealing the rear tires with tread marks, and sped away. Tombak only caught a partial glimpse at the license plate. He suspected the black SUV was government issued.

"Well, that was almost worth the run. So, what do you think? FBI? NSA? CIA? DHS? A new fed agency we don't know about yet?" remarked Dr. Watkins.

Dr. Swindon replied,

"I don't know, but the FBI would be my best guess. All this attention suggests there is more to this story. This case has me psyched! Let's analyze these specimens and let the data unravel this case."

They walked and talked as they approached the molecular laboratory building, which was an impressive six-story architectural marvel. The inside of the research facility was like nothing anyone has ever seen before.

As they entered the building, they passed glass enclosed cases lining the hallway, showcasing medical tools that ranged from a simple monocular microscope to a compact nucleic acid sequencer the size of a USB thumb drive. All descriptive place-cards detailed and dated the exhibits in precise chronological order.

At the end of the hallway, the inner amphitheater-like room awaited, filled with towering, lighted instrumentation everywhere. Sophisticated, roaming robots crossed one's path, feeding data to the hungry instruments. A plethora of state-of-the-art computers orchestrated all duties. As one continued on the marked path, stacks of folders and secure file cabinets surrounded by glass enclosed offices were visible as far as the eye could see.

The building comprised six floors and held a couple hundred white coat laboratory professionals, concentrating on a vast array of complex testing with accompanying computer-integrated instruments. Robotics and artificial intelligence (AI) controlled most of the workflow and even the test results interpretation.

The most impressive part of the facility was the highly secured biocontainment floor. This area comprised multiple separated rooms designated as Biosafety Level 3 (BSL-3) and a separate, highly restricted area comprising a Biosafety Level 4 (BSL-4). Like the one at CDC, it is one of a handful existing in the United States today.

Each BSL-3 room had an attached ante-room (i.e., secure entrance area) that led into another hermetically sealed, larger testing room. Every room had a dedicated HEPA filtered airflow system, and to maintain absolute containment, each BSL was independently sealed from others and the building at-large.

All BLS rooms contained a pass-through door for specimens, as well as a separate double-door pass through autoclave for sterilizing contaminated materials. Each person working in these rooms adorned themselves in protective gear from head to toe before entering the room. Especially prominent was the encased headgear, somewhat like a 'beekeeper' head enclosure, and often with an attached, self-contained air supply.

Dr. Watkins thought to himself,

"If we can't unravel this case with the best state-of-the-art technology, no one can."

Dr. Swindon placed the box containing the specimens from the ME's office in the hands of one of the many Assistant Research Scientists (ARSs). The ARS passed the specimen box into one of the BSL-3 rooms through the secure pass-through door, gowned up and entered the suite through the anteroom. Now in full body protective gear, the ARS carefully unpackaged the specimens and prepared them for processing and testing.

Because of their potential biohazardous nature, all unknown specimens are handled under a special biosafety cabinet. The BSL room chosen depends upon the level of biocontainment required, based upon the assessed risk. Here, because the risk is high, a BSL-3 with strict containment protocols was chosen. The potential risk is unknown, but it could be chemical (e.g., toxin) or biological (e.g., viral, bacterial or some other microbe). Risk assessment protocols always prioritize considering radioactive risk, and they have already ruled it out.

The next step in the protocol was to inactivate a portion of the specimen, making it safe to continue the testing outside the high risk BSL-3 containment area.

Dr. Watkins headed back to his office, asking Dr. Swindon to join him. His office was spacious, with a spectacular view overlooking Lake Pontchartrain. He moved some towering folders occupying his desk, sat down, and opened his laptop. A keystroke on the computer took him into the microbial and toxicology databases. He was ready for action. He then looked up and addressed Dr. Swindon,

"I'm thinking of mass spectroscopy (MS), metagenomic sequencing (Meta), and whole genome sequencing (WGS) testing to start. MS can cover the toxins and Meta, followed by WGS, will give us some idea of the microbial content. What do you think?"

"I Agree." said Dr. Swindon. "We can continue testing from there."

An abrupt announcement echoing from his office phone suddenly interrupted them.

"Dr. Watkins, the PHL Director, Dr. Whinnier, is on line 2, and he says it's critical."

Dr. Watkins paused in his discussion with Dr. Swindon,

"Excuse me. This might be the test results from Dr. Whinnier."

"Greetings, Dr. Whinnier. I understand you have some important information."

Dr. Satchel Whinnier and Dr. Watkins have been friends and professional colleagues ever since their post-doctoral training at the University of Chicago. Since that memorable time, they have collaborated many times together over recent years.

"Yes, I do, my dear friend Dr. Watkins. This bizarre cluster of deaths has become even more challenging. CDC states that the CSF specimens from both meningoencephalitis patients appear to contain a rickettsia-like bacteria. It is like the bacteria that causes rocky mountain spotted fever (RMSF). Rickettsia in New Orleans? Kind of unexpected, isn't it? This would explain the CSF findings, but not the blood results."

"Agree. It is rare, but reports have showed cases of RMSF in the state of Louisiana. However, you need an infected tick for transmission. The medical charts did not mention ticks or their presence during the autopsies in these cases, as far as I know. How does the patient's pneumonia fit into this picture? We are dealing with a whole new type of animal here." Replied Dr. Watkins.

"What a challenging case. We've collaborated on extraordinary cases, but this one could surpass them all! I will call you when I know more, Tombak. Great talking to you, my friend," replied Dr. Whinnier as he hung up the phone.

# CHAPTER 3 – VOODOO QUEEN OF NEW ORLEANS

Wednesday, April 24, 9:36 P.M.

Maia Revalue residence

St. Roch neighborhood

New Orleans

Maia Revalue, the indisputable Voodoo queen of New Orleans, stood swaying and chanting in her spacious, lofty walled and dimly candle-lit kitchen. Supernaturally, her eyes seemed to roll back in her head during her worshipful incantation. This is a ritual she had recently performed after completing the same 'black magic' incarnation about a week earlier.

Haitian by birth, she appeared gracefully aged at 58 years old. She appeared adorned with a beautifully chiseled light-brown face, ravaging dark blue eyes, an aristocratical nose and blood-red lipstick on her wide, slender lips. She wore a tightly bound cranberry headdress that hid most of her dense, curly peppered grey hair. Her brilliant, stark white, lengthy dress all but covered her bare feet as her body swayed in the voodoo ritual.

Those who are searching for a seasoned practitioner of black magic may find more than they wish for with her. Queen Maia is one of the most powerful black magicians anyone could ever encounter, with devastating powers.

Tonight, her ritual began at dusk with the consecration of another gris-gris bag. This bag was remarkably like the one she used in her other ritual a week ago. Both were truly 'black magic' or, as the saying goes, 'the left hand of voodoo'. Voodoo of the New Orleans variety is more commonly referred to as voodoo-hoodoo. Voodoo-hoodoo practitioners mostly use this religion as a positive benefit to help and heal the intended recipient in daily life matters. Queen Maia believes it is time for a 'black magic reckoning' because of countless unaccounted atrocities by drug felons.

"I will hold these villains accountable to the power of voodoo!" she spoke aloud to herself.

Traditionally, the ritual was to be performed in front of a voodoo altar. Essential for every voodoo altar is the representation of the four elements aligned in a compass-like arrangement. South is "earth", which is closest to the practitioner and on her altar contains soil and dust from St. Louis #1 cemetery graveyard and gravestones. Counterclockwise, the practitioner arranges "air" in the east with burning incense, followed by placing the carefully chosen 7-knob black jinxing candle signifying "fire" in the north, and finally representing "water" in the west with a small bowl of holy water. They properly adorned the voodoo altar. In the voodoo religion, the four elements are all connected and not unidirectional with an end.

A gris-gris bag (i.e., charm bag) is essential for the success of a spell. Queen Maia's gris-gris bag comprised a small 2 x 3-inch hemp drawstring, black flannel pouch. The contents included five objects representing the specific spell: a coin, a braid of human hair, a razor blade, a brass shell casing, and a tiny drinking straw. As she placed each object in the bag, she blessed it by anointing it with St. Jude oil. These paraphernalia represent the illicit cocaine drug trafficking plague unleashed upon greater New Orleans. However, a talisman (i.e., amulet) is needed to consecrate the contents of the gris-gris bag, activate the satchel, and finally bring the bag to life.

Queen Maia finished her incantation and was now preparing to consecrate the talisman. She arranged three white candles in a triangle on her kitchen counter altar, in front of a wall adorned with selected pictures of Catholic saints. She respectfully lit each of the three candles. The enormous room brightened with the flickering flames from the ignited candle wicks. It was now time to inscribe the "magical alphabet" onto the parchment paper, which will serve as the talisman. Queen Maia inscribed the following words:

"Isaiah 48:22 — There is no peace, saith the LORD, unto the wicked."

She consecrated the talisman by placing the inscribed parchment paper in the center of the candlelit triangle and sprinkled it with salt. Queen Maia then recited the words,

"I compel the spirits to appear and serve my needs. Offer an aura of protection for the person who holds you....", as she continued the consecration with the proverbial phrases for the four elements. Then, placing both hands over the talisman, she visualized the white light above and spoke the words,

"I charge this amulet...." and finished the ritual by pinching out each of the three candle flames with her fingers.

Only the 7th knob on the black candle flaming wick now flickered wildly as a breeze enveloped the room. She proceeded to the 'fixing of the gris-gris bag'. Now that she has consecrated and secured the talisman in the bag, she had to activate and bring the gris-gris satchel to life. Queen Maia smudged the bag with incense and spoke the following words over it.

"These are words of power that I employ you, oh spiritual loas. I seek you as the intermediary to the Bon Dieu to swiftly trigger the spell contained, but I implore protection for the holder of the bag."

Finally, she breathed over the gris-gris bag to 'give it life'.

"Now it was alive." Queen Maia softly spoke to herself.

Following that, she recited selected psalms repeatedly.

She began with Psalm 94: Verse 1 as she spoke the words:

"The lord is a God who punishes.

God, show your greatness and punish!

Rise, Judge of the earth,

And give the proud what they deserve.
How long will the wicked be happy?
How long, Lord?"

Her ritual continued uninterrupted until the jinxing candle flame consumed the rest of the candle's body into a puddle of molten black wax. Finally, the last 7th knob on the seven-day candle vanished with the last flicker of the flame. Once again, she would cast another deadly spell upon unsuspecting victims for a second time in the past week.

Queen Maia Revalue orchestrated a similar spell about a week earlier at the time of the French Quarter Festival. However, this weekend was different because it was the 'Jazz Fest'. This festival was the New Orleans highlight of the year, the coveted New Orleans Jazz & Heritage Festival (i.e., 'Jazz Fest' or just 'Fest'). The first of two weekends are now. The Jazz Fest will have another consecutive second event next weekend.

"How marvelous. I will have another spell to consummate the evildoers at next week's Jazz Fest," Queen Maia thought to herself.

Again, this intended, deadly spell seemed justifiable for all those who had not yet accepted spiritual guidance and self-restraint from their despicable, drug ridden lifestyle. Her plan was to impose this spell upon the end-user of the drug, orchestrated through the drug peddler and the dealer.

"Their unaccountable actions have continued unchecked far too long and have hurt far too many innocent people. Paying for their actions was not on the horizon until now! I serve the saints and ask them to intercede to Bon Dieu for me, as I also revere my ancestors today." She softly spoke upon completing the deadly spell.

The ritual consumed every trace of energy from her entire body. Her kitchen was now completely dark, and it was time for sleep. An unforgettable day awaited her.
Thursday, April 25, 7:32 A.M.
Maia Revalue residence
St. Roch neighborhood

New Orleans

Queen Maia awoke rejuvenated and after completing her morning routine, she would prepare her incarnation handy ware and head to the Fair Grounds Racecourse. This location was center stage for the New Orleans Jazz & Heritage Festival. Less than a couple of miles away, she could easily walk there by North Miro Street in less than an hour. This early in the morning, the weather was perfect for a walk in the placid heat, which she loved.

She already carefully arranged the paraphernalia on her kitchen counter to complete the spell. She retrieved the gris-gris pouch, the small cloth bag filled with magical ingredients, and the ampule containing cemetery dust from the adorned Voodoo altar. The last task at hand was to place all the ashes and molten wax from the ritual in a small brown paper bag. She would then transport the bag to the center of a distant crossroads that she would encounter on her way to the Fair Grounds Racecourse for disposal.

Queen Maia carefully hid the gris-gris bag on her person. One should never expose a gris-gris bag in public. Opening the tall, bright green-colored, paint flaking front door to her house, she stepped onto the raised, cracked sidewalk leading to the street. Her next-door neighbor's cat, Gumbo, thin, with filthy fur and bony legs, stamped out of her way with a lingering hiss. She was now on her way with another deadly mission of 'black magic'.

Thursday, April 25, 9:16 A.M.

Fair Grounds Racecourse

1751 Gentilly Boulevard

New Orleans

Streaming grey clouds splattered the sky against a light blue background in the humid morning air as she approached the Fair Grounds Racecourse. Soon, summer will engulf the city and bring with it excruciating heat and thunderstorms. However, today there was a slight breeze along with the peaking morning sun, which was ideal for carrying out such a spell, she thought to herself.

Multicolored food stands, sweeping stages offering a vast array of genres, and dense crowds as far as one could see riddled the sweeping fair grounds. Waves of spectators were streaming in and out from all directions. The fair grounds resounded with the sounds of music genres coming from every direction, resembling a colossal symphony. For Queen Maia, there was only inner silence and a riveting focus on finding the target location for the completion of her spell.

Queen Maia was quite knowledgeable about every 'nook and cranny' of New Orleans. She could even tell you about a person she never met before simply by appearance and mannerism with astonishing accuracy. Now, she was searching the landscape for a well-known New Orleans drug lord, Rafael Nacket. He was one of New Orleans most notorious and illusive drug dealers. Finding him was paramount to fulfilling the spell.

This was 'big business' for Rafael Nacket every year. Cocaine was his specialty, and he was a master at targeting and stealthily selling his product to those tourists addicted to cocaine. For him, it was more lucrative in New Orleans than the crowded fentanyl drug trade. Rafael was a New Orleans self-proclaimed 'cocaine drug lord' with his loyal lieutenants and an army of street distributors.

Queen Maia's mission was to locate Nacket. The spell targeted the drug users. However, it was to be delivered from the chain-of-command to the end-user, beginning with the drug lord, Rafael Nacket.

The size of the crowd was rapidly escalating, and Queen Maia was still frantically searching for Rafael or any of his henchmen. She was aware of Rafael's music obsession with New Orleans jazz, so she checked out the infamous Royal Blue Jazz Tent. This was one of the largest and always the most congested tents of the Fest.

She entered the tent. It was elbow-to-elbow for at least thirty yards before a break-off into smaller groups. She was determined to find the closest seat to the stage performers.

"Now, it was a simple matter of observation for inattentive music lovers. Those seeking their 'high' before jazz infusion." Queen Maia spoke softly to herself.

Many of the groups were truly enjoying the ambiance of the moment. However, there was one group that appeared to be more interested in handshakes and 'give me five' than the usual greeting of friends. As she got closer, she noticed the tall, slender, bearded face with dark sunglasses of Rafael Nacket hiding in the shadows next to the suspicious crowd.

Rafael Nacket, blending into the crowd, but he cannot hide from Queen Maia, she whispered to herself.

It had to be just the right time to complete the spell. The suspicious crowd was still tending to their reprehensible drug business. The music was also in full swing. This allowed Queen Maia to prepare stealthily and cautiously to retrieve the ampule filled with dust. She removed the cap and poured the powdery mix into her palm.

"Perfect timing." She muttered to herself.

The music reached an astounding lull in cords as the crowd stood and clapped incessantly with waving hands and loud cheers. This was the moment, Queen Maia thought to herself. She deliberately stood upwind from both Rafael and the suspicious crowd. Now she was strategically situated and vigorously heaved the dust into the air. The dust spread evenly over the unsuspecting crowd. The crowd was so mesmerized by the performance that the dust cloud went unnoticed.

"My spell is complete." Leaving the fairgrounds, her face aglow with delight, she headed for home.

# CHAPTER 4 - THE JAZZ FEST

Thursday, April 25, 3:45 P.M.
Federal Bureau of Investigation Headquarters
2901 Leon C Simon Drive
New Orleans

The FBI Headquarters was abuzz with activity as agents prepared for the city's annual Jazz Fest surveillance. Team leaders gathered in a briefing room, studying maps, and coordinating with local law enforcement to ensure a seamless operation.

"I'm on my cellphone right now with the agent in charge at the Jazz Fest, sir," the team agent informed Special Agent Jack Lawins.

"We have secured the festival grounds, and our agents are in position, ready to monitor the crowd for any potential threats of criminal activity."

"Need a status update now!" replied Special Agent Lawins.

"Sir, no suspicious activity reported to the agent in charge by any of the field agents embedded in the festival crowd."

"Any news on the suspects from our list?" Special Agent Lawins asked.

"No, sir!"

"Nothing at all? No suspicious behavior?" Special Agent Lawins asked.

"Only a little dust cloud blowing around in the Royal Blue Jazz Tent. Not high on the suspicion list, sir."

"Dust cloud?"

"That's right. That's what the agents on the ground reported. I didn't think it was important."

"That's not your call. Find out more information about this 'dust' and call me."

"Yes, sir!"

The team agent made a call to the agents at the festival grounds, as Special Agent Lawins considered the significance of a harmless 'dust cloud'. He shared his thoughts aloud with the team,

"Was it just typical New Orleans festival activity? It was under a tent, but the floor was asphalt in the Royal Blue Jazz Tent. New Orleans humidity should generate 'wet dirt'. This dust had to be carried into the tent by someone."

"Agent Johnson. Agent Adams. Let's go."

Special Agent Lawins and his team hurried on their way to the festival grounds.

He called ahead to his ground team of agents, scanning the crowd at the jazz festival.

"Try to discover the source and the person responsible for generating that dust bloom."

"You also need to intensify your search to see if you can pick up any clues to the whereabouts and activities of our suspects on the list."

It should be noted that the list included pictures and brief descriptions of the most wanted terrorists at-large in the southeastern US. The list also included other persons-of-interest.

Special Agent Lawins thought to himself,

"These festivals are prime targets for any would-be terrorist. A dense gathering of unsuspecting, often loopy party goers. Mix the residents in with the tourists. Voilà! A recipe for unadulterated chaos. Now, it is a race against time to prevent any catastrophic event."

"Something is brewing, I just know it, but I don't think we're dealing with a terrorist," he mumbled to himself.

This is what Special Agent Lawins calls 'mind dilemmas'.

He hates the term gut feeling, because he knows best. After all, he has training and history as one of the best agents in the FBI. He knows the line, where DHS or other agencies need to get involved. After all, this will secure the credit for him, and the FBI, over those other scavenging agencies.

"Close, but I am not yet convinced that a terrorist is involved.", he spoke.

It is a known fact that if the government agencies could cooperate and share their 'sandbox', 911 may have been partially or even completely averted. In retrospect, the 911 Commission Report alluded to this.

Thursday, April 25, 5:48 P.M.

Fairgrounds Racecourse

1751 Gentilly Boulevard

New Orleans

It was the first weekend of the Jazz and Heritage Festival. The locals call it, 'Jazz Fest'. This phenomenal, one-of-a-kind event captivates its audience for two long weekends. Visitors could find tasty Cajun food and every other imaginable Louisiana heritage delicacy there. Alluring, colorful food stands splattered the entire fairgrounds, each one as enticing as the next.

There were fourteen stages, offering a vast range of Louisiana genre and beyond. One could hear a symphony of music in the background. It included music icons and locals such as Jimmy Buffett, Stevie Nicks, J. Monque, and D Blues Revue.

The crowd displayed spectacular density, and the expected attendance was in the thousands. An aerial view showed the fairgrounds as a maze of colored dots. These 'dots' represented almost every color of umbrella possible. Each served as a heat shield for its holder from the intense New Orleans sun.

Special Agent Lawins arrived at the fairgrounds entrance and flashed his credentials. He scanned the populated crowd in front of him as he moved forward. Now he had to trust his instincts to scrutinize the crowd for suspects from the list, while moving towards the Royal Blue Jazz Tent.

He focused his attention on a middle-aged man with a bright red, long-sleeved shirt, sports cap, pulled over his forehead to hide his face. The man had a suspicious bulge in his back pocket. The 'person-of-interest' did not resemble anyone on the list, but the man drew his attention. As Special Agent Lawins approached, he observed the man's movements, noting how he seemed to scan the area as well. On a closer look, he noticed the pocket bulge was only an oversize harmonica as the man entered the Royal Blue Jazz Tent in front of him.

He entered the Royal Blue Jazz Tent behind the 'person-of-interest'. The colossal interior of the tent was now packed with jazz enthusiasts. Most of them were sitting, exhausted from walking in the heat. He was trying to find the agent that reported the dust bloom. Snaking his way through the seated crowd, he finally located the agent at the far end of the enormous enclosure.

"I need to know more detail about this dust cloud. Was it generated by one person? A fan or AC unit out of control? Was it only under this tent?" Special Agent Lawins asked the agent.

"Sir, we checked on the source of the dust. It appeared to be a local, older, middle-aged woman who was involved. When she stood up with the crowd to applaud the performer, her hands were also in the air. However, she threw dust or dirt in her hand-clapping motion. No other person was taking part in this odd action. Honestly, sir, the tent was too dimly lit and the crowd too dense with the applause to notice anything else. This was all I could observe."

"Thanks for your help, agent."

Special Agent Lawins turned to answer his cellphone,

"Sir, this is Agent Johnson at headquarters. I have further information on the status of the woman with the dust."

"Great timing Johnson."

"They have identified her as Maia Revalue, a local voodoo queen practitioner. She was born in New Orleans and has a notable reputation for practicing voodoo-hoodoo."

"Any local address?"

"She lives only about a mile or so from the festival grounds in the St. Roch neighborhood. An agent saw her on camera leaving the fairgrounds a short time ago and heading toward her home."

"Good work, agent. Keep me updated. I'm going to pay a visit to Queen Maia."

Thursday, April 25, 7:23 P.M.
Maia Revalue residence
St. Roch neighborhood
New Orleans

The St. Roch neighborhood had a history as one of the country's largest populations of free people of color before the civil war. Then, in the 1920s, it transitioned into a racially mixed residential section of New Orleans. St. Roch was home to many Creole and black families. Today, after constructing Interstate 10, it is predominantly Afro-American.

In 1867, the inhabitants at the time turned to Saint Roch, the patron of good health, for help and prayer because the yellow fever epidemic was on the rise. They named it "St. Roch" after turning to the patron of good health, Saint Roch, for help and prayer because of the rising yellow fever epidemic. In that year, they erected a shrine and cemetery in honor of Saint Roch.

The New Orleans form of voodoo, voodoo-hoodoo, is still active in St. Roch and the greater New Orleans area.

The St. Roch neighborhood was historic in New Orleans. A spattering of colored houses, blue, turquoise, burgundy, and yellow. Tall in appearance, with high ceilings.

Special Agent Lawins along with Dr. Margie Starters arrived at the home of Maia Revalue. Special Agent Lawins, deliberating and appearing authoritative, knocked on the tall, bright green front door.

"FBI. We need to speak to Maia Revalue on an urgent matter." Special Agent Lawins said in a loud, stern voice.

There was no reply, even though Dr. Starters could see the shadow of someone inside the house. Dr. Starters walked around to the front porch window. The window was clouded with dirt and a draped curtain hung inside, blocking any attempt at visibility.

Again, Special Agent Lawins knocked. This time more forcibly, "Maia Revalue, we need to talk. Now or later at the FBI Headquarters. Your choice."

Silence ensued, but after a few minutes, the door cracked, and Queen Maia peeked through the narrow opening. In a soft, timid voice, she spoke, "Who are you?"

"FBI", with Special Agent Lawins and Dr. Starters displaying their agency credentials,

"Can we come in? We would like to ask you some questions."

Reluctantly, she allowed them to enter and pointed at the dingy gray sofa.

"Please sit. Why do you come to my house at this hour?"

"We have some questions about your presence and actions at the Jazz & Heritage Festival today." replied Special Agent Lawins.

"Please understand that the FBI is often present at large events for public safety reasons. We noticed you were interested in jazz and wondered if you enjoyed the event?"

"I am watched. Why? Is this because my religion is not acceptable to such authority?" Replied Queen Maia.

"No, ma'am, this has nothing to do with your religion. Your brief stay and actions were suspicious behavior by our agent. It is our duty to follow up on all reports."

"Please leave! You have insulted me and desecrated my house. Leave!"

"We have other questions, if you please."

Queen Maia's rapport changed to one of anger. Her eyes widened, her face scowled, and her voice became intense.

"No more questions. Leave now!"

Looking at each other in disbelief, their eyes signaled, "it's time to depart". Both agents rose from the worn couch and left the house. Queen Maia punched the heavy door shut and bolted it behind the two agents.

Looking behind themselves, they noticed a shadow of a figure slowly moving the draped curtain aside, as if to insure their departure.

"This is your area of expertise, Dr. Starters. What is your take on this behavior?" asked Special Agent Lawins.

She closed her eyes as if to choose the response.

As a psychology profiler, this approach was quite useful in revisiting the scene. It often elicited new information that was hidden within the subconscious.

Dr. Starters answered his question,

"We alluded to her voodoo-hoodoo religion being practiced at the festival, which irritated her. She knows we saw her throw some type of dust or dirt and knew that we just refrained from asking her about the reason for the dispersal. The most logical explanation is that it was part of a voodoo spell or ritual."

"We were too close to discover the truth, so she used anger as a defense to stop the conversation before giving out any clues."

"So, the question is whether this is a harmless practice or something of concern? It is implicit that we know the content of the dust." replied Special Agent Lawins.

"Yes, I agree. We have no probable cause and only a 'person-of-interest'. Identifying dust containing a dangerous component within the mixture would be a probable cause. We need additional information from the agents on the ground. Likewise, finding another suspect or suspects from our list might help rule out Queen Maia."

"Meanwhile, it's a delicate situation with her and her accusation of religious persecution on our part. We need to leave her be for now unless we have more incriminating evidence of her involvement."

Friday, April 26, 7:37 A.M.
Federal Bureau of Investigation Headquarters
2901 Leon C Simon Drive
New Orleans

Special Agent Lawins and his team had just arrived at the office, eager to search for more information about a potential terrorist their surveillance might have uncovered.

Their excitement was palpable as they gathered around the conference table, ready to delve deeper into Maia Revalue's background and where any pertinent clues might lead them.

After a lot of paper shuffling and coffee refills, the team gathered in the main conference room for the early morning report. As they settled in, the flickering glow of monitors filled the room, casting an eerie light on the determined expressions of the agents.

Special Agent Lawins began with an opening statement:

"Some believe we may be dealing with an alleged terrorist in New Orleans. I'm not convinced that is the case. Therefore, I believe other agencies need not be involved until we gain more information."

"We have briefed all of you on the suspicious deaths surrounding the French Quarter Festival. Now we want to make sure we don't have the same scenario at this week's Jazz Fest."

"Any suspicious information from yesterday's surveillance at the Fest is a prime concern at this point. We should discuss any such information from yesterday's surveillance at the Fest in this morning's debriefing."

"Let's start the discussion, agents."

Agent Anderson, being the agent in charge of the Jazz Fest surveillance, led the debriefing.

"Maia Revalue, a well-known, prominent voodoo-hoodoo queen in the greater New Orleans area, is the only 'person-of-interest'. During one of the jazz accolades, observers saw Maia Revalue throwing an unknown substance, dirt, or dust into the air. It could be a part of a well-planned, elaborate voodoo-hoodoo spell."

"It was also noticed that she had a definite interest in our local drug lord, Rafael Nacket. Our agents identified her, seeking him out from the crowd and keeping in close contact with him and his bodyguards until she left the grounds."

"Mr. Nacket was overseeing his illicit drug trade and paying little attention to Ms. Revalue at the Fest. The DEA observed money for drug exchanges but did not act upon it because of a 'stand down' order. Could there be an association between him and Ms. Revalue? We don't know, but that is under investigation."

"Agents. That's my report for now."

Agent Anderson wrapped up the debriefing and returned to his seat at the table.

Special Agent Lawins cleared his throat and stepped forward.

"We need to track both Maia Revalue and Rafael Nacket and gather more intel. It is imperative that we get a sample of the dust Maia Revalue used at the Jazz Fest. As for Rafael Nacket, maybe DEA can share some intel with us?" he stated, shaking his head and displaying a dubious facial expression.

"Agent Starters and I paid a visit to Ms. Revalue. She became very irritated at the point of making us leave when we asked questions about her actions at the Jazz Fest. We have our suspicion, and she is a 'person-of-interest'. Unfortunately, we don't have probable cause at this point to take this matter much further. We believe she has a connection to our investigation. This new information only strengthens the need for careful surveillance."

"Continue your efforts and keep me informed of any other suspicious subjects. We will coordinate with the DEA to gather as much information as possible."

Special Agent Lawins stopped speaking and refocused his gaze, shifting from one team member to the other. One by one, the team members exchanged worried glances as they realized the gravity of their next move.

"Foremost are those high-value felons on our suspect list."

"Thanks for your attention, everyone."

Back in his office, Special Agent Lawins stared at Agent Starters and proclaimed,

"Place a 24-hour surveillance on Ms. Revalue and continue

the one on Dr. Watkins. I am not getting surprised with any of this! As for Rafael Nacket, maybe the DEA can share some intel with us?"

"Yes sir. Anything else?"

"No, but is this voodoo-hoodoo for real?"

Agent Starters replied,

"It is a religion. All religion is based upon faith in a supreme entity. Those who practice New Orleans voodoo-hoodoo almost always have the intention of benefiting the bequeathed. However, practitioners of New Orleans voodoo-hoodoo sometimes engage in left-handed voodoo, known as 'black magic', intending to cause harm to the recipient. In documented cases, the intended victim received a toxin or poison, resulting in death from a spell. This could explain the current cases. Maybe it is nightshade or some other exotic poison?"

The conversation weighed on Special Agent Lawins as he pondered the potential risks posed by the elusive threat of voodoo-hoodoo.

Agent Starters continued,

"I cannot understand how you could achieve this, with ten different individuals being spread out at different times and in different areas at the French Quarter Festival."

"Agreed," sighed Special Agent Lawins, leaning back in his chair.

"It is paramount that we know what was in that dust or dirt she expelled into the air."

"We need it tested for biological agents, toxins, and poisons. The foremost question is: How do we find the alleged substance when there are no victims at this current event?"

"Yet!"

# CHAPTER 5 - FALLOUT

Friday, April 26, 9:30 A.M.
Office of Dr. Catechin
New Orleans Medical Examiner
3001 Earhart Boulevard
Dr. Catechin was sitting at his desk and checking his email when he noticed a message from the Forensic Lab entitled "Particulate matter, left lung, lower lobe ID: 00348.22."

The Forensic Lab summary report read:

"The particulate matter submitted consists mostly of airborne dust and unknown microbial content. This is consistent with dust found in the greater New Orleans region during the current atmospheric conditions. No further analysis was performed."

He quickly instructed the secretary to contact Dr. Watkins office.

"Sir, Dr. Watkins is on line 2."

"Dr. Watkins, this is Dr. Catechin. I just forwarded to you the report on the dust autopsy sample from the forensic lab."

"Thanks for the prompt response, Dr. Catechin. Give me a minute.... Can you explain this to me, I mean the underlying pathology?"

"I'm not concerned about the dust, but I would like to rule out any microbial pathogen, and that is your area of expertise with your high-capacity DNA sequencing. Any update on the samples?"

"So far, no toxin or poison involved using mass spectrometry. The DNA sequencing is still in progress. I will call you as soon as I know more about the testing."

"Thanks for your help, Tombak."

Dr. Catechin's next call was to Special Agent Lawins. Dr. Catechin received an order to provide any progress on the cases to Special Agent Lawins at FBI headquarters immediately.

"Why the secrecy? We should all be working together. Right?" he muttered to himself in disbelief.

Friday, April 26, 1:30 P.M.

Ochsner Medical Center (OMC), Intensive Care Unit

1514 Jefferson Hwy

New Orleans

Dr. Whinnier from the New Orleans PHL abruptly exited the elevator and hurried to the meeting room at the end of the hallway. He arrived late to a meeting with Dr.'s Watkins, Swindon, and Millirem at the OMC conference room. This was a medical debriefing on recent pneumonia cases in New Orleans.

Dr. Millirem began the session, saying,

"Greeting everyone and glad you could join us, glaring specifically at Dr. Whinnier with a cocked head and partial smile. Dr. Catechin at the medical examiner's office has already brought me up to speed. We all know each other from past case consults, so let's begin."

"I invited Dr. Rhone Eckman, Medical Laboratory Director, and Dr. Yahara Hearne, an Infectious Disease physician at OMC. Dr. Hearne, has been the main consult on all these cases."

Following doctors Hearne and Eckman's introductions to the group, Dr. Hearne briefly reviewed the case histories.

"Within the past week, we admitted six patients who experienced a sudden onset of severe shortness of breath (SOB), critical respiratory values, and accompanying radiology indicative of pneumonia."

"All patients were adults from both sexes, ranging in age from 23 to 53 years. They have an unremarkable history; no known contact with Covid-19 or other respiratory pathogen infected individuals, and no contact with persons from areas reporting recent severe pneumonia. Some were visitors and others were longtime residents of New Orleans. However, all six patients attended our recent French Quarter Festival."

"In reviewing their charts, we noticed an abnormally high cell count for WBCs, specifically for neutrophils, in the bloodwork. The clinical laboratory report suggests that some type of infectious agent, likely bacterial, infected the six patients, based on the abnormally high cell count for WBCs, specifically for neutrophils, in their bloodwork. Over the next 48 hours, post-symptom onset, all six patients experienced deteriorating vitals, leading to septic shock. All patients have since expired."

Dr. Eckman followed the chart review with a summary of the microbiology infectious disease testing results,

"All microbiology testing conducted so far for microbes has yielded negative results. This includes antigen tests, culture, and even syndromic molecular panels for blood and respiratory pathogens. I have used all our available testing here at OMC. Therefore, as a medical consultant, I strongly recommend employing more advanced molecular testing."

Dr. Hearne, an expert in infectious disease, provided her medical diagnosis for the cases,

"This is most likely a deadly microbe, not highly transmissible, but capable of eliciting an immune response that even our most potent antibacterial, antiviral and anti-fungal pharmaceuticals cannot overcome."

Dr. Watkins contemplated the implications of her statement, knowing the impact on OMC and the potential fallout for other hospitals and health care organizations citywide. He then delivered a summary of his laboratory findings:

"At this time, we have found no sign of a toxin or poison using MS analysis. Our DNA sequencing is a lengthier process which requires multiple steps to confirm specific classes and species of microbes. However, the initial results of our PCR testing show bacteria. Viruses and other microbes have yet to be ruled out."

Dr. Whinnier then interjected his findings from the PHL Forensic Laboratory,

"We were interested in the particulate matter observed in the tissue found at autopsy. Testing showed dust with unknown microbial content normally found in the atmosphere at this time in the greater New Orleans area."

Dr. Millirem thanked everyone for their summary statements and added the following finding from CDC's testing:

"Dr. Whinnier submitted CSF specimens to CDC for testing from two patients with meningoencephalitis at Lakeside Hospital. Both CSF specimens appear to contain a rickettsia-type bacteria, like the Rocky Mountain spotted fever rickettsia. The doctors diagnosed the other two patients with pneumonia only, and they did not have CSF available for testing."

"So far, OMC has only six patients with pneumonia who have subsequently expired. However, you need to be on alert for the possibility of meningoencephalitis in all these cases."

"I want you to know that CDC guidelines classify this cluster as a stage one event, which is a serious health emergency."

"We are on a tight schedule today, so thank you for your support in these cases. We will continue the investigation with those invited to the meeting at Lakeside Hospital promptly today at 4:00 PM."

Everyone arose to leave the room. Leaving the meeting, Dr. Millirem stared at Dr. Whinnier and nodded, as if to reprimand him for his tardiness.

Friday, April 26, 4:00 P.M.

Lakeside Hospital (LSH) (Previously Tulane Medical Center)

1415 Tulane Avenue

New Orleans

Tulane Medical Center is a 235-bed academic hospital that was renamed in 2005 as Lakeside Hospital. Today it is a part of a multi-hospital system, the Tulane Health System.

The meeting with CDC started promptly at 4:00 PM in the LSH Boardroom. Dr. Millirem and other members included Drs' Watkins, Swindon and Whinnier. LSH staff included Dr. Ian Cleat and Dr. Jilin Slocum, Infectious disease physicians, and Dr.

Roosa Willing, RN, DPN, Nurse Practitioner.

Dr. Millirem spoke,

"Ladies and gentlemen, we are here to discuss the fallout from our recent cluster of deaths in New Orleans. There were ten pneumonia patients, six brought to OMH and four to LSH. I briefly reviewed your four patient charts and can state with a good certainty their medical history is almost identical to the six OMC pneumonia cases. Therefore, I would like to focus on the two meningoencephalitis cases."

"Let's look at the meningoencephalitis cases more closely."

"Dr. Cleat, please summarize the findings from your team."

Dr. Ian Cleat is a short, distinguished looking, Harvard trained infectious disease physician known for his love of patient care. He has an avid interest in translational medicine and serves as the Primary Investigator (PI) in multiple clinical trials. He has been a member of the medical staff at Tulane Medical Center for decades, before joining the Tulane Health System at Lakeside Hospital.

Dr. Cleat arose from his seat and approached the podium. He brought up information from the medical reference database on his laptop and explained the gravity of the cases by summarizing the chart reviews.

"The four male and female patients ranged in age from 24 to 57 years. All four patients initially presented with severe pneumonia and quickly progressed to septic shock and death. Our best efforts using antibacterial and antiviral therapy did not slow the course of disease, patient deterioration sped up, and death quickly ensued."

"However, two patients, the 24-year-old male and the 57-year-old female, also had a concurrent meningoencephalitis. A rare co-morbidity combination."

Dr. Millirem interrupted,

"Dr. Cleat. Please focus on these cases and explain why they differ from the other two cases."

Dr. Cleat continued,

"The two pneumonia cases, a 34-year-old female and a 45-year-old male, that were not associated with meningoencephalitis, were previously healthy individuals with no known risk factors from the medical history."

"In contrast, the medical history of the other two patients revealed a history of an immunocompromised state. The 24-year-old male was HIV positive, but had an undetectable viral load controlled by highly active antiretroviral therapy (HAART). The 57-year-old female was a Stage III Non-Hodgkin lymphoma patient, currently in remission following chemotherapy and radiation."

"Dr. Millirem. Your finding of rickettsia in the CSF from both patients seems to fit the medical history. However, it is highly unusual for rickettsia to cause meningoencephalitis. I must admit, the rickettsia finding surprised me. However, we know that there is a case reported in our literature search."

"The perplexing question is: Do we have one microbe causing this infection, or multiple microbes? Multiple pathogens are my choice because rickettsia is unlikely to be causing the pneumonia, so that leaves another bacterium, virus, or other type of deadly microbe."

Dr. Millirem, in summarizing the meeting, spoke,

"The specimen testing pre-mortem and post-mortem are key to every investigation."

"The more we delve into molecular testing, the better."

"Dr. Watkins and Dr. Swindon, your phenomenal molecular expertise is much appreciated. We must find the root cause of the deaths as quickly as possible. Today, we have a 'molecular toolbox' like no other in the history of infectious disease diagnostics. Time to use everything at our disposal expeditiously."

"This concludes our meeting, and I would like to thank everyone for your reports."

[

# CHAPTER 6 - PUBLIC HEALTH AND THE MEDIA

Friday, April 26, 7:15 P.M.
Lakeside Hospital, Emergency Department (ED)
1415 Tulane Ave
New Orleans

Lares Turncock, a New Orleans newspaper reporter with an unconventional satirical personality, lies in wait at the Lakeside Hospital ED for a press briefing,

"Friday night and no disappointment at the Emergency Department. 'Keep those gunshot victims rolling into the ED like a Vegas roulette on steroids', thought Lares Turncock, senior reporter for the New Orleans Tribune. It's Hotel California again for some. You can check in, but you can never leave. Alive that is!"

"Save that thought," he thought, because he just spotted Dr. Whinnier through the hazy glass doors, surrounded by a flurry of doctors, nurses, and medical staff. Lares cameraman zoomed in, capturing the chaos. Sirens wailed in the background as Lares shouted.

"Dr. Whinnier! Lares Turncock, New Orleans Tribune. A couple of questions if you please...."

Lares stood out from the cast of reporters, his voice booming over the wailing sirens. He hurriedly made his way towards Dr. Whinnier.

"Isn't pneumonia in the heat of this late spring rare?

Are we currently experiencing an outbreak? Is this the start of another COVID-19 and could New Orleans be ground zero?"

"Are we talking about the beginning of another deadly pandemic? I'm hearing that we already have multiple fatalities?"

Dr. Whinnier replied,

"Patients succumb to pneumonia, regardless of the season. Depending on the patient, even early detection and treatment might still result in a greater than 50% mortality. There are some pneumonia cases with death, but we are still early in the investigation."

"Dr. Whinnier, why did the CDC decide to come here if this is not considered an outbreak?" Dr. Whinnier began walking away, but replied,

"Thank you all for your attention. We will keep you updated as we know more information."

He twisted as he walked from the crowd, saying,

"Please keep in mind that we believe the public is not in any eminent health risk currently."

"Dr. Whinnier...." Shouted a torrent of reporters with loud voices and blurred questions filling the air.

The doctor paid no attention and hurried to his car, being followed by an unruly assemblage of shouting reporters and flashing cameras.

Lares was a seasoned reporter who knew the importance of the impending tedious task of quickly gathering more information about these suspicious cases. However, do not allow yourself to be misled. Mr. Lares Turncock is New Orleans finest. Nothing will stop him from digging to 'hell and back' to unearth the truth.

Lares is a handsome fellow with a likable personality. At 47 years old, he is still worthy of, as the locals say, "pass a good time". He frequents Pat O'Brien's with a hurricane or two and 'Pinch the tail and suck the head' at any of the local restaurants while eating crawfish. Of course, he could not resist a hardy dinner at Mr. B's or Commander's Palace for the local Cajun special, but only after breaking this story.

Lares softly says aloud,

"Next stop, Dr. Catechin and the City Morgue."

Monday, April 29, 9:15 A.M.

New Orleans Coroner's Office

3001 Earhart Boulevard

On the surface, the Coroner's Office presents itself as a beautiful three-story medical facility, but inside, it disguises itself as a tomb where mortals are prepared for all eternity. It houses an autopsy suite, four stations and a separate room for decomposed bodies to confine the 'gag-inducing stench'.

With determination in his eyes, Lares approached the foreboding doors of the autopsy suite (i.e., morgue). He took a deep breath, pushing aside any lingering nerves, and cautiously opened one of the heavy glass doors. A sudden surge of formalin-saturated air causes his eyes to burn. His jaw dropped at what he saw as he slowly shuffled into the crowded suite.

The room was dimly lit except for the autopsy tables, with the overhead fluorescent lighting casting an eerie glow on the stainless-steel tables lined with medical instruments. Pathologists in blood spattered, white bodysuits were crouching over pale blue bodies in various stages of dissection. However, what was unusual, when they stood upright, was that each bodysuit contained sealed headgear with an attached air supply. They looked more like astronauts exploring an alien world rather than physicians performing an autopsy. It became more gruesome, seeing the blood-dowsed gloves dripping, red tinged fluid with every movement. The scene showed tissue being extracted from the lifeless bodies. This tissue was being placed into nearby containers and carefully sealed.

The ultimate in horror was the line of corpses on nearby gurneys. A stark white sheet covering a shimmering stainless-steel gurney heartlessly outlined the contour of each body.

"What have I uncovered?" He thought to himself.

The glimpse of a shadow suddenly interrupted this fleeting thought, moving from a dark corner of the room. This fleeting figure emerged from the darkness; its outline faintly illuminated by the overhead lights. Squinting, he tried to make out the identity of the mysterious figure. It was to no avail. Suddenly, as if stung by a vicious bee, he encountered total darkness, collapsed, and laid helplessly unconscious on the frigid morgue floor.

Monday, April 29, 11:53 A.M.

New Orleans Coroner's Office Parking Lot

3001 Earhart Boulevard

An approaching siren abruptly awakened Lares as he clenched the steering wheel of his car.

"What the hell happened?" he shouted out loud.

His head was aching and his neck stiff, but he stumbled out of his car. The intense sunlight without sunglasses was blinding as he walked over to the Coroner's Office building massive front doors. He headed straight to the office of Dr. Melvin Catechin.

Dr. Catechin's secretary knew Lares, and before he could even speak, she said,

"Mr. Turncock, if you please. Dr. Catechin is at lunch and will be at meetings for the rest of the day. Would you like to leave a message?"

Surprised by the scripted message, Lares replied,

"I have an urgent matter to discuss with him. Please relay that message. Was Dr. Catechin presiding over an autopsy this morning?"

"Mr. Turncock. You know that his schedule is private."

"Thank you for that information. Again, it's an urgent matter!"

"I will make sure he knows about the urgency of the matter. Can I help you with anything else, Lares?"

"No, thank you."

Turning abruptly, he departed.

He had the distinct impression he was being stonewalled by the office secretary.

Monday, April 29, 1:39 P.M.

New Orleans Tribune, Office of Lares Turncock

2317 Esplanade Avenue

Lares stormed into the office of Shepard Althorn, Editor-in-Chief, New Orleans Tribune, and paced in front of his desk. Shepard, a short, stout fellow approaching the sole wrenching age of 60, was never at a loss for words. He looked up at Lares, saying,

"Lares, stop with the incessant pacing. Either speak or get out of my office!"

Lares mind was racing with thoughts of aliens or some kind of bioterrorism agent or the like, being autopsied at the morgue. Was this a hallucination or an atrocious nightmare? He was literally speechless but stammered out a few words.

"Shepard, I think I just witnessed a horrific, colossal postmortem operation at the city morgue. Some sort of scene out of a fiction novel."

"Lares. Do you think or do you know about the event? You need to clarify this for me."

"That part remains sketchy. I believe I may have had a blackout after witnessing it and somehow, I must have made it back to my car before passing out."

"I was following up on a lead at the Coroner's office with Dr. Catechin after Dr. Whinnier's news interview at Lakeside Hospital."

"Something didn't set right after Dr. Whinnier didn't answer my question about why the CDC was here and if the cluster of pneumonia deaths is now considered an outbreak."

"So, I visited the morgue to see if Dr. Catechin was performing the autopsies. Unbelievable! I stepped into a room packed with cadavers and pathologists in full biohazard mode, bodysuits, air supplies, and the whole enchilada!"

"The last thing I remembered was a bee sting on the back of my neck, and it propelled me to the cold morgue floor."

"No, it was not a dream! It's likely that someone drugged me."

"I then tried to find Dr. Catechin, but his gatekeeper secretary was too guarding. She told me he would not be available for the rest of the day, even before I spoke. Meetings?"

Lares deliberately did not mention the unknown figure. He couldn't shake off the uneasiness that haunted him. He knew better than to mention the unknown figure in the shadow. This might be too much information for Shepard right now.

"Lares. You could be onto something. It's worth a follow up. However, I want you to update me on your every move for this one. I know this is unusual, but this is an order. Understand!"

"Yes, sir!"

"This was not like Shepard.", Lares thought to himself as he headed out, closing the door somewhat abruptly.

As soon as the door closed, Shepard forcefully grabbed his phone and muttered five words, "He just left my office" and hung up.

Monday, April 29, 2:43 P.M.

New Orleans Tribune, Parking Lot

2317 Esplanade Avenue

Lares took a deep breath as he stepped out of the building and walked towards his car. Surveying the surroundings of the parking lot, he noticed a figure in the shadow of a nearby tree. However, in a fleeting moment, while fumbling with his car keys, the figure disappeared.

Am I being followed, or am I just imagining another unknown figure? This only made him more cautious as he quickly unlocked his car and yelled,

"Laissez les bons temps rouler" (i.e., let the good times roll)

Confused and his mind racing in all directions, he squealed his tires as he raced away.

# CHAPTER 7 - BIG BROTHER IS WATCHING

Monday, April 29, 3:07 P.M.
New Orleans Tribune
2317 Esplanade Avenue

Lares was back in his office, staring at a blank computer screen in disbelief. He couldn't shake off the eerie feeling that someone was watching him. Possibly, even monitoring his every move.

As usual, he would glance around the room to help his thought process. However, this time, Lares noticed the subtle flicker of a tiny blue light in the room's air vent. He took out his cellphone and stealthily took a picture of the vent. He noticed that a hidden camera was targeting his desk. This confirmed his suspicion, but he used this surveillance camera to his advantage.

Lares thought carefully,

"It's not logical to assume that the Chief is unaware. Right? Why is someone snooping on me? It must be the pneumonia deaths story. After all, I am the best in the city known as the "Big Easy."

His desk was always an 'organized mess', but this was his idea of a filing system. He could always find even a solitary, isolated, stickynote of interest when needed.

Unfortunately, today was different because his 'organized mess' was in disarray. Someone has clearly been rummaging through his papers.

"Why? What are they looking for in my notes?"

Lares had a clear view of Shepard's office from his desk. Suddenly, he noticed that his office seemed unusually busy. There were three individuals in suits with their backs to him in deep conversation with Shepard. The erratic arm waving and hand gestures were obviously expletive without speaking words. It was also rare to see Shepard's intimidating glass enclosed, spacious office door closed on any day.

The heated discussion in Shepard's office was short-lived. The men left as quickly as they arrived. Lares barely caught a glimpse of their faces, but all of them appeared in suits and ties. Government or attorneys, he thought to himself as he bolted towards Shepard's office.

"Hey chief. Do you have a minute to talk?"

Slumped over on his desk with his hands supporting his head, Shepard glanced up with a surprised look on his face.

"Lares, it's you."

"Yes chief. Are you ok?"

Shepard appeared confused and glowing red in the face. "I'm fine!"

Lares continued,

"I left something out in our earlier conversation. I believe I may be under some type of surveillance. I saw someone just now, more like a shadow of a person, as I was going to my car to retrieve my briefcase. This figure quickly disappeared before I could get a better look. I suspect it may be linked to my CDC question at the ED and morgue investigation."

Shepard was unusually quiet and kept staring at his desk, which revealed a vast array of disheveled documents.

This was not the chief I knew at that moment.

"Lares! If your imagination continues to consume your investigative skills on this story, I will replace it with a more factual one. Understand!"

"Yes sir. I will focus on clear, documented facts and leave the spooky shadows out."

"Fine but keep me totally and timely informed at every step of your investigation."

As he headed back to his office, Lares became convinced that this investigation was going to be one of his most challenging.

"Shepard has his marching orders, and I have my own. This one is big, and it may even be my Pulitzer prize story."

Monday, April 29, 4:35 P.M.
Federal Bureau of Investigation Headquarters
2901 Leon C Simon Drive
New Orleans

The agency formally assigned Special Agent Lawins as the lead agent on the pneumonia mortality cases of unknown cause. The FBI Director was expecting swift action and decisive results. Special Agent Lawins knew the weight of this investigation and was determined to uncover the source.

Special Agent Lawins thought the investigation was weakly suspicious about bioterrorism. A more likely possibility was an underlying religious motive involving New Orleans voodoo-hoodoo. Therefore, at this time, he decided not to involve Slogger Mortlake, Regional Director, Department of Homeland Security (DHS). He felt the FBI was more than capable of handling Queen Maia Revalue's voodoo-hoodoo.

Just then, his office phone rang.

"Lawins!"

It was the FBI field agent overseeing the New Orleans Jazz Fest.

"Sir. We are seeing nothing more than the usual cocaine dealings. However, I heard earlier today, Ochsner Medical Center admitted a couple of people who attended the festival on Thursday to the Intensive Care Unit. I do not have any other information. HIPAA, you know."

"I'm on it!" replied Special Agent Lawins as he slapped the phone down and fled for the door.

April 29, 6:12 P.M.
Ochsner Medical Center (OMC)
Intensive Care Unit (ICU)
1514 Jefferson Highway

New Orleans

Special Agent Lawins approached the ICU nursing station and flashed his badge, immediately grabbing the attention of the nurse on duty.

"I understand you have recently admitted two critical patients exhibiting pneumonia. I need to speak to the attending in charge."

"Yes, absolutely, Special Agent Lawins."

In reviewing the patient charts, she replied,

"That would be Dr. Yahara Hearne, DO, PhD, an infectious disease physician here at OMC. She is also the primary attending physician for both patients."

"Interesting. I'm not medical, but why is an ID specialist the primary healthcare provider rather than an internist or hospitalist?"

"I'm not sure, it seems unusual because ID is usually by consult. I can tell you that Dr. Hearne was also the consultant for the other unusual pneumonia cases this week. Unfortunately, all those patients' conditions deteriorated rapidly, and they subsequently expired."

"Let me page Dr. Hearne for you."

"Very intriguing", thought Special Agent Lawins.

"Special Agent Lawins. Dr. Hearne is seeing another patient, but she will be here shortly."

Just moments later, the overhead speakers blared, "Code blue, room 633. Code blue, room 633."

Special Agent Lawins abruptly moved aside as the medical staff flooded the room. He was only steps away from entering.

He glanced through the glass window and saw a team of doctors and nurses frantically performing CPR on a lifeless patient lying on the hospital bed. The doctors lifted the crash pads several times but did not provide resuscitation. Now he could see the team dispersing.

"I'm calling it at 7:07 P.M.", he could hear one doctor stating in an emphatic voice.

Another doctor raced past him and into the room with a

very concerned look on her face. Grabbing the chart and shaking her head. She muttered to herself,

"Not another one. What is going on in this city?"

"Special Agent Lawins." spoke Nurse Wilson as he was staring into the room.

"That is Doctor Hearne. She is the infectious disease physician you were asking about."

He strolled to the entrance of the patient's room and introduced himself to Dr. Hearne.

"I am FBI Special Agent Lawins. I need your medical expertise. It appears this patient may be another unfortunate victim?"

"Special Agent Lawins, this is another pneumonia case, and the patient has expired. We have seen more of these unusual cases recently. I've been called in as a consult on them. It is unusual at this time of the year to see critical pneumonia cases, especially where the very young or old are not involved."

"Dr. Hearne. Are you the primary caregiver or the consult on this case?"

"I suppose, the primary?" Dr. Hearne replied to Special Agent Lawins as she flipped through the patient's chart.

"I notice here in the chart that a Doctor Tod Firehall appears to be the primary physician in this case. I don't believe I've ever met that physician."

Dr. Hearne stepped out of the room and went to the nursing station to see if Dr. Firehall was on the medical staff.

Stepping back into the patient's room, she replied,

"No one knows Dr. Tod Firehall, which is quite unusual. He might be a new hospitalist or internal medicine doctor."

"Special Agent Lawins, would you mind accompanying me to the room of the other pneumonia patient that came in shortly after this 24-year-old male that just expired?"

"Lead the way, Dr. Hearne."

"This other patient is a 36-year-old female, that is also in a critical state.", Dr. Hearne explained as she was walking down the corridor to the other side of the ICU with Special Agent

Lawins.

Entering the room, Dr. Hearne quickly noticed that the patient was unresponsive. Dr. Hearne checked the IV pack and noticed that someone appeared to have tampered with it at the port site.

"How strange!"

Looking everywhere in the room, she also noticed that the medical chart for this patient was not to be found. She left the room and headed to check for the chart at the nursing station.

"Excuse me, do you have the chart for room 603?"

"No, Dr. Hearn, but Dr. Firehall was reviewing it earlier. Oh, there he is, walking down the hallway."

Special Agent Lawins overheard the conversation with Dr. Hearne and the nurse and quickly turned to follow Dr. Firehall.

Dr. Firehall noticed his approach and began pushing medicine and food carts and even shoved people behind him as he ran towards the sixth-floor exit.

Special Agent Lawins was quickly in pursuit.

Dr. Firehall made it to the exit door and ran frantically down the staircase, throwing his white coat behind him as he tried to escape.

Special Agent Lawins was now on the first floor and flung the street level exit door open, running into the street. Lawins scanned the busy street, searching for any sign of Dr. Firehall. Dr. Tod Firehall was nowhere to be found. He seemed to have vanished.

Special Agent Lawins immediately called his office, giving a full description of Dr. Tod Firehall, for immediate apprehension.

Returning to the ICU floor, he found Dr. Hearne writing notes into the patient's chart. He realized he missed all the action because this patient also expired while he was chasing Dr. Firehall.

Dr. Hearn informed Special Agent Lawins that she had another urgent case and had to leave. However, she mentioned that this patient appeared to have died from a heart attack.

"An autopsy will be more definitive, Special Agent Lawins.", she spoke as she ran down the hallway.

Special Agent Lawins raced back to his office in pursuit of information on the suspect, Dr. Tod Firehall. This could be the break he was looking for in the case.

Monday, April 29, 7:38 P.M.

FBI Headquarters

2901 Leon C Simon Drive

New Orleans

It was early evening, but Special Agent Lawins was determined to stay late at the office to gather as much information as possible on Dr. Tod Firehall.

He got a copy of the hospital video surveillance before leaving Ochsner Medical Center. The footage showed Dr. Firehall attempting to leave the hospital discreetly through a side exit. The facial evidence was perfect for face recognition software.

Searching the criminal database should reveal a hit. Not so, including several other databases, as well as Interpol.

He now presumed that alias Dr. Tod Firehall was a highly trained professional. He also suspected that an autopsy on the second patient would not reveal a natural cause of death, but a homicide.

"Of course. It all makes sense now.", he said out loud. "He is a ghost!"

# CHAPTER 8 - THE BREAKTHROUGH

Tuesday, April 30, 8:16 A.M.

Watkins & Swindon Medical Diagnostics, LLC (WSMD)

Mandeville, Louisiana

The lab was operating at warp speed, even at this early hour. Anyone walking through the massive hallways could feel the analytical power exuding from the vast array of medical instrumentation. It intensified with every step, like a crescendo in the most captivating scene of a Don Giovanni opera. Robotics whirred and pipettes clicked as technologists hurried to analyze the latest batch of samples.

Dr. Watkins and Dr. Swindon were in the main conference room with their staff, reviewing a mound of test results. These represented data and reports from testing the pneumonia victim's specimens. The nucleic acid sequencing methods in use employed complex algorithms using the most power-driven computers. They were tedious protocols, even with the use of the most sophisticated state-of-the-art instrumentation.

The world renown laboratory of Watkins & Swindon Medical Diagnostics, LLC (WSMD) achieved its notoriety by such groundbreaking molecular methods. Now it was the goal of the medical professionals at WSMD to finish the task.

Dr. Swindon stated,

"The answer lies within this voluminous amount of data. We possess the technology, the molecular expertise, and the vast investigative experience to assemble this molecular puzzle into the elusive picture. Let's do it!"

The two doctors and the team of professionals pored over the data, silently contemplating the implications of the findings.

Dr. Swindon stated it more bluntly,

"You know the old saying, it's like finding a needle in a haystack."

The data analysis presented them with an enormous list of microbes. It was a heroic undertaking to separate the potential pathogens from the harmless bystanders. Let alone finding the culprit causing the recent deaths. If it exists? The initial focus was to match the molecular test results with the autopsy and medical record findings. Potential pathogens associated with pneumonia will be first on the list, along with those known to cause meningoencephalitis.

The clock on the wall ticked loudly, incessantly, emphasizing the urgency of their task.

Dr. Watkins addressed the team.

"Finding a potential pathogen or pathogens in common with all victims would be ideal. He paused, allowing the weight of the situation to sink in before continuing. We need to act fast."

The team nodded in agreement, realizing the importance of narrowing down the list of potential pathogens to identify the root cause of the deaths. All evidence so far implicates a deadly microbe.

He continued,

"So far, the DNA of the specimens reveals bacteria that scientists would consider 'normal' in the human body."

"This DNA probably represents DNA fragments rather than live bacteria. Blood and CSF should be sterile. However, sterility implies dead microbes, but nucleic acid sequencing detects both dead and alive."

"Since nucleic acid sequencing methods can detect whole genomes or fragments of dead bacteria, viruses, or other microbes, many of these represent microbes destroyed by a healthy immune system. This is called innate immunity."

Dr. Watkins continued.

"We are finding DNA and RNA fragments that match various viral groups. Using such a sensitive technology, we expect to find these fragments."

The executive assistant bellowing an announcement over the intercom system interrupted the exhaustive data analysis:

"Dr. Watkins, you have a call on line 3."

Dr. Watkins excused himself and hurried to his office to take the call.

"Dr. Watkins, it's Dr. Whinnier. Some of the more sophisticated test results are back from the forensic lab for the autopsy specimens from the pneumonia patients."

"We now know why the toxicology on the blood and urine did not detect narcotics. The toxicology on the blood and urine did not detect any narcotics because they collected and tested the specimens too late in the course of illness."

"We discovered cocaine in the first four hair samples tested. We need to test the others, but my suspicion is that we will find it in all of them."

Dr. Watkins commented,

"Of course, the body eliminates cocaine from the blood and urine relatively quickly, but it can still be detected in hair for at least a month."

Dr. Swindon quickly sat up straight and interjected,

"This changes everything. There is a possibility that we are dealing with cocaine that is 'tainted'! Sniffing cocaine provides direct entry into the lungs along with any microbes."

"If it became contaminated with a microbe, such as a bacterium or virus. The microbe would then have direct access to the respiratory track."

Dr. Watkins added,

"A large gathering such as our world-famous festivals provides an ideal environment for using cocaine. Have you heard the saying in New Orleans, 'Laissez les bons temps rouler' (i.e., let the good times roll)? It would also explain the patient age range encountered."

Dr. Whinnier replied,

"Agreed. How is the testing coming along for the remaining samples?"

"It's a tedious process, but I will have some results for you later today. Talk later."

Dr. Watkins thought to himself.

"Now is it time to have a serious discussion with our friends at the FBI. I will let Dr. Whinnier handle that part for now. I'm sure their agents have contacted him, considering his reaction to our earlier discussion."

Tuesday, April 30, 11:14 A.M.

Federal Bureau of Investigation Headquarters

2901 Leon C Simon Drive

New Orleans

FBI Agent Sanchez greeted Dr. Whinnier as he entered the FBI headquarters. The metal detector beeped as Dr. Whinnier passed through the intimidating horseshoe structure. Wanding him recovered a lost pen from his shirt pocket. He was visibly nervous.

Dr. Whinnier arrived at a conference room in the bustling headquarters, where Special Agent Lawins greeted him.

"Dr. Whinnier. I'm glad you could make it. Please, have a seat."

"I understand from our phone conversation that cocaine use is now on the table for the pneumonia deaths."

"Yes, but not for all the victims yet."

"Pneumonia followed by death from cocaine. Really?"

Dr. Whinnier replied in a subservient tone of voice,

"The medical record evidence is pointing to cocaine use as a contributing factor. Probably acting as a vehicle for introducing an infectious agent. Dr. Watkins is working on that part."

"That's all for now, doctor. Agent Sanchez will show you out."

Dr. Whinnier left the conference room with a sense of unease.

Clearly disturbed by the involvement of Dr. Watkins in the

case, Special Agent Lawins snatched his coat and hurried out of the office.

Tuesday, April 30, 1:34 P.M.

Watkins & Swindon Medical Diagnostics, LLC

Mandeville, Louisiana

Special Agent Lawins stepped into the bustling laboratory building, the tension from the earlier meeting lingering in his mind. He flashed his credentials to the receptionist, and the receptionist escorted him to Dr. Watkins' office.

Both Doctors' Watkins and Swindon sat waiting for him, looking rather nervous.

"Please, have a seat, Special Agent Lawins," said Dr. Watkins.

"What part of our meeting earlier was not clear? There is to be no undermining on my watch. Understand!"

In a somewhat calm retort, Dr. Watkins replied,

"We were invited and accepted this case by the New Orleans Department of Health, specifically by the Director, Dr. Whinnier. This is not our first case consultation with the New Orleans PHL, as you probably already know. How about a truce and a public-private sharing of information?"

Special Agent Lawins sighed and looked at the two doctors, considering their offer.

"This comes with strict conditions. First, I know what you know immediately, along with Dr. Whinnier. Second, any obstruction and the deal's off. Agreed!"

"What will you share with us to support our findings?"

"Whatever I can, if it is not classified."

"Agreed," replied Dr. Watkins and Dr. Swindon.

"You already know about the cocaine." We are still analyzing the samples at the lab to get concrete results, and once we have them, we will inform all parties."

"What can you share with us, Special Agent Lawins?"

Special Agent Lawins replied,

"We have a suspect under surveillance. A voodoo-hoodoo practitioner that is suspicious, but not even probable cause currently for a search warrant."

Special Agent Lawins thought for a moment as he was leaving the office, and added,

"However, we believe she might be involved in the deaths."

Dr. Watkins replied.

"Yes sir. As soon as we have more answers."

Dr. Swindon remarked,

"The voodoo practitioner may be involved in the distribution of the tainted cocaine. If the cocaine is tainted, the voodoo practitioner may be involved in its distribution."

"This is becoming more intriguing by the minute, but how does it all fit?" Dr. Watkins thought to himself.

A loud knocking on the glass door of the office startled both. It was one of the technical assistants.

"You have to see this!"

# CHAPTER 9 - WHAT ABOUT AFRICA?

Tuesday, April 30, 1:46 P.M.
Watkins & Swindon Medical Diagnostics, LLC (WSMD)
Mandeville, Louisiana

Special Agent Lawins, as if by habit, looked back at the glass enclosed office of Dr. Watkins as he departed. He noticed a definite exuberance in the mannerism of the technical assistant as she addressed the two doctors with papers waving in the air.

"It could be the break we need in this case. No doubt this will be an interesting day," he thought as he reached for his cell phone to make a call.

"Starters. Any update on the Maia Revalue surveillance?"

"No sir. The only oddity was candlelight glowing in the late evening hours. I would have expected lamp lighting in the house. It's probably not unusual considering the voodoo-hoodoo cultural beliefs."

"Possibly? How about some photo surveillance? Cautiously, of course."

"Tried it. The curtain sheers blurred the digital photos to the point of being unrecognizable."

"Understood. Call if anything changes."

As he hung up the phone, Special Agent Lawins felt a niggling sense of unease at the lack of progress on the Maia Revalue surveillance.

"I still believe we will find probable cause. I can just feel it!" Special Agent Lawins thought to himself.

Meanwhile, back in Dr. Watkins office.

He captured several papers in midair that were waved in front of him by the technical assistant. She was excited with the newly found data.

"Thank you, Ashley. That's all for now."

Quickly perusing the documents, Dr. Watkins could see patterns emerging in the data, but something about it felt elusive, like puzzle pieces not quite fitting together.

Turning to Dr. Swindon, he remarked,

"This sequencing report shows quite an impressive list of microbes. There are many that I am not familiar with at all. No wonder Ashley was so excited."

"Bacteria, viruses and even parasites? How bizarre is that Dr. Swindon?"

He handed the report over to Dr. Swindon.

Following the words on each page of the detailed report with her finger as a guide, she snapped.

"You're not kidding. This is wild. Please allow me a minute more to absorb the details of the results."

"I am speechless! Look at this bacterium, Geobacillus thermoglucosidasius. Haven't run across this one ever. No doubt by the name, it is a heat loving, thermophilic bacterium. The Big Easy is humid, but this bacterium could probably survive in one of the hot geysers at Yellowstone."

"As we say in New Orleans, the data reports at this point are just 'gumbo ya-ya' until we unravel the mysteries of this case."

"That's hilarious, Dr. Swindon. Now, that's the spirit...so off we go!"

Tuesday, April 30, 3:24 P.M.

FOX 8 WVUE TV Station Studios

1025 South Norman C. Francis Pkwy

New Orleans

Jenna Samps, FOX 8 TV meteorologist, was always in love with the weather. Her passion for weather started at a young age and continued to grow throughout her life, shaping her career and bringing her to FOX 8 TV in New Orleans.

Even when a 'big game' was interrupted with a brief weather alert, Jenna, one of those captivating southern gals, could calm even the most extreme sports fanatic.

Everyone knew Jenna for her cheerful demeanor and in-depth weather forecasts, as she was tall, blond, attractive, and always sported her signature smile with flickering blue eyes. She was the indisputable "TV weather goddess" of New Orleans.

There she sat, mesmerized by the multimillion-dollar weather program starring her in the face on her triple-screen displays. She realized there were only a couple of hours remaining to prepare for the evening broadcast, but she was use to the rush. She thrived on it, sometimes finishing within seconds of airtime.

Her focus on the 'Special Topic' tonight would be on the trendy, air quality report. Meteorology was her college major, but she also had a minor in both atmospheric chemistry and physics. Her keen expertise in meteorology, combined with her love for the weather, paved the way for her success in delivering comprehensive and insightful forecasts. No doubt, New Orleans had attracted the best.

In tonight's prime-time report, Jenna would describe a massive dust cloud that was overlaying the greater New Orleans area. Her exhaustive research and expertise led her to believe that this massive pollutant appeared to exhibit the same characteristics as the one in the summer of 2017. However, there was a difference. Today's dust cloud had arrived much earlier this year.

In 2017, the dust cloud had caused widespread respiratory issues and reduced visibility, so Jenna was concerned about the same potential impact. The obvious question, could the source of today's dust cloud be identical to the 2017 massive pollutant? Could this be another Sahara dust storm, or possibly a new, unknown source?

Jenna's mind raced with questions as she prepared her report, her extensive background in chemistry and physics giving her unique insights. As she sat down to compile her findings, she couldn't help but wonder if this new dust cloud was just the beginning of a series of environmental challenges. The national weather service formally listed the dust cloud as a Sahara dust storm based on satellite evidence.

"What a great time to be the hottest meteorologist in this fine city of New Orleans," she thought to herself.

"Ms. Samps, twenty minutes to airtime.", proclaimed Hal, the Production Assistant.

Scurrying off to makeup with papers in hand, she was again taunting the final countdown to airtime.

It's five, four, three, two and one, spoken softer with each numeral and climaxing to a whisper at one, along with a solitary finger targeting Jenna. She took a deep breath, adjusted her posture, and faced the camera.

"Where Y'At New Orleans! Awrite, and now for the weather." Spoke Jenna Samps as she gracefully pointed to the virtual weather map on her left side. As if in a Russian ballet, she performed her magic weather song and dance, then delivered the special report to her mesmerized audience.

"Springtime, in our fine city, is a little darker recently during the day because of an unusually dense dust cloud traveling through our area. The general term used for this event according to the national weather service is the 'Sahara dust storm'. As the name implies, its origin is the Sahara Desert in North Africa. Historically, this is like the one that appeared on July 4, 2017, in our fine city, but it has arrived much earlier this year."

"What ya need to do is watch for our special alerts. If you have respiratory or heart problems, stay indoors until the air is clear. Thanks for watching, New Orleans."

Jenna concluded her weather report with a warm smile, her eyes conveying reassurance to the viewers. As the camera panned away, Jenna made her way out of the studio and down the bustling hallway towards her office.

"Why is this earlier this year? According to the satellite maps, it also appears to be quite extensive, and could last, for weeks, if not longer." Jenna thought to herself.

As she pondered the unusual early arrival and extended duration of the Sahara dust storm, Jenna couldn't help but feel a sense of unease, to the point of grave concern.

Tuesday, April 30, 6:32 P.M.

Watkins & Swindon Medical Diagnostics, LLC (WSMD)

Mandeville, Louisiana

Dr. Watkins was the last to leave the conference room, looking back at stacks of documents and glowing computer screens. The brightly lit room suddenly turned dark as the automatic system sensed everyone departed from the area. Walking back towards his office, he could hear conversations about a weather report and concern for some type of approaching storm front.

"Excuse me, Dr. Ying. What is this? I'm hearing about a storm?"

"Oh, Dr. Watkins. Good evening. Everyone is talking about a special weather report by Jenna Samps at FOX 8 WVUE TV. There is a Sahara dust storm developing in the greater New Orleans area. Looks like special alerts will be forthcoming, depending on the severity of the dust storm."

"Really? I'm not an expert on meteorology, but why the big deal?"

"She talked about a similar event in 2017, and how it had impacted certain health conditions in some people by the sheer density of the cloud."

"I remember that Sahara dust storm back in 2017, Dr. Ying. It was not pleasant!"

The phenomenon caught the attention of both doctors as they continued discussing the potential health implications of the incoming dust storm.

"Thanks Dr. Ying."

Dr. Watkins quickly turned about and headed back to the conference room in a frenzy. The lights illuminated the entire room as he targeted one of the computer terminals, sat, and pulled up data on the previous Sahara dust storm.

"Amazing!", as he read site after site on the web

with accelerating interest, about this remarkable, natural phenomenon. The more he read, the more he realized the potential impact on public health, prompting him to dig deeper into the research for clues about the current cases.

Grabbing a nearby pen, he took notes the old fashion way on a nearby legal pad.

He pieced together snippets of information that may be important in solving the current pneumonia cases. The checklist notes were exhaustive.

Winds disperse several billion tons of mineral dust from arid and semi-arid areas of the world globally every year.

The main hotspots are in North Africa, comprising 50 to 70% of the global dust.

This dust reaches remote areas of the world: North America, South America, Europe, and the Middle East.

It mostly occurs during the spring and summer, but there is even documentation of wintertime dust.

The smaller particles travel the longest distance. If this particulate matter crosses the Atlantic, we are looking at about 5000 miles (ca. 8,047 km).

Dr. Watkins talked to himself, "...so many questions, but it is possible that we may have microbes tagging along with this mineral dust that could be pathogenic or even opportunistic?"

"If so, are they alive when they reach their destination?"

"They would also have to be small enough to tagalong at that distance?"

He continued to sift through the notes, searching for any potential clues that could shed light on the mysterious pneumonia cases.

"Why only a handful of patients when this dust storm is everywhere? It could be sporadic right now, since it is the beginning of this Sahara dust storm. Where does the cocaine fit in? Again, more questions than answers."

"Yes, computers are always slow," he mumbled to himself as he frantically searched the web for links between dust clouds and human illness.

"Voilà, there it is, evidence of the link between dust and human disease."

It was a recently published article, a meta-analysis, revealing dust related microbiomes and human disease. The paper compilation provided evidence for pathogens and opportunists being carried by desert dust clouds. They caused pneumonia, respiratory tract infections, COVID-19 infections, tuberculosis, and even a fungal infection, coccidioidomycosis.

The staggering implications pointed to the potential for the dust storm to spread a wide range of illnesses beyond what had currently been identified.

"I have to call Dr. Swindon right now."

Leaving the conference room and heading towards the elevator, he called Dr. Swinton on her cell phone and left an urgent message.

"I don't know if you listened to the local weather report on FOX 8 WVUE TV tonight, but we are expecting another 2017-like Sahara dust storm. We may have an answer for our sequencing data, which could help us understand this series of pneumonia deaths. This could be groundbreaking!"

In the parking lot next to the laboratory building, and unbeknown to Dr. Watkins, was a black sedan parked in the shadows with a suspicious onlooker. His telephoto camera targeted Dr. Watkins, every move as he entered his car and drove away.

# CHAPTER 10 - FIFOLET

Wednesday, May 1, 6:00 A.M.

Dr. Tombak Watkins residence

St. Charles Avenue and Tulane University of Louisiana neighborhood

The preset alarm woke Tombak precisely at 6 A.M., resembling the sound of Zydeco music booming over a Harman Kardon speaker.

"Beats that old bell.", he muttered aloud as he arose and prepared for his morning ritual, joined by his faithful companion, Corona. He greeted the morning with a stretch and a yawn as Corona wagged her tail, anticipating a playful day.

It was a long night for him with his on-line research of the Sahara Dust Storm. Thankfully, his sacrifice of sleep allowed him to gather enough background information on the topic to spark a fruitful discussion with Dr. Swindon and colleagues at the lab this morning.

A piece of buttered toast and a hardy cup of strong, black chicory coffee were for breakfast after a quick shower. Of course, Corona received her morning breakfast as well, before the dog walker arrived.

Eileen rang the doorbell and retrieved Corona with a hardy smile and open arms.

"Off you go, girl. Be a good girl and I'll see you soon. Thanks, Eileen."

Tombak gathered his printed documents, shut down his computer, and searched around his desk area for his briefcase.

"Found it!", but the computer screen was still brightly lit.

"That's odd. I must have tapped the wrong keys."

The second attempt worked, but it took a few minutes. It

was a new computer, and it took some getting used to for now.

He secured the house and locked all the doors before finally heading out for the lab.

Wednesday, May 1, 7:28 A.M.

Watkins & Swindon Medical Diagnostics, LLC (WSMD)

Mandeville, Louisiana

Upon arrival at the lab, Dr. Watkins met his colleagues who had already immersed themselves in their work.

As he headed down the brightly illuminated corridor towards the densely packed conference room, he noticed that Dr. Swindon displayed visible signs of distress. She was fiercely tapping on the computer keyboard, to no avail.

Quietly entering the room, he peered from behind her and saw a frozen, flashing computer screen. One by one, others in the room encountered the same phenomenon.

"All computers off! Now!"

"Call anybody in communications. Move!" shouted Dr. Watkins.

"The backups are also not responding," Dr. Swindon reported, her fingers flying across her phone screen as she dialed the IT department.

Minutes later, the entire floor was on backup power lighting, and the screens were dark. The remaining floors appeared unaffected, except for the computer network. Someone had breached multiple firewalls.

Separate circuits and firewalls secured every floor, all containment rooms, and most of the instrumentation as protection from such an event.

"Why only this floor and the computer network? Asked Dr. Watkins, directing his question to Vicky, director of the IT department."

"Dr. Watkins, I don't have an answer yet, but this was the handiwork of a very sophisticated hacker. This is one of a handful in an elite group."

Vicky emphasized the need to isolate and counter their attack quickly while monitoring her team's efforts to regain control.

"While IT is investigating the problem, let's continue reviewing the paper backup documents, but first...." Said Dr. Watkins.

"We seem to have a Sahara dust storm passing through our fine city, as reported by our own Jenna Samps at FOX 8 WVUE TV last evening. I believe our dust sequencing results may be that of Sahara dust."

"And if that's true," Dr. Watkins pondered, "it could have significant implications for our ongoing cases."

"I spent a considerable amount of time last night searching the literature and the Web for evidence. Today, I want everyone to focus on analyzing the sequence data for the microbe list. Hopefully, a good match in the microbial data will provide credible evidence of the dust originating from the Sahara."

"Why do we care about the dust from the Sahara? It might explain the particulate matter found in the autopsies from the diseased lung tissue specimens. If we dig far enough into the sequencing data, we could identify the infectious agent or agents contributing to these horrific deaths."

"Let's see if there are any correlations between recent health records and potential pathogens that may have been brought in by the dust storm."

Vicky was out in the hallway, tapping on the conference room glass door to attract Dr. Watkins' attention.

Gently nudging the door a bit, she said,

"You're back on-line and the firewalls are back up and safe. We are still working on the cause and any fallout from the intrusion, but I will keep you updated."

Dr. Watkins nodded, grateful for Vicky's diligence.

Turning to Dr. Swindon, he asked, "How do you think cocaine fits into this picture?"

"I believe the process could introduce a lethal infectious agent directly into the respiratory system of a cocaine user by snorting cocaine from a flat surface that may contain Sahara dust from the atmosphere."

Dr. Watkins remarked,

"This is a logical and workable explanation, but where is the origin of the infectious agent? Is it in the cocaine or in the Sahara dust? If it's in the cocaine, do we have a contamination by the drug dealer or a deliberate introduction of a lethal agent, for nefarious intent? Likewise, if it's in the Sahara dust, is it a natural event, or possibly some new, unrecognized form of bioterrorism?"

Dr. Swindon abruptly hurled her body from her chair and shouted,

"Oh, my God, if you're right, this could have unforeseen consequences for massive death tolls!"

Wednesday, May 1, 10:13 A.M.

Federal Bureau of Investigation Headquarters

2901 Leon C Simon Drive

New Orleans

There was a whirlwind of activity in the FBI offices this morning following the local news media reporting the series of pneumonia deaths in the city with an unknown cause. Each media source had their interpretation of the findings. The word "bioterrorism" mentioned by some reporters had quickly alarmed the Director of the FBI, who immediately called for an emergency meeting with the city's top officials.

"Lawins!" shouted the Director. "A word in my office. Now!"

"The news is fresh on the trail of the pneumonia deaths, and they want an answer. Now a couple of reporters are mentioning bioterrorism. I am under pressure, and I must hold an emergency meeting with the mayor and other officials this morning."

"Have we included Homeland in any remote chance of a bioterrorism event yet?

"No, sir, we didn't." Looking at the evidence so far, I can't see how a bioterrorism event is possible. As you know, we have a couple of persons-of-interest under surveillance, Queen Maia, and drug lord Nacket. As mentioned in my report, the DEA asked me to stand down on Nacket, and we need a stronger case to establish probable cause for Queen Maia."

"I'm awaiting the autopsy report on the latest victim at Ochsner. I suspect this may be a murder by the escaped suspect."

"Lawins, I will downplay the bioterrorism for now, but I hope you're right. That's all."

Walking back to his office, Special Agent Lawins thought to himself,

"I know I'm right. I damn well need that probable cause of Queen Maia, and now!"

He glanced at the evidence board in his office, determined to find the missing piece that would incriminate Queen Maia. This is the last week of the Jazz Fest this weekend, but he would like to avoid any further victims if possible. He thought,

"Even with the surveillance on Queen Maia, she must know we're following her every move, and she may not act again. The other possibility is that she is innocent and believes in a voodoo-hoodoo spell that someone else is possibly orchestrating for her. The got away at the hospital is involved, and he may even be a part of some drug scheme with drug lord Nacket?"

Special Agent Lawins thoughts were suddenly interrupted by a phone call.

"Lawins."

"This is Dr. Catechin. I have the autopsy report on the 36-year-old female from Ochsner. Interesting report. She had findings consistent with the other cases of pneumonia, but her death was because of cardiac arrest, cause unknown. I'm not saying that she wouldn't have died from the pneumonia, but maybe her respiratory system and the overwhelming infection may have caused the cardiac arrest? Another possibility is that the trace of cocaine found in her urine could have contributed to her death."

"Dr. Catechin. Your autopsy report is more than interesting. It is exactly as I expected. Thanks for the call."

Special Agent Lawins quickly arranged a meeting with his team to share the findings. At the end of the debriefing, he added,

"Keep the surveillance going on Queen Maia and Nacket. I have this gut feeling that they are involved, someway, somehow. Anything, and I mean anything, out of the ordinary for these two, I want you to call me immediately."

"Is there any information on the alias Dr. Tod Firehall yet?"

Agent Collins replied,

"We ran the facial image through every database we have access to. Nothing. We're onto our confidential informants (CIs), and it's only a matter of time. My feeling is we're talking about a 'ghost'."

Special Agent Lawins replied,

"I agree. Collins, I need the real name of alias Firehall today. Understand!"

"Yes, sir."

Wednesday, May 1, 8:43 P.M.
Queen Maia Revalue residence
St. Roch neighborhood
New Orleans

Queen Maia sat peacefully in front of her exquisitely adorned voodoo-hoodoo altar, with both of her arms firmly propped in the finely woven Watton armchair. Both eyes were closed as she sat motionless, meditating over this weekend's last spell. She realized that both the FBI and drug lord Nacket would most likely be following her every move at the Jazz Fest. This was not an obstacle to her plan because she would always have the protection of Bon Dieu, the saints, and her ancestors.

Parked at a short distance from Queen Maia's house was a black sedan hidden in the darkness of a nearby tree with two occupants. The reflected light from a cell phone revealed a man with a well-manicured mustache and dark, burley eyebrows in the passenger seat. The driver was an attractive, red-headed woman sporting an emotionless, as if frozen in time, facial expression.

"It's almost nine o'clock, and we're still seeing a dim light in the house and not the usual flickering candlelight. Every night, like clockwork, the lights go off at 8:30 and the candles are lit. Something is not right. I think we need to inspect." Said FBI Agent Thomas to his partner, Agent O'Riley.

They carefully approached the house in separate directions, signaling each other using only hand gestures in the dimly lit front yard. Agent Thomas covered the front door, while Agent O'Riley peered in the window through the narrow opening of the delicate sheers.

There she sat in the dim room light, Queen Maia. Motionless, as if in a meditating state or some type of trance. Her posture in the chair was perfect, almost as if she were deliberately posing for a portrait.

"How odd," Agent O'Riley thought to herself as she hand-signaled Agent Thomas to knock on the front door.

He knocked three times somewhat forcefully. There was no response, and Agent O'Riley shook her head, showing Queen Maia showed no response. Again, he knocked three times more forcefully while saying,

"FBI, Queen Maia. Open the door!"

Again, Agent O'Riley shook her head.

"Queen Maia, we are coming in. Stay where you are and don't move."

The two agents cautiously entered her house, one by one, after unlocking the door. She was still motionless in her chair as the "All clear." from the agents secured the house.

Agent O'Riley approached Queen Maia cautiously and noticed her eyes were closed and her body was rigid.

"Queen Maia, can you hear me?" No response, so she checked for a pulse.

"She is dead."

The words hung heavy in the air, sending a chill down Agent O'Riley's spine.

"Call it in, Thomas, and I'll start securing the area."

Wednesday, May 1, 9:54 P.M.
Watkins & Swindon Medical Diagnostics, LLC (WSMD)
Mandeville, Louisiana
It was a late night for everyone at the Lab, including Dr. Watkins and Dr. Swindon. The team was coming close to compiling an extensive list of the microbes found in the particulate matter from the autopsy specimen sequencing data.

Vicki was also frantically working with her team on the IT issue and the identity of the unknown hacker. It was paramount that she located a source and the extent of the intrusion as quickly as possible.

Dr. Watkins was in deep thought when his cell phone vibrated. A quick glance told him it was Special Agent Lawins from the FBI.

"Dr. Watkins, I have good news and bad news. It's possible that we have a break in the case, which is good news. The bad news is that two of our agents found our prime suspect, Queen Maia, dead in her house. The crime scene is currently being processed. We will process most of the evidence at Quantico, but I will send you a couple of items for your state-of-the-art sequencing".

"Special Agent Lawins, this is very disturbing. Do you have any other information you can share with me?"

"No but keep your cell phone nearby." And he hung up.

Dr. Watkins garnered the immediate attention of the team and spoke,

"The FBI discovered that the prime suspect in the case was dead in her home. We were told that we will receive a couple of pieces of evidence for sequencing, and that is about all."

Vicky deflected his attention, tapping on the glass door to the conference room. Waving her hand was a definite signal that she has new information. Dr. Watkins returned the gesture for her to enter the room.

"Dr. Watkins and Dr. Swindon. I believe we have found the root cause of the breach. First, I need to ask Dr. Watkins a quick question."

"Yes, of course Vicky, please proceed unless it is confidential?"

"Dr. Watkins, did you notice anything out of the ordinary on your home office computer within the last 24 hours?"

"Nothing unusual, only a little difficulty in shutting down my laptop before leaving home. Is that a problem?"

"Normally, it is not an issue. However, we traced the breach back to your neighborhood and specifically to the IP address of your laptop."

"I had no idea that my computer was compromised."

"Whoever was involved in the intrusion is an extremely knowledgeable hacker, and the person has access to highly sophisticated equipment. Our multiple layers of firewall did not prevent the breach. I believe we have it under control now, but everyone needs to be acutely aware of anything unusual and overly diligent."

"Now for the most shocking news. We painfully traced the source of the breach to a government agency, NSA."

Dr. Watkins eyes widened, and his head slowly shook.

"I believe this case got a lot more challenging now that the government is involved."

Wednesday, May 1, 10:38 P.M.

Deep in the Louisiana Bayou

Ascension Parish

Gonzalez, Louisiana

There are three million acres of marshland in Louisiana. Some say that the human eyes have not seen a substantial portion of this marshland.

Gonzalez remains hidden deep in the Louisiana bayou and the bayou is filled with folklore. The Cajun culture in the Louisiana bayou nurtures a deep appreciation of the amazing tales passed down to the born and bred residents. This is best portrayed by the 'swamp fairies' or 'feu follet or fifolet'.

The history of fifolet dates to the mid-1,700's and the migration of Acadian, Catholic families from persecution by the British. Cajuns are the designation given to these migrants, who now live in Louisiana.

According to the folklore, people saw the fifolet at a distance in the swampland and described them as glowing orbs or dancing candle flames. Parents warned their children not to follow these "swamp fairies" or "fifolet" into the swamp because they would never return.

So, what is the fifolet? Can it be the peace-loving ancestors visiting and possibly bringing with them good fortune? Just the opposite may also be true, an evil force setting a trap in the swamp, leading to one's own demise. What does it mean when you observe the fifolet?

The belief in the supernatural is an integral part of the Cajun culture, passed down from generation to generation. Folklore or credible premonition, it is as real as one's own belief.

Rafael Nacket found that the Gonzalez bayou was the ideal location for a stash house. This desolate location served as the perfect place for safe packaging and storing his cocaine contraband. Swampland, where every natural sound was familiar and any deviation from the norm surrounded it, could show intruders. No Wi-Fi camera could do a better job.

Nacket felt safe with his henchmen, observing the dark swamp under the starry sky with insects serenading.

Then it appeared in the distance. The fifolet, glowing and flickering in the distance, as if challenging him to follow. At first, he thought it was a reflection from the airboat in the distant dock. Somewhat horrified by the sight, he screamed aloud,

"Fifolet, fifolet,"

It disappeared as quickly as it appeared. Two of his bodyguards ran to him at the sound of his voice with their semiautomatic weapons drawn,

"Rafael, where!"

"Stand down boys, it is only a gator!"

Inside, Nacket was terrified at the thought of something bad was going to happen.

Just then, the sound of his cellphone startled him, ringing. It was an 'unknown caller'.

He answered the call but remained silent. A broken voice at the other end said,

"S...is dead...now...beware."

The caller hung up.

# CHAPTER 11 - MORE THAN DRUGS

Thursday, May 2, 7:28 A.M.

New Orleans Tribune

2317 Esplanade Avenue

The news that Maia Revalue, the most respected voodoo-hoodoo queen in New Orleans, had been discovered dead in her house last evening was buzzing in the Tribune office. Lares, along with an entourage of reporters and camera crews from other media outlets, was at the scene last night. Even with his exceptional news reporting skill, he could only find out scanty information on the circumstances of her death. His usual contacts at the local police headquarters and even the FBI were of very little use.

"How unusual. They are lacking credible evidence at this point or withholding information on a need-to-know basis only for law-enforcement personnel." Lares thought to himself.

Some witnesses claimed to have seen a mysterious figure leaving her house around the time of her death. The exact details of the description of the mysterious person were relatively sketchy, but the witnesses seemed credible and consistent in describing a tall, middle-aged white man with dark clothing. One witness mentioned, seeing a small bluish, red-colored skin discoloration on the back of the man's neck. The witness claimed it could have been a small tattoo or a birthmark. A facial description was not clear, except for his dark-colored hair with streaks of gray.

Deep in thought, Lares mulled over the information he had gathered. He realized he was probably being observed by the overhead camera that he found in his office earlier. Therefore, he deliberately shuffled papers and notes as a distraction for the intruder. Even better, he could go across to Shepard's office and see if he could extract any more information from his editor-in-chief.

Lares finished tidying his desk, making sure every document was inconspicuous and unnoticed by the camera lens. He pushed back the chair from his desk. He loved that chair. The wheels made him feel like he was in a race car. That's why he often inadvertently bumped into the bookcase behind him. Off he walked to Shepard's office, thinking how he would approach him with the opening discourse.

Shepherd noticed Lares coming down the hallway and waved him in as he peered through the massive glass doors. He had an obvious look of concern on his face as Lares began pacing in front of his desk.

"Sit down Lares! Stop the incessant pacing and tell me what's on your mind."

Lares used this tactic regularly with Shepard, hoping to find out more information on a case that he might've missed, and Shepard may have unknowingly withheld.

"I'll get right to the point. Do you think Maia Revalue could've been a target for some person or organization? Could her death be a homicide?"

Shepard appeared visibly nervous as he answered,

"Wow! Do you have any evidence supporting the claim?"

"I would like to know if you think that is actually possible?"

"A meteor destroying the earth is possible, climate change is possible, but I think you're reaching on this one, Lares."

"I'll get myself to work on evidence," Lares murmured under his breath, his mind racing with ideas.

He then noticed a business card by Shepard's phone with the address, 1515 Poydras. Other information on the card was not legible because some paperwork on his desk was obstructing his view.

"Thanks boss. Just thinking out loud, and I thought I'd run some ideas past you."

Lares told himself, "The next stop is to check out 1515 Poydras."

Thursday, May 2, 8:00 A.M.

Queen Maia Revalue residence

St. Roch neighborhood

New Orleans

The scene at Queen Maia's house was one of busy activity, with police officers cordoning off the area and reporters clamoring for any information they could get. Special Agent Lawins was in charge. The New Orleans Police Department (NOPD) officers were under his jurisdiction as the ranking officer of the FBI.

The bright yellow 'Police Line - Do Not Cross' barrier tape was secured by an officer. It surrounded the landscape and the house like a sprawling, yellow python, ready to strike any trespasser. The officials declared the area a potential crime scene and secured it. The FBI assumed jurisdiction because of Maia Revalue, their 'person-of-interest' of Interest' in an alleged mass murder case.

Homicide Detective Shaky Ottavino was first on the scene from the NOPD. The FBI summoned his presence, along with other officers, at Detective Ottavino's discretion, because of the suspicious nature of the victim's death.

Detective Ottavino was one of NOPD's most decorated officers. His case success rate rivals even the best homicide detectives from San Francisco or New York. He always followed the evidence and made no assumptions that were not borne out in hard, credible facts. He often portrays a nice guy persona when interrogating suspects but could come down on them with forceful rhetoric.

The FBI agent leading the investigation gestured for Detective Ottavino to join him near the house.

Detective Ottavino slowly walked toward Special Agent Lawins, meticulously scrutinizing the landscape along his path for any potential evidence that might be useful in the case.

"Detective. I understand you were born and raised in

New Orleans. I would very much value your thoughts on this unfortunate scene. Would you share with me what you know about Maia Revalue?"

"Dat for sure. Aint kidding. A little New Orleans slang, Special Agent Lawins."

"I appreciate the humor, detective, but can we get serious?"

"Absolutely. I'm always willing to support our fellow brother officers. Let's agree that we have a mutual understanding of sharing the evidence in this case. I know the heartbeat of the Big Easy and I love this city. Agree?"

"Detective Ottavino, it will be a pleasure working with you. Just keep in mind who makes the calls."

"Understood. Now, back to your original question about Maia Revalue."

"Almost everyone in New Orleans knows Queen Maia. She is quite a celebrity among the voodoo-hoodoo crowd and often outspoken at Congo Square gatherings. From what I've heard, she earns reverence for her good deeds in the practice of the voodoo-hoodoo religion. Queen Maia has been a controversial yet influential figure in New Orleans for years. By this, I mean she could have also practiced black magic, but I am not aware of cases brought forward to the NOPD."

Special Agent Lawins expressed a great deal of interest in Detective Ottavino's comments. He was especially alert with an inquisitive facial expression at the mention of 'black magic'.

"Why the interest? Are you just searching for background information, special agent?"

"Just trying to put all the pieces together for this investigation."

"Interesting. Join me inside, detective!"

Detective Ottavino entered the crime scene, his sharp eyes scanning the room for any clues. He was very familiar with the voodoo-hoodoo decor and rituals surrounding the practice of this blend of religion and magic. Despite the strict confidentiality of the traditions among family members, each practitioner typically follows a common thread. This always serves as the guiding compass in these cases for Detective Ottavino.

Within moments, Detective Ottavino spotted an intricately carved amulet hidden beneath a floorboard. He carefully removed the amulet by its chain, using a pen from his shirt pocket. Hidden beneath the amulet, he uncovered two other objects; a small, ancient-looking vessel and a petite flannel bag, secured by a raggedy cord. By its bulky appearance, the bag obviously contained something.

"Special Agent Lawins. Chop chop. I found some items that may be of great interest in the case."

"I'm coming!" Special Agent Lawins called out as he hurried into the room, his gaze immediately drawn to the amulet and the exquisitely designed vessel.

"Well, what do we have here? Does it appear to be some type of contraband? There was definitely a good reason for hiding these. Safekeeping? Maybe even an attempt at hiding evidence?"

"Special Agent Lawins, I believe we have discovered paraphernalia used in the practice of black magic. This makes perfect sense, considering the voodoo-hoodoo altar and the plethora of articles found throughout this house so far."

"Indeed, detective, it makes perfect sense," frowned Special Agent Lawins.

Detective Ottavino commented they would need to conduct further investigation to determine if these items are connected to any recent incidents.

The look on Special Agent Lawins face was priceless. His look fulfilled the intent of the classic saying, 'the cat that swallowed the canary.'

Detective Ottavino did not totally trust the FBI. Experience taught him it was relatively common practice to withhold information from the NOPD. When you ask why, your reply is usually, 'It's on a need-to-know basis.' This really caused his 'blood to boil' every time he heard it. Lucky for him, he was always quick enough to spot a cover-up and abruptly confront it head-on.

"Tell me something, Special Agent Lawins, can you share with me why and how long you have considered Maia Revalue as a "person-of-interest"?"

"I beg of you, please don't tell me, 'It's on a need-to-know'. Communication is crucial for us to work together effectively."

After a lengthy pause, and with a very stern look on his face, Special Agent Lawins replied.

"You are pretty ballsy and direct, detective! I like that attitude."

"Maia Revalue is a person-of-interest in the pneumonia deaths that have recently plagued our fine city. I can share some information with you, but I need to verify other facts before discussing it further."

"Right now, it is time critical to process this fresh evidence and check the status of the autopsy being performed on Maia Revalue."

Detective Ottavino's suspicions deepened as Special Agent Lawins response confirmed his worst fears.

"Bet you, king muffin man (i.e., reference to a drug lord) is involved in this scene."

Thursday, May 2, 9:28 A.M.

1515 Poydras

New Orleans

1515 Poydras is a 29-story skyscraper residing in the Central Business District of New Orleans. Formerly known as the Gulf Building, it houses 24 office floors with a three-floor parking garage. The building offers an eclectic collection of client services, including legal services with attorneys, physician offices, news media services, and technical professional offices. It is in an ideal business location, residing within the vicinity of the greater New Orleans Biosciences Economic Development District (GNOBEDD) and near the infamous, 'Caesars Superdome.'

Lares entered the parking structure at 1515 Poydras, not

having a plan of action but knowing he had to play it cool. He then made his way to the main entrance and located the tenant's directories.

"There are at least 100 offices! What's the plan, Lares? Think! Surveillance, of course," he muttered to himself.

He located a cafe near the entrance to the building and found a suitable table, so he could observe anyone entering the building. He sat down and watched the flow of people coming in and out, keeping a close eye on anyone who seemed to resemble the witnesses' description.

It was near lunchtime when he saw the tall man matching the suspect's description walk through the front entryway and head for the elevators. To avoid attention, he took pictures of the man by pretending to take a selfie. Quickly reviewing the pictures, he noticed the bluish-red skin discoloration on the man's neck as he was standing by the elevator.

The elevator doors quickly closed so he couldn't board with the suspect. He was lucky there were only three people in the elevator. He quickly pushed the up button and diligently watched which floors registered on the overhead illuminated numbers. Only floors, 17 and 19, registered. The elevator reversed course and was now on a nonstop, downward descent back to the first floor.

Lares hastily reviewed the clients listed on the directories for floors 17 and 19.

"Beaucoup!" (New Orleans slang for "a lot."), Lares mumbled to himself.

Which floor would be first, because he had two choices, 17 or 19? For some odd reason, maybe because of his uncanny news reporter intuition, he believed the 19th floor would be a good place to start. He realized he may lose his chance to track the suspect if he were mistaken, but dat just the way it goes.

He barely made it onto the same elevator before the doors closed. More people boarded on this run. In fact, it was so crowded that he had to ask the person closest to the floor panel to please press floor 19. Lights were flashing on other floors, but at least floor 19 was the last stop.

Lares always thought that he had a touch of vertigo because he instinctively stared at the floor whenever he rode in an elevator. This time, he noticed a small business card on the floor below the button panel. Curiosity got the best of him, so he picked it up and read the salutation.

'Gregor Osseo, Chief Executive Officer (CEO), Roster Pharmaceuticals, Inc., San Jose, Costa Rica,'

Lares recalled seeing Roster Pharmaceuticals, Inc. listed in the directories on the first floor.

There it was again on the 19th floor, listed on the directories by the elevator,

Suite 1906 is the location of Roster Pharmaceuticals, Inc., which serves as the headquarters in New Orleans.

The pieces were coming together in Lares mind as he exited the elevator on the 19th floor. This was the corporate office for a pharmaceutical company plant in Costa Rica.

As Lares scanned the hallway, he noticed the logo of Roster Pharmaceuticals, Inc. on the glass enclosure of suite 1906. People in business attire hurriedly walked in the corridor as he stumbled into a vacant waiting room.

The receptionist was a well-groomed southern gentleman, garnishing a petite black mustache, oily hair, and a thin tie to match his business suit. He appeared very concerned with Lares uncontrolled entrance,

"Cher. Y'all right?" He spoke with a bona fide (i.e., genuine) concern.

"Dat door is tricky. I'm good, only embarrassed."

"Cher. What can I do for y'all?"

"I don't have a scheduled appointment, but I would like to speak to Mr. Osseo."

"Oh, my Cher. You are in the wrong office. Mr. Osseo's main office is at the research facility in Costa Rica."

"I'm sorry, but who are you?"

"How rude of me. My flinging entrance must have interrupted my manners. I'm Lares Turncock, a newspaper journalist from the New Orleans Tribune."

"Cher. No apology necessary. I'm impressed."

"Please sit, and I'll see if anyone else is available."

Lares waited in the pristine waiting room, feeling slightly out of place among the sophisticated decor.

The receptionist smiled affectionately at Lares in the waiting room, picked up the phone and called Dr. John Roster, the owner and founder of Roster Pharmaceuticals.

"Dr. Roster, I believe that the individual you were expecting is sitting in the waiting room."

"Thank you, Devon. Let him wait for now. I am at a conference."

Hanging up the phone, Dr. Roster continued his discussion with Art Lifehold in his office.

"You were correct in your character judgment of our friend, Lares. The business card you left in the elevator brought him directly to our office. Now, what should we do?"

"Find out what he knows so far and take the appropriate steps. Bring him in and have a discussion. I'll leave by the back entrance."

Shortly after, a tall, distinguished man with salt-and-pepper hair approached Lares in the waiting room.

"Mr. Lares Turncock? It is a privilege to meet you. I understand you are one of New Orleans finest journalists. Allow me to introduce myself. I am Dr. John Roster, owner, and founder of Roster Pharmaceuticals. Please, join me in my office."

Lares rose from his chair, feeling a mix of curiosity and apprehension as he followed Dr. Roster to his office.

"Mr. Turncock, how can I be of help?"

"I'm writing a piece on the current research trends in New Orleans. You know we're very proud of our Greater New Orleans Biosciences Economic Development District (GNOBEDD). I'd like to understand how your company fits into this district?"

"Well, Mr. Turncock, we don't. Our office is the headquarters for a research facility based in Costa Rica. I'm sure you can understand that our research is confidential and proprietary. What I can tell you is that it will be a significant and innovative advancement."

"Dr. Roster, why Costa Rica and not New Orleans?"

"Mr. Turncock, you know it all comes down to profit and the board. It's simple: we would not survive here in New Orleans with the cost of supplies and labor. Any more questions?"

"Only one Dr. Roster. Would you mind if I talked to Gregor Osseo?"

"Not at all, Mr. Turncock. So, you know Gregor?"

"I believed we've met in the past. Where, I can't really recall."

"However, we may have a slight problem, Mr. Turncock, because Gregor is currently in Costa Rica."

"Dr. Roster, I'm sitting here thinking that it may be a good idea to include your company in my story, even though you're not a part of GNOBDD. Would it be possible for me to pay a brief visit to your Costa Rica facility?"

"Absolutely! I'm always up for good PR."

"I can arrange for you to visit our facility in Costa Rica and speak with our team there. Devon will call you shortly with the details."

As Lares left his office, Dr. Roster abruptly grabbed his cell phone and spoke.

"You were right. I believe he knows too much. Meet him in Costa Rica. I'll call you when the plane departs."

# CHAPTER 12 – CAUSE OF DEATH

Thursday, May 2, 5:21 P.M.
New Orleans Coroner's Office
3001 Earhart Boulevard

Dr. Melvin Catechin stood in the morgue examination room, peering down at the lifeless body on the table. It was difficult for him to perform the autopsy on one of New Orleans most revered voodoo-hoodoo icons, Maia Revalue. He had known her personally, having witnessed her impact on the local community over the years. As a voodoo-hoodoo practitioner, he always believed that her religion was for the good of New Orleans. Here she lies, lifeless, and now it was his responsibility as a medical examiner to determine the cause.

He adjusted his glasses and began preparing his equipment, a heavy sense of duty weighing on him as he meticulously started examining the body. There was no visible evidence of foul play.

He continued with the lengthy process of precision cutting, before examining and weighing body organs, including collecting blood and tissue specimens. Closure was incomplete until the body cavity of the cadaver was closed with knit sutures. As he meticulously finished the process of surgical repair of the body, a somber atmosphere enveloped the room.

It was indeed an endless night when he finished. The paperwork that followed was meticulous, a vital part of the process of determining the cause of death.

Dr. Catechin dictated his preliminary findings for the

pathology autopsy report,

"As the medical examiner, it is my finding from this autopsy that Maia Revalue died from natural causes. The cause of death was most likely the result of acute cardiac arrest. These findings are preliminary, pending completing the pathology testing of the blood and tissue specimens."

Following the customary chain-of-custody, he carefully labeled the blood and tissue specimens. Then, he transported them to Pathology, where Dr. Sullivan, a second-year pathology resident, signed for receipt of the specimens. Likewise, he will transport the specimens to the forensics laboratory and Dr. Watkins' laboratory for specialized testing.

Friday, May 3, 7:22 A.M.
Watkins & Swindon Medical Diagnostics, LLC (WSMD)
Mandeville, Louisiana

Detective Ottavino was waiting in the lobby, tapping his foot impatiently and checking his watch. He was very familiar with WSMD, as well as knowing Dr. Watkins and Dr. Swindon by his work on past cases. However, this case was different since the FBI was involved, and he suspected he didn't have all the information on the case. He hoped to get briefed by Dr. Watkins himself as soon as the results were available.

Dr. Watkins emerged from the hallway, an air of urgency about him as he briskly made his way to Detective Ottavino.

Detective Ottavino, "it's always a pleasure to see you."

Dr. Swindon sat in Dr. Watkins office while reviewing a stack of laboratory results. Her eyes scanned the pages methodically, her brow furrowing as she absorbed the data before her.

Slowly looking up from her paperwork, she generated a lovely half-smile for Detective Ottavino,

"It's been a while detective, how are you?"

"Dr. Swindon, what can I say? Laissez les bons temps rouler!"

"Doctors, I'm investigating the pneumonia death cases, and Special Agent Lawins informed me yesterday at the Maia Revalue crime scene, the FBI has authority over the NOPD."

"I was hoping you could share information with me. Any

details would be useful in my investigation. Mind you, I don't mind working with the FBI, I do! You know, those feds, they like no one playing in their sandbox unless they control that little yellow plastic shovel and everyone else is in that little red bucket."

"Understood, Detective Ottavino.", replied Dr. Watkins.

"Unfortunately, we are under that same 'need to know' directive as you and your NOPD. What I can tell you is that Special Agent Lawins sent us evidence from the scene. It appears to be a powder or dust from some type of vessel found at the scene."

"Dr. Watkins."

"I found voodoo-hoodoo paraphernalia in the house, an amulet, and an exquisitely designed vessel. I suspect you are analyzing the contents of that vessel."

"Detective Ottavino. Tell you what, I will contact Special Agent Lawins and ask if we can all play in the same sandbox. I like that analogy. Very appropriate."

"Dr. Watkins, your help is appreciated. We will be in touch," as Detective Ottavino left the office.

Dr. Swindon was silent during the entire conversation, but she made a mental note to monitor the detective.

"Elise, what's up with the silence? This is totally out of character for you."

"Something is just not right. Look, we have FBI agents paying the special visit to you at your house and asking you not to interfere in the case. Then we have a selective request for an analysis of evidence. Now we have Detective Ottavino wedging us in the middle of the FBI and NOPD."

"My medical intuition tells me there's a lot more to this case than the pneumonia deaths."

Dr. Watkins narrowed his eyes thoughtfully and leaned back in his chair, absorbing Elise's words.

He slowly nodded his head in agreement, and they headed into the lab.

Friday, May 3, 10:00 A.M.

Federal Bureau of Investigation Headquarters
2901 Leon C Simon Drive
New Orleans

As Special Agent Lawins made his way towards the conference room, the bright morning sunbathed the glass enclosed offices of the FBI headquarters in a warm glow. The enormous, exquisitely polished, cherry-wood table encircled the agents who were anxiously expecting the update on the pneumonia cases. The air was heavy with a softly muddled conversation among the agents as he approached the head of the table. Special Agent Lawins cleared his throat in a boisterous, authoritative manner, capturing the attention of the agents.

"Agents Thomas and O'Riley found our 'person-of-interest', Maia Revalue, dead at her residence on Wednesday during our surveillance. We immediately secured the scene, and local law-enforcement arrived shortly thereafter. The NOPD investigation was under the leadership of Detective Shaky Ottavino. The investigators currently list the cause of her death as 'natural causes' until they complete the autopsy and pathology testing."

"I made it clear to Detective Ottavino that the FBI has jurisdiction over this local death, even though it is not considered a homicide. As of now, NOPD knows the FBI has an interest in Ms. Revalue's death. We informed NOPD that we are investigating the recent pneumonia deaths, which could be connected to Maia Revalue's actions."

"Currently, we are processing the evidence collected at the scene, and we also sent some evidence to Quantico and Dr. Watkins at WSMD."

"In particular, I want to draw your attention to three pieces of evidence that are of special interest: an amulet, an ancient-looking vessel, and a small flannel bag."

"Detective Ottavino, being a native-born citizen of New Orleans, believes these articles are a part of traditional paraphernalia used in the art of New Orleans voodoo-hoodoo, black magic. For the record, I'm not a believer in magical voodoo spells and their spiritual ability to impose harm, or even death, upon the intended victim. However, I believe that a poison may be involved in some of these stories to bring about death from a voodoo spell."

Agent Evans abruptly appeared on the outside of the glass-enclosed conference room, slowly nodding his head and pointing to a paper fluttering in his hand. Special Agent Lawins acknowledged his action and waved him into the room.

"I apologize for the interruption, sir, but testing results have just arrived from the forensic lab. It may be pertinent to your case discussion."

He handed over the document to Special Agent Lawins, submissively nodding his head, and exits the room.

Special Agent Lawins scans the document, shakes his head in disbelief, and addresses his agents with the news.

"Well, we have just received confirmation that Maia Revalue may have been in possession of cocaine. Two swabs taken at the scene show residual cocaine on both the voodoo-hoodoo altar surface and the kitchen table. She is now considered a suspect, along with Rafael Nacket and the elusive Dr. Tod Firehall, in the pneumonia death cases."

Special Agent Lawins gathered his notes and signaled Agent Gonzalez to deliver her report on the surveillance status at the Jazz Fest.

"It is 'status quo' at the Jazz Fest. In my estimation, even with the unprecedented crowds, there is no sign of unusual or nefarious activity. Allow me to clarify. We're only seeing the usual petty stuff, along with the expected cocaine trading activity by Rafael Nacket and his crowd. I also checked the local hospitals, and there's no sign of new patient admissions with life-threatening pneumonia. Our surveillance is tight. If there is any unusual activity, we will take swift action. That's all I have for now, sir."

"Thank you, Agent Gonzalez. Keep me updated on any developments," replied Special Agent Lawins, as he turned to Agent Gonzalez standing by the door.

"This debriefing has now concluded. Let's close for now and

reconvene when we have more information."

Friday, May 3, 1:13 P.M.

Watkins & Swindon Medical Diagnostics, LLC (WSMD)

Mandeville, Louisiana

Dr. Dana Merrily, the chief pathologist, was just putting away a specimen when her phone buzzed with a high-priority message.

"Dana, it's Tombak. Do you have any results on the autopsy blood specimen from Maia Revalue, WS30125?"

"Tombak, your telepathy is remarkable! I was just reviewing the results from the mass spectrometry (MS) on that blood specimen. I found a significantly sized peak on the readout. What is strange is that it's not matching in any of our database searches. I'm not finding any other foreign substances in the blood sample."

"It may be wise to call our esteemed colleagues at NIH. I'll send you the MS file shortly."

Tombak replied,

"You are the best!"

"Thank you, Dana. I'll contact NIH right away and keep you posted on any further instructions."

Dr. Tombak arranged stacks of papers in very neat piles along his lengthy desktop, representing various stages of testing results in the pneumonia cases. He spent the better half of this morning discussing and theorizing about the results with Dr. Swindon.

Stretching across his desk, he leaned over to the autopsy file reports on the far-right corner, and pulled out the file folder entitled, 'Maia Revalue'. There was a new report in the file that he just received less than an hour ago. So far, he only had a chance for a cursory review. Even with that scanty perusal of the documents, what stood out in the preliminary report was the cause-of-death description, "natural causes".

The phone call from Dr. Merrily provided hope for finding new evidence amidst the overwhelming information.

The thought just stuck in his head. Dr. Merrily's finding did not coincide with the preliminary autopsy report. Flipping page-by-page, he now diligently read every line of the report.

The unidentified substance detected by MS was indeed suspicious. Intuitively, he wanted to label it as an unknown toxin or poison.

Especially concerning was the mention of abnormal rigor mortis in the autopsy report. The report stated,

"Rigor mortis appears strong, considering the time of death."

He pondered the intent of this statement, while staring at the wall across from his desk, displaying a shrine of medical credentials and award plaques.

Then Dr. Watkins mumbled softly to himself,

"This has to be relevant to Ms. Revalue's death."

Interrupting his thoughts, the computer screen flickered to life and displayed an email icon, blinking with urgency. It was the copy of the MS report from Dr. Merrily. He quickly opened the file, reviewed, and confirmed the results described by Dr. Merrily, 'No Match'.

Completing the review, he sent a copy to his colleague at NIH/NIAID, Dr. Kaaren Zama Penrith, MD, PhD, physician and NIAID research fellow. Her current fellowship in toxicology provided an ideal starting point. Dr. Penrith had access to one of the most extensive digital libraries in the world, the NIH MS global database.

Finishing the delivery of his message, he noticed that Dr. Swindon was deep in thought over the sequence data. She was still deciphering the list of microbes detected in the autopsy pneumonia case samples. He distracted her from the sequencing list by placing an empty file folder over her documents.

"Elise, you need to refocus. Let's discuss the MS data mystery posed by Dr. Merrily."

"OK, Tombak, you've got my attention."

Connecting the dots in her mind, Dr. Swindon supported Dr. Watkins conjecture that the abnormal rigor mortis might show foul play. Identifying the unknown entity in the blood specimen would certainly provide an answer. The autopsy report was preliminary, but it still provides valuable observations on the physiology of the cadaver following death.

"Tombak, please hand me the preliminary autopsy report you just received on Maia Revalue."

She spent a year in forensic pathology at Cooke County Hospital in Chicago. Dr. Swindon could assess the autopsy report with a critical eye. Her expertise in infectious disease and forensic pathology gave her unique insight into the case. She read the autopsy report with vigor, absorbing every word with a pleasurable look on her face. Feeling a sense of urgency, she noted possible discrepancies and missing details that could be crucial in unraveling the mystery behind Maia Revalue's sudden death.

"Tombak, this report does not represent Dr. Catechin's usual fine art of autopsy. It's far too general, even as a preliminary report. There is one part that stands out. This is the same rigor mortis description that caught your eye. I have enough training in forensic pathology to know paralysis from rigor mortis in a cadaver. If it turns out to be paralysis, the clinical pathology on tissue and blood results, and especially on brain histology samples, should be quite interesting. In my professional opinion, considering the mass spectrometry revealed an unidentified compound, is that we will identify some type of toxin or poison on the NIH databases."

"Elise, I agree. Allow me to further support your opinion. I reviewed the NOPD report from Detective Ottavino. It described Ms. Revalue's appearance at the scene unusually, 'as rigid as a stone statue sitting on the chair in front of her voodoo-hoodoo altar.' Interesting, Dr. Catechin did not even mention this finding in his preliminary autopsy report."

"Tombak, did NOPD or the FBI send us swab samples of the armchair surfaces on which she was sitting at the time of death?"

"I'm not sure. Let's look at the chain-of-custody forms."

"Yes, they sent us two swabs as evidence for analysis."

"Great! Run the mass spectrometry and let's see what we can

find out from those swabs."

"Good call, Dr. Swindon."

As he spoke, he kept his eyes fixed on Dr. Swindon, but he couldn't help but notice the computer screen flickering. Once again, it was showing an email icon that blinked with urgency.

Dr. Penrith sent the message entitled, 'MS results WS30125'.

He opened the encrypted attachment.

'WS30125 mass spectrometry identification of peak 215.31 shows a 99.2% identity match on the NIH MS global databases to the following compound:

Batrachotoxin: $C_{31}H_{42}N_2O_6$

Molar mass 538.685 g·mol$-1$

CAS Registry Number® 23509-16-2

Source: Phyllobates terribilis (Golden poison frog, golden poison arrow frog, poison dart frog) endemic amphibian found in the rainforests of Colombia, South America.'

"Elise, you never fail to amaze me with your forensic pathology expertise. You were right, the death of Maia Revalue was probably a homicide, and the instrument of death, batrachotoxin, according to our friends at NIH."

Dr. Swindon's attention to the details of Dr. Watkins' reading of the MS report was priceless. Her eyes widened, her shoulders and head plunged forward, and her voice blared out in a high-pitch tone.

"Alright! That year of forensic rotation really paid off in this case."

"Tombak, obviously, Maia Revalue can't be the only person involved in the deaths. We already know, from the FBI, there are at least two other persons-of-interest in the picture. We need to increase the suspect list and find out who had access to that deadly toxin. I hope the FBI can play nice with us by finding this crucial piece of evidence?"

"This new finding aligns with the preliminary autopsy and police reports."

"I'll bet anything that the rigor mortis was paralysis and the stoic posture of Maia Revalue in the armchair was caused by batrachotoxin poisoning," she said confidently, "fitting perfectly with the preliminary autopsy and police reports."

"If I recall correctly, batrachotoxin permanently blocks nerve signal transmission to the muscles. It's one of those nasty toxins that irreversibly opens the sodium channels of nerve cells and prevents them from closing. Hence, the muscles remain in an inactive state of contraction, leading to paralysis, heart fibrillation, heart failure, and ultimately death."

"Tombak, what do you think the swab samples from the chair will tell us?"

"Elise, I know exactly where you're going with this train of thought because we think alike. It is likely that someone contaminated the armchair with batrachotoxin. Maybe a hidden drop of toxin or even a small needle laced with toxin?"

"I'm just now reviewing the medical literature on the web for more information on the batrachotoxin."

"What I can tell you from my research so far is that batrachotoxin is the king of toxins! Poison arrow frogs can produce other toxins, but batrachotoxins and pumiliotoxins are the most toxic, followed by histrionicotoxins and gephyrotoxins."

"Phyllobates terribilis, the golden poison arrow frog, is endemic to the humid forests of the Pacific coast of Colombia, specifically to the Cauca and Valle del Cauca Departments in the Chocó Rainforest."

"Even more interesting, the diet of this tiny frog is the key to production of the batrachotoxin. If you try to raise the frog in captivity, it fails to produce the lethal toxin."

"This is our break in this case because we have linked someone from South America, or one of the bordering countries, to the toxin."

"Now, for the critical question, how does this fit into our case?"

"I also found more pertinent information on the lethal power of batrachotoxin."

"Experts estimate as little as 2 µg, which is equivalent to

1/1000 of a milligram, can fatally poison a human. The golden poison arrow frog in its natural habitat, the rainforest, contains about one milligram (i.e., 0.00003527396 ounce) of toxin. This tiny amount can kill between 10 and 20 humans, or even two African bull elephants. Yes, it is truly the king of toxins."

"Terrifying, and quite diabolical,"

"Tombak, in your research, did you find any information on introducing the batrachotoxin into the victim's bloodstream at the time of death in the victim?"

"Not yet, but my suspicion would be, it depends upon the quantity and route of toxin introduction into the blood. As you so eloquently described earlier, the mechanism of action is irreversible, meaning, 'no antidote' would be possible."

"Dr. Swindon, I think it's time to have a discussion with our friends at the FBI."

Without hesitation, Dr. Watkins pressed a button on his cell phone and the screen lit up with a name.

'Special Agent Lawins, from the Federal Bureau of Investigation in New Orleans.'

Staring at Dr. Swindon in complete silence, he pressed the speaker 'on' button on his cell phone. It rang twice and a voice abruptly answered.

"Lawins!"

"Special Agent Lawins, this is Dr. Watkins. We have some important findings on the autopsy blood sample from Maia Revalue. Her blood contained a rare toxin that could be involved in her death. If you are available now, Dr. Swindon and I could be on our way to your office."

There were a few seconds of silence at the other end of the call, but then Special Agent Lawins spoke in a gruff voice,

"Am I to believe that our medical examiner's preliminary report is an error? Have you confirmed the finding?"

"Sir, it is real and substantiated by our expert at the National Institute of Health (NIH) laboratory in Bethesda, Maryland."

"Dr. Watkins, I will expect both you and Dr. Swindon at my office within the hour for debriefing."

Friday, May 3, 4:13 P.M.
Federal Bureau of Investigation Headquarters
2901 Leon C Simon Drive
New Orleans

Traffic was heavy on this humid Friday afternoon. It took almost one and a half hour's travel for the 50-mile trip from Mandeville to the FBI headquarters.

Dr. Watkins sent a text message to Special Agent Lawins notifying him of the delay. The text did not please him, considering the urgency of the matter.

Dr. Watkins and Dr. Swindon were escorted to Special Agent Lawins' office upon their arrival at the FBI headquarters. At the door, his steely gaze and a curt nod greeted them. Turning to Dr. Watkins with a steady stare, he said,

"Dr. Watkins, the floor is all yours."

Dr. Watkins took a deep breath, recognizing the gravity of the situation. He handed Special Agent Lawins the documents, describing the mass spectrometry reports from his laboratory and Dr. Penrith's at NIH.

"I realize there's a lot of technical information in those reports, but the important finding is batrachotoxin in the deceased blood."

Special Agent Lawins studied the documents with intense scrutiny. He then looked up and replied,

"This changes everything."

"We have already determined that Maia Revalue, Rafael Nacket, and alias Dr. Tod Firehall are suspects, elevated from persons-of-interest. This happened when we found cocaine in two places at the crime scene. Deductively, there had to be a link between the suspects."

"Why Maia Revalue is now a homicide victim presents a very challenging twist to the entire case of the pneumonia deaths."

Dr. Watkins and Dr. Swindon slowly nodded their heads in agreement.

The two medical investigators exchanged a worried glance.

Then Dr. Watkins spoke in a stern voice,

"We're keep you updated, Special Agent Lawins. I'm sure you will also alert us to any pertinent information on your behalf."

"Doc, what can I say? It's always on a need-to-know basis. I'll keep you informed."

"Thank you, Special Agent Lawins," Dr. Watkins replied with a nod as they left the office, escorted by another agent.

They were now outside at the entrance to the FBI building, where they could speak more freely to each other.

"Elise, what do you think?"

"Tombak, I think I found the answer in the sequencing data. This pathogen even caught me off-guard! I will fill you in later at the lab when we can review the documents together."

Tombak was truly at a loss for words as they strolled to the parking garage.

# CHAPTER 13 – TROJAN HORSE

Friday, May 3, 6:38 P.M.
Watkins & Swindon Medical Diagnostics, LLC (WSMD)
Mandeville, Louisiana

The laboratory parking area was nearly empty, with only a few cars scattered across the lot. A pleasant smile enveloped on Dr. Watkins and Dr. Swindon's faces as they arrived at their laboratory. The discovery of the alleged pathogen in the sequencing data overjoyed the doctors. Tombak spent the better part of the return trip from the FBI headquarters discussing the implications of such a pathogen in a pneumonia case with Elise.

As they made their way to the entrance, Dr. Watkins glanced at his smartphone and noticed an unusual alert from the lab's security system. He quickly unlocked his smartphone and tapped on the alert to open it, feeling a sense of foreboding. The message revealed an unauthorized access attempt to the lab's servers, originating from an unfamiliar IP address.

Within seconds, his smartphone played the William Tell overture, his custom alert for the WSMD IT Director.

"Dr. Watkins, please verify your identity."

Since the recent hacking incident compromising their laboratory computer network and his personal laptop, Dr. Watkins started the use of special code phrases. All staff members are now required to use these codes following any special smartphone alert.

Dr. Watkins quickly replied with his code phrase,

"Have you walked my dog Corona today?"

"Dr. Watkins, it's Vicky from IT. Our new firewalls successfully averted the unauthorized access attempt. However, it was a unique IP address from the recent hacking. Please hold on for a second. I'm being waved over by one of the IT specialists."

"Clyde is a genius."

"He traced it back to a different government site. It appears to be originating from the Pentagon, specifically from within the Department of Defense (DoD)!"

"Thank you, Vicky. Dr. Swindon and I are in the parking lot, and we will be in my office shortly."

"Elise, now the case has just been elevated to the highest level possible, the DoD."

"Tombak, you know what I'm thinking, but let me say it out loud. We need to notify the FBI immediately and let them handle this from here on out. Do you seriously want to be involved in military gamesmanship?"

"Dr. Swindon, how can I say this? We are already involved, and now with the new information, it will no doubt add a level of danger to our investigation. I'm not too sure about notifying the FBI at this point. You know how well communication works between the different agencies. Usually, not very well at all."

"You're right. I'm not thinking this through too clearly. For now, let's review the sequencing data."

"Agreed. Let's focus on gathering as much evidence as we can before deciding."

As they walked into the conference room, folders in hand, they noticed a flickering tab on one computer. There was new sequencing data available on the contents of the powder found in the vessel at the crime scene. Dr. Swindon paused and said,

"We need to approach this with caution. The deeper we dig into the sequencing results, the more significant our discoveries may become. Let's cross-reference any new data with existing evidence before jumping to conclusions."

"Elise, you know our motto, follow the data. It rarely lies."

"I know you're right, but I'm concerned about how far this

might lead into the rabbit hole. You can't help but think the CIA might also be involved, and they don't leave any loose ends."

The doctors were deeply worried and had valid reasons to feel that way. Little did they know, the CIA was involved in a way they would never imagine. The flickering tab was a subtle clue to a deep-seated cyber intrusion, one that had quietly seeded itself within the very heart of their laboratory network.

Dr. Swindon was sure she found the pathogen causing the pneumonia deaths from the autopsy sequencing data. Now, she had an epiphany about comparing the new sequencing data from the crime scene powder to the autopsy dust results.

"Tombak, I just reviewed the crime scene powder results to compare the sequence data with the autopsy samples. You won't believe this!"

"They match at about 95%. The additional 5% comprises microbial sequences that are unique to the autopsy samples. I am calling this 'subtractive DNA deduction', because it tells us that Maia Revalue's powder did not contain the suspected pathogens."

"Elise, correct me if I'm wrong, but I believe you're saying she is a diversion with her black magic from the actual murderer?"

"Yes, that is precisely what I'm saying," Elise replied with a discerning look on her face.

"But it goes even deeper than that. This has the makings of the CIA and the involvement of drug cartels." said Dr. Watkins.

With a surge of energy, Dr. Swindon pulled Dr. Watkins over to the stacks of sequencing data, starting a lengthy discussion to support her conclusion. Frantically flipping pages and highlighting key results, she finally revealed the most likely pathogen,

"Tombak, I hope you agree with this fascinating microbe. It is a free-living amoeba, Balamuthia mandrillaris."

"Elise, I can't believe we were looking so intensely for bacteria or a virus, when we should've been focusing more on other microbes, such as this parasite."

Tombak was deep in thought about their discussion on the

way back to his office. Why would one consider a parasite, Balamuthia mandrillaris, a free-living amoeba, in a differential diagnosis when it presents with signs and symptoms of pneumonia? Of course, he did not have the experience with patients. He was not the infectious disease physician; it was Dr. Swindon.

"Elise, why Balamuthia mandrillaris? Pneumonia? You're the physician, but I am not aware of any case in the literature where this free-living amoeba has caused pneumonia in a patient. I always thought it was associated with granulomatous amoebic encephalitis?"

"What if this is not just a regular case of pneumonia?"

"You must explore unconventional solutions on this one."

"Elise, why Balamuthia mandrillaris out of the extensive list of microbial choices?"

"Excellent question. Think about it like this. We have all the patients dying from life-threatening pneumonia, and only two patients with meningoencephalitis. The difference is, they were immunocompromised. However, if you check the sequencing data, you find the rickettsia was present in all patient samples tested. This is precisely why I would not consider the rickettsia as the primary pathogen."

"Elise, if I understand what you're saying, you are no doubt one of the most remarkable diagnosticians. I believe you suggest that the free-living amoeba, Balamuthia, is a Trojan horse for the rickettsia."

"Yes, that is precisely what I'm thinking. The interesting question is whether the Balamuthia mandrillaris is the primary cause of the life-threatening pneumonia? I think we need to dig deeper into the sequencing data, along with help from our esteemed colleagues at NIH."

"Agreed."

"I'll notify Dr. Dhyana and Dr. Smithcraft about our visit. Given the urgency and critical nature of our findings, I'm confident they'll meet with us, even on a Saturday."

"We will head to Washington, DC, on the first flight out

tomorrow morning."

Saturday, May 4, 11:48 A.M.

National Institutes of Health (NIH)

National Institute of Allergy and Infectious Disease (NIAID)

9000 Rockville Pike

Bethesda, Maryland

Upon reaching NIH, Dr. Ewan Smithcraft, Ph.D., NIAID Director, Division of Microbiology and Disease, greeted Elise and Tombak.

"Tombak. Elise. It's always a pleasure. I hope your flight and travel from Washington National was uneventful."

They both appeared tired but conjured up authentic enthusiasm for the visit. Tombak smiled at the sight of his friend.

"Ewan, seeing you again brings back fond memories of my postdoctoral fellowship days at this beautiful campus."

Elise added her greeting.

"Ewan, you look happy. I'm delighted to see you again."

Dr. Smithcraft's warm smile flickered for a moment before he replied, "It's great to see both of you."

The NIH dates to the 1880s. Today, it is part of the United States Department of Health and Human Services (HHS). The NIH conducts its research through an intramural research program, funding non-NIH research facilities. The campus is reminiscent of a small town, employing almost 20,000 professionals and staff workers, and 27 institutes and centers. It is the largest biomedical research institute on the face of the earth.

As they made their way through the impressive campus, Ewan filled them in on the latest developments in infectious disease research.

"Tombak, Elise, our team has discovered some groundbreaking information on the transmission patterns of a new strain of influenza," Ewan said, as they made their way through the maze of the hallways to one of the many NIAID conference rooms. There, they joined Dr. Darnell Dhyana, M.D., physician and NIAID, Director, Vaccine Research Center,

Emerging Virus Center.

In the past, Dr. Dhyana served as a consultant for Dr. Watkins and Dr. Swindon on complex cases. However, today's case will take precedence over any other case from the past.

"Welcome, my dear friends and colleagues. I don't mean to be curt, but I am extremely concerned about your findings. I reviewed the documents, reports, and summations. Ironically, I am an expert on free-living amoeba, along with Dr. Smithcraft's area of expertise."

Dr. Smithcraft began with a concise description of free-living-amoeba and clinical disease,

"Clinically, we are concerned with three types of free-living-amoeba; Naegleria, Acanthamoeba, and Balamuthia. Naegleria and Acanthamoeba can cause encephalitis. Acanthamoeba, causes ocular infections that may lead to blindness or even death sometimes. Balamuthia is the most concerning, causing granulomatous amoebic encephalitis. I believe we have a good understanding of the transmission for Naegleria and Acanthamoeba, but Balamuthia remains a mystery."

"If I may speak for Dr. Dhyana, we are both fascinated with this case. This may offer insight into a new portal of entry for Balamuthia transmission. Obviously, this is based upon the assumption Balamuthia mandrillaris is the true pathogen in the pneumonia cases."

Dr. Swindon interjected,

"We have been working tirelessly to gather more information, but one piece of the puzzle still eludes us."

"Why pneumonia and not a neurologic outcome leading to death?"

After considerable deliberation, Dr. Dhyana commented on the discussion,

"Why can't Balamuthia target a different organ in the body? As you so eloquently wrote in your notes, Dr. Swindon, this free-living-amoeba could be a Trojan horse. I like the idea, and there is evidence in the literature to support the carriage of rickettsia by free-living-amoeba. However, let's not stop here.

Let's ask; What else is carried in that tiny unicellular protozoan, Balamuthia?"

"Here is where we tease out the remaining 5% from the sequencing data. My impression is that we're going to find the actual cause of the deadly pneumonia in that cluster."

Intrigued by the thought of Balamuthia potentially acting as a Trojan horse, the team delved deeper into the study of the sequencing results.

Finally, after a couple of hours, a real possibility for the respiratory pathogen emerged from the mound of DNA sequences. The data pointed to unexpected genetic material typically associated with anecdotal accounts of viral infection related to laboratory accidents. It was associated with the recent interest in giant viruses, and their symbiotic relationship with protozoa.

Acanthamoeba polyphaga mimivirus (APM) was the first giant DNA virus discovered living in the free-living amoeba, Acanthamoeba polyphaga. In 1992, researchers mistakenly identified it as a bacterium from a water-cooling tower in Bradford, England. Scientists announced in 2003 that it was a virus. Today, it is one of many species belonging to a group of large viruses. It is in the same group as the poxviruses. The giant virus is called the missing link, as it carries its own genetic material to produce proteins and enzymes instead of relying on the host. There is evidence from a laboratory event, the mimivirus can cause respiratory disease in humans.

Dr. Dhyana and Dr. Smithcraft knew they had found the underlying pathogen, along with Dr. Watkins and Dr. Swindon. The DNA sequence supported a giant virus genetic makeup, but it differed from other large virus sequences in their massive databases. Why?

Dr. Watkins provided the summation.

"The carrier or vector, so to speak, is Balamuthia mandrillaris. The victim most likely inhaled Balamuthia mandrillaris in the environmentally resistant cyst form from cloud dust, making it the carrier or vector, so-to-speak.

According to DNA sequencing, this free-living amoeba harbors rickettsia and a giant 'mimivirus'. The rickettsia caused neurologic disease in the immunocompromised patients but spared the immunocompetent ones. Likewise, this new giant virus caused pneumonia and death in all patients. We would suggest that the possibility of genetic manipulation might have contributed to the virulence of this virus."

The team was in full agreement with Dr. Watkins' summation.

This finding raised concerns by the team about the potential for genetically modified viruses to create catastrophic health impacts.

Dr. Watkins and Dr. Swindon gave a heartfelt farewell to their colleagues at NIH and headed back to Reagan National Airport.

Saturday, May 4, 4:28 P.M.

Ronald Reagan Washington National Airport

Arlington County, Virginia

As they made their way through the bustling airport, Dr. Swindon had the impression they were being followed.

"Tombak, don't look behind you, but I think we're being followed by two men, dressed in dark business suits and carrying briefcases."

"Elise, I think you've become a little paranoid, but I'll play along. Let's split up and see what happens. I'll meet you at the gate in a few minutes."

Tombak quickly pulled out his cellphone and hit the selfie button. As soon as they split up, he noticed the man followed Elise, and the other was on his tail. He mumbled softly to himself,

"Elise is always right. I hate that!"

Thinking fast, he dived into the food court and immersed himself in the crowd. He quickly removed his coat, bound it up in his hands, and placed sunglasses on his face. He lost the man in the crowd.

Likewise, she was in luck. Elise used a similar evasive tactic and ran into him in the narrow hallway. They both walked swiftly towards the exit, flagged down an oncoming cab, and headed towards Washington Dulles International Airport for their departure back to New Orleans.

Meanwhile, back at Reagan National Airport, the two men reconnected in the busy terminal and realized they had lost their chance at tracking down the two doctors. CIA Case Officer Art Lifehold turned to his partner with a disgusted, self-absorbed, frustrated look, and said,

"Letting them slip through our fingers was a rookie move."

"Now, I'm convinced they know too much. It's time for a reckoning."

Saturday, May 4, 5:37 P.M.

Federal Bureau of Investigation Headquarters

2901 Leon C Simon Drive

New Orleans

Special Agent Lawins received a call from the lead agent at the Jazz Fest. Their team observed suspicious behavior by two individuals matching descriptions on the most wanted list. He ordered the agent to only observe, and not to intercept, the suspicious individuals.

Surveillance became more difficult on this last weekend of the Jazz Fest, not only because of the phenomenal crowd but also with the increase in the Mardi Gras party goers. The crowd stretched the agents thin and made them tired. So far, they have found no other credible activity.

Shortly after reporting the suspicious individuals, the lead agent called again,

"Sir. The two unsub's we were just tracking are a no-go. I'll keep you updated, sir."

Special Agent Lawins smartphone rang again. However, this time, the call was from Dr. Watkins.

"Lawins."

"This is Dr. Watkins, and I have little time for discussion because our plane is about to depart. We believe we have found the agent causing the pneumonia deaths. We also have evidence

107

that the powder found at Ms. Revalue's crime scene is dust, the kind you might find in the atmosphere lately because of the Sahara dust storm."

"I will provide you with more details tomorrow if you can meet us at WSMD around 9 AM."

"I apologize, but I must leave. The plane is closing the boarding door."

"Doc. I'll be at your lab around 9 AM tomorrow."

# CHAPTER 14 – COSTA RICA

Sunday, May 5, 8:50 A.M.
Watkins & Swindon Medical Diagnostics, LLC (WSMD)
Mandeville, Louisiana

Special Agent Lawins sat in the reception area, scanning through some files he compiled on the pneumonia deaths and Maia Revalue's crime scene. It was conceptually easier for him to visualize the cases outlined on the storyboard at the office. However, he frequently used his process, resembling shorthand, in which he jotted down keywords and relied on them as mental triggers to flawlessly recall events in a case. It worked well for him over the years and complemented his intuitive ability to solve cases. His persistence and love of solving puzzles as a child was a potent driving force for his success in solving even the most diabolical cases.

The distant sound of a familiar feminine voice suddenly pierced the peaceful silence of the reception area, calling his name.

"Special Agent Lawins, we appreciate you meeting us at the laboratory instead of at your office. It is easier to explain the details of the recent evidence in this case with access to our laboratory network."

"Dr. Watkins is waiting for us in his office."

"If you please, follow me," said Dr. Swindon.

"We'll update you on the analysis of the recent evidence," she said, leading the way past the display of medical instruments.

If one closes their eyes, one could even imagine these

humming technological marvels communicating in their language. A language they could only understand. This technology was so advanced that only a single laboratory specialist was required to oversee the testing in an area the size of a high school gymnasium.

Dr. Watkins was waiting at his office door entrance. He appeared eager to greet the special agent.

"Special Agent Lawins, I believe you know, Detective Ottavino from the NOPD. Dr. Swindon and I have worked with the detective on many cases over the years. He recently requested that we share some of our findings with him."

"I invited him to our meeting so that we could all be on the same page with the evidence. Especially in what we are about to present."

Detective Ottavino visibly irritated Special Agent Lawins. After a moment of silent reflection, he spoke in a calm but stern voice,

"I'm sure Detective Ottavino mentioned the FBI oversees the case, and not NOPD. You know what that means. You're an intelligent man, a doctor. I don't appreciate being blind-sighted like this. Ever!"

"Special Agent Lawins, that was not my intention. I want to maintain active communication between us. I know very well that you are in charge, and I respect that position. My entire lab operates on teamwork, and that's how I approach every interaction, including interactions with outside parties."

"Dr. Watkins. I believe we both have a clear understanding. Let's get on with the matter at hand."

The foursome left Dr. Watkins's office and proceeded down the hallway, entering a semi-lit conference room. Dr. Swindon approached the front podium, and the others made themselves comfortable on three front chairs along the lengthy conference table.

"Dr. Swindon, could you please present the summation of our findings in the case."

The tedious, weeklong effort by a multitude of clinical

laboratory staff and investigators, terabytes of sequencing data, and a voluminous stack of paper documentation culminated in a twenty-minute PowerPoint presentation.

"Let me begin by describing each item of evidence from the autopsy cases, and those articles from Maia Revalue's crime scene."

Dr. Swindon was flawless in her description of each piece of evidence. Her mannerism and verbal description of the evidence was reminiscent of a prosecuting attorney presenting the case evidence in a courtroom.

The next part was more difficult because she had to describe the molecular diagnostic findings in layman's terms to the officers of the law in the audience. She began by describing the basic principles of infectious disease. For example, she described the rationale for referring to a microbe as beneficial or pathogenic.

"Microbes are everywhere. How do we know which microbe is a threat to humans, and the cause of disease or death? It's not a simple matter because it requires the expertise of a professional. Sure, there are simple ones like the measles virus or the tuberculosis bacterium. We know they will invariably cause disease. Other microbes are more challenging, and their infectious potential will often depend on the health of the individual."

"Today, it's a unique time in infectious disease diagnostics. We have introduced molecular sequencing technology. Unlike culture, this technology detects the DNA of dead and alive microbes in the sample tested. This presents our laboratory investigators with a unique challenge, while sifting through the multitude of microbes detected in a sample. How do we find the pathogen, the infectious agent, causing the disease?"

"You also need to understand that culture is never 100%. Why? Some microbes evade cultivation, while the human immune system eliminates others before they can proliferate in culture."

"Allow me to cut to the chase. Finding the infectious agent

is a balance between the digital world and human ingenuity. We are successful in our molecular approach because of our expertise and training in medical microbiology and infectious disease diagnostics. This is a team effort on behalf of Dr. Watkins, our laboratory staff, me, and our colleagues at NIH. Now, here are the results from our efforts."

"All the autopsy samples from the victims revealed the same molecular sequencing results. We have concluded that the prime agent is a parasite, a free-living amoeba, Balamuthia mandrillaris. This is a simple microscopic animal, tiny, but mighty. It creeps along eating bacteria, but when it runs out of food or encounters a harsh environment, it turns into a highly resistant form, the cyst."

"However, Balamuthia is not actually causing the pneumonia, it's only serving as a 'vector', or if you prefer, a Trojan horse for delivery of the true infectious agents."

"Yes, there is more than one pathogen involved. One belongs to a 'giant virus' group, mimivirus."

"The other is a rickettsia bacterium, similar to the bacterium that causes Rocky Mountain spotted fever."

"We believe atmospheric dust, known as Sahara dust, here in New Orleans, delivered Balamuthia to these patients."

"The Balamuthia protects the virus and the bacterium by being transported as an environmentally resistant cyst. We do not understand how it ended up infecting only these select patients. This is now the major question in the investigation."

Dr. Watkins mentioned to Special Agent Lawins that Maia Revalue may not be the actual killer.

"Our testing shows the crime scene dust from her residence did not contain these microbes."

"Now, it is up to you, our law-enforcement officials, to determine her role in the case."

"Thank you for your attention. You had no questions as I gave the talk. I assume the findings are clear?"

The summation impressed Special Agent Lawins and Detective Ottavino and showed they understood the results by a simple nod.

The foursome continued a discussion for a few minutes, and then the law-enforcement officers left the building.

In the parking lot, Special Agent Lawins commented to Detective Ottavino,

"The cocaine connection is the key. I know it in my gut. I'll be in touch, Ottavino."

Sunday, May 5, 10:20 P.M.

New Orleans Tribune

2317 Esplanade Avenue

Cinco de Mayo commemorates the Mexican victory in the Battle of Puebla against the French in 1862. When you think of New Orleans, you often think of Mardi Gras and Cajun music rather than Cinco de Mayo. However, over the past 20 years, the Mexican population has blossomed in New Orleans.

Today, the people of New Orleans and the surrounding area celebrate Cinco de Mayo, along with other ethnic festivals. Now, after five years, the Cinco de Mayo Fest has become a regular annual event. The celebration takes place on May 5th at Fat City Park, which is less than 5 miles (ca. 8 km) northwest of New Orleans in Metairie, Louisiana.

The Editor-in-Chief of the New Orleans Tribune, Shepard Althorn, assigned Lares to cover exclusively the Cinco de Mayo Fest. His journalistic style is beyond reproach for coverage of festivals, especially the Mardi Gras. His ability to capture the atmosphere and essence of cultural celebrations had earned him a reputation as the 'go-to festival reporter'.

It is a late Sunday night in the darkened, silent Tribune office of Lares Turncock. This is the way he likes it, because it is most conducive to arousing his journalistic talent. Tonight, the office ambience was exquisitely seductive for writing his editorial on the Cinco de Mayo Fest.

Paragraph after paragraph flowed onto his laptop, articulately describing the event in vivid detail. In his poetic words, Lares skillfully captured the vibrancy of the festival, the lively music, and the colorful decorations.

"Done. Another masterpiece, if I must say," Lares spoke softly to himself as he emailed his masterpiece to Shepard.

Lares sat there, motionless on his office chair, with a smug look on his face.

He said to himself, "I must have beaten my record." It took me less than an hour to complete this piece of excellence.

"Now, for my other work at hand."

The death of Queen Maia consumed Lares, and he became convinced that foul-play was to blame. After encountering Dr. Roster at Roster Pharmaceuticals headquarters, Lares swore he would not stop investigating until he uncovered the truth.

Dr. Roster's executive assistant, Devin, was prompt in emailing the itinerary to him last Friday for the Roster Pharmaceuticals Costa Rica research facility visit. With such short notice, Lares now had to scramble to secure a plane ticket to San Jose, Costa Rica.

This unexpected, and somewhat aggressive, approach by Dr. Roster for an expedited visit to Costa Rica incited suspicion and concern for Lares. Could this be a clever PR business strategy ploy by Dr. Roster because he believed Lares fabricated a story for the visit? Maybe Dr. Roster wants to convince Lares that his company was legitimate, and this visit could expel any concerns of nefarious activity? Of course, the most dreaded concern would be, Dr. Roster was luring him to a foreign country to ensure that he is silenced. Lares didn't know the reason, but his burning curiosity as a journalist had to be fulfilled.

"I am a great investigative journalist. I have published stories before under more threatening circumstances. Why should this story be any different?" Lares thought to himself.

He knew he had to keep this trip in confidence, especially from Shepard and whoever was monitoring the surveillance camera hidden in his office ceiling. He orchestrated a diversionary tactic for the eye of the camera. All it took was a straightforward task: place a phony itinerary calendar where the camera could see it on the desk. Hopefully, that would keep the unknown individual less interested in his whereabouts over the coming days.

As for Shepard, Lares would send an email, informing him he will take a few well-deserved days off for the award-winning article on this weekend's Cinco de Mayo Fest.

Lights off, and the door closed behind him, Lares headed home to pack for his journalistic expedition to uncover the mystery behind Roster Pharmaceuticals, Costa Rica.

Monday, May 6, 6:20 A.M.

Louis Armstrong International Airport

New Orleans

When viewed from a satellite, the scene at the international terminal resembled packed grains of sand on a beach. The dense crowd of visitors was returning home after their exuberant celebration at the Jazz Fest and Cinco de Mayo. The partying always culminated in a motionless stupor for most visitors waiting in the winding airport lines.

Lares moved cautiously through the crowd. He always loved the feeling of flashing his press credentials at security. This gave him a genuine sense of power with priority passage through the security area. He sighed with relief when he saw the open area leading to the airport gates.

Lares, not being a religious man, softly spoke, "Thank you, God, for making me a journalist."

An announcement overhead informed that "Air Canada, flight AC 3992 will board in 30 minutes for San Jose, Costa Rica at gate A13."

Lares had already slipped through the security area, and now he made his way to the gate, feeling the growing pulse of excitement for the adventure that lay ahead.

In his fury to make the flight, Lares failed to notice that he was being followed at a distance through the dense airport crowd.

A sky marshal, U.S. Marshal Edith Floral, was close in pursuit of Lares every move. Yesterday, Washington DC sent a special authorization email letter to the US Marshal's office in New Orleans, Louisiana, assigning U.S. Marshal Edith Floral to Air

Canada flight AC3992.
Monday, May 6, 8:30 P.M.
Juan Santamaria International Airport (SJO)
San Jose, Costa Rica

San Jose is the capital of Costa Rica, with a population of approximately 300,000. It is the largest canton (i.e., local government serving as a municipality) in the Republic of Costa Rica. Nicaragua is to the north and Panama borders this Central America country to the southeast. It is a sovereign, democratic country, and one of the few nations without a standing army.

Costa Rica is an attractive location for many types of companies, ranging from financial and medical to the service industry. Many of these foreign companies operate in Costa Rica because of the Free Trade Zones (FTZs). This is a worthwhile investment for any company, because of the tax incentives. Recently, the Alajuela FTZ parks have attracted heavy industrial companies, especially those manufacturing medical devices. One such company is Roster Pharmaceuticals Inc. Their headquarters are in New Orleans, but the research and manufacturing facility is in the Alajuela district of Costa Rica.

Lares was in transit on the long flight to Costa Rica. Fourteen hours later, and two stops, Washington, Virginia, followed by Toronto, Ontario, Air Canada flight 4391 finally approached Juan Santamaria International Airport in San Jose, Costa Rica.

Lares secured a window seat on the last leg from Toronto. Unfortunately, even with earplugs and a window to lean on, he couldn't manage a moment of sleep on the flight.

An overhead announcement echoing throughout the cabin in Spanish, then English, suddenly startled the passengers and reminded them of their responsibility as the plane approached the airport. No matter, Lares was excited because he never visited Costa Rica in any of his travels.

He kept staring out the window into the ominous darkness with only a glimpse of light below, peeking through the dense tropical, jungle foliage. Suddenly, he experienced a rapid descent, followed by an awkwardly bumpy approach through the cloud cover. Even now, he could still not see the telltale lights of an airport.

There was another overhead announcement, this time only in Spanish, with static in the background. The cabin temperature felt warm, and he was feeling hot and sweating. He kept staring out the window, this time with a noticeable concern. His eyes widened, protruding white, and his sweating increased as tiny drops of sweat rolled down his face.

He reluctantly managed one quick look out the window.

All Lares could think about now is, "This may be my last."

Within seconds, the dark, dense jungle setting magically turned onto an asphalt runway. The plane bounced several times, and a couple of overheads opened, releasing some of their contents on unsuspecting passengers below. He could hear the squealing of massive rubber tires, and the plane abruptly stopped on the cracked, barely illuminated tarmac.

Passengers lunged forward from their seats, some applauded, and a few even shouted in Spanish, "Gracias a Dios para un aterrizaje saguaro" (i.e., "Thank you, God, for a safe landing"). He was later told this response was not uncommon to most of the frequent flyers.

Again, the overhead speakers bellowed with the welcome announcement, signifying a safe landing in San Jose, Costa Rica.

Lares was a seasoned journalist. He was always aware of his surroundings, especially other people, and their mannerisms. He couldn't help the gnawing feeling that he was not alone on this adventure. However, he did not recognize anyone acting suspiciously on this long flight. He was especially concerned about the whereabouts of the unknown male he followed in New Orleans at Roster Pharmaceuticals headquarters.

Lares intuitive feeling was genuine because U.S. Sky Marshal Edith Floral was monitoring his every move on the entire flight. Marshal Floral was a master of disguise. Even though she was tall and masculine in appearance, she had alluring facial features that could entice any man. On the flight, she wore an expensive, two-piece business suit, the type one might associate with a female company executive. Recognizing her as a US sky marshal would be out of the question.

"It's going according to plan," Marshal Floral thought to herself as Lares stepped into the arranged limo at the airport, heading to the hotel.

Tuesday, May 7, 7:58 A.M.

Grano de Oro Hotel

Calle 30, Aves, 2/4

San Jose, Costa Rica

Grano de Oro is an elegant, Canadian run-hotel in a leafy district just 20 minutes walking time from downtown San Jose. It caters to the rich, with its exquisite artwork, renown musical entertainment, and gourmet, French-inspired, Costa Rican fusion cuisine.

"Devon, you single-handedly destroyed my personal budget on this trip. I'm impressed." Lares softly spoke to himself as he flagged down a taxi for the Alajuela district and Roster Pharmaceuticals.

U.S. Sky Marshal Floral was not far behind in a black Jeep Cherokee, but keeping a safe, unobtrusive distance.

Tuesday, May 7, 8:43 A.M.

Roster Pharmaceuticals Instalacion

Alajuela, Costa Rica

Roster Pharmaceuticals Instalacion serves as a manufacturing and research facility (i.e., Sp., Instalacion). Locally, Costa Rica produces approximately 25% of the registered pharmaceuticals, with about 56% of them being prescription drugs and almost all the remaining production dedicated to antiserum. The COVID-19 pandemic has taken a toll on the world, especially hard hit was the pharmaceutical supply chain. Roster Pharmaceuticals Inc. expanded its production of pharmaceuticals because of the COVID-19 pandemic.

On the way, Lares read about this company overview in one of the local commercial listings. His journalistic instinct told him that there was a lot more to this company than manufacturing pharmaceuticals. He just couldn't figure out what it was yet. Thinking out loud,

"The mission statement is committed to serving the people of Costa Rica, but what about the research they conduct?"

"Señor. We are here."

Roster Pharmaceuticals Instalacion was not a single building, but a small campus. There were five buildings in total. The one dedicated to research was the tallest and probably the newest. It was a five-story modern-looking brick structure comprising darkly tinted windows, but there were only windows on the first and fifth floors.

"Odd, but no doubt this building secures their research from those evil industrial spies. Maybe there's another reason this research is in another country?" Lares will find out, as he always does.

Lares couldn't help but feel a tingling anticipation as he entered the building and made his way to the reception area. Upon entering the spacious, rotunda-like room, he faced two armed militia guarding the massive room. Two M15 combat rifles crossed his path directly in front of his face as he tried to step forward to the reception desk. A very subtle hand wave by the receptionist prompted the armed officers to stand down.

The presence of armed officers was relatively common in places of historical or financial importance in Costa Rica, such as banks and government buildings. In a country without a standing army, one would expect the police officers to increase their presence.

Lares curiosity only heightened as he watched the receptionist discreetly guide him towards the secured conference room on the top floor of the building. The massive surge of adrenaline heightened his emotions, vacillating between curiosity and fear, as the receptionist left him in the silence of a spacious room. Only his thoughts kept him company at that moment,

"Something must be special at Roster to deserve this type of security. What next?"

# CHAPTER 15 – ON FILE
# AT THE COMPANY

Tuesday, May 7, 9:30 A.M.
Roster Pharmaceuticals Instalacion
John Roster Centro de Investigation
Alajuela, Costa Rica

After escorting Lares to a spacious, penthouse-like room, they abandoned him with only his thoughts as company. Darkly tinted windows surrounded the fifth-floor room of the John Roster Centro de Investigation floor.

The room held a sprawling, teak-crafted conference table in the center encased by dozens of plush, executive-style chairs. The back of the room displayed an enormous library with artistic mahogany craftsmanship stretching from wall to wall and ceiling. A tall ladder, guided by a rail system, allowed one to retrieve even the most well-hidden book on the highest shelf.

Lares felt as if someone had placed him in solitary confinement. Close to an hour has passed in the silence of the empty room. He tried his best to keep any thoughts away from his actual feelings, his fear of a dreadful outcome or even death.

The abrupt opening of the double-sided, key card secured door interrupted his daydream reflections. A distinguished man of Eastern European descent, in his early sixties, stepped slowly into the room. He appeared handsome for his age, revealing dense, black hair with streaks of grey, and a finely manicured grey beard.

He muttered authoritatively, in his native country accent,

"Mr. Turncock, your background precedes you. I am Gregor

Osseo, the Chief Executive Officer of Roster Pharmaceuticals. Welcome to my home, away from home."

Shaking hands, Lares replied,

"It's a pleasure to meet you and thank you for your kind words. I'm also appreciative of Dr. Roster for the invitation and making the trip arrangements."

"Lares, I hope it's OK with you, if I address you as Lares."

"Please sit and tell me why you're here."

The bold approach of Mr. Osseo caught Lares by surprise. He was thinking, Dr. Roster should have discussed the reason for his visit, after all, he made the arrangements. His concern was that he had told Dr. Roster he met Gregor Osseo before at a meeting, but he was not truthful.

Lares spoke, but his words were obviously a telltale sign of being nervous.

"As I mentioned to Dr. Roster, I'm writing a special piece," sighing.

"Let me rephrase that. My article is on the current research trends in New Orleans. Your story will nicely complement the Greater New Orleans Biosciences Economic Development District (GNOBEDD) special edition."

"Lares, if I recall this correctly, didn't we discuss GNOBEDD at a recent meeting?"

Lares was silent for a moment. Again, showing a telltale sign of nervousness to Gregor.

"I believe you are correct. I recall the conversation, but now we need to fill in the details."

Gregor knew Lares was lying, and the actual intent of his visit was to gather details about his company. After all, he has a reputation for being an investigative reporter.

Gregor just smiled and gave a nod of agreement. He was in the game for only one reason: to win.

"Lares, thank you for including us in the story. The PR Department will be delighted."

"Allow me to bring in our team, and we can get this started."

Gregor left the room and secured the door behind him.

Lares felt relieved. He stood up and surveyed the beauty of the Costa Rican landscape from both sides of the room through the tinted windows.

After about 20 minutes, he could hear activity with talking on the other side of the door. Gregor Osseo, along with an entourage of executive types, entered the room, and sat, as if by assignment, along the front of the conference table.

Gregor Osseo introduced Lares to the executives seated across from him at the table and started the meeting.

"Allow me to describe our company and our mission."

"Dr. John Roster is our founder and established Roster Pharmaceuticals, Inc. approximately 10 years ago. We manufacture many types of drugs and vaccines, as well as supporting an active research arm for the company. Our mission is to support the health and well-being of Costa Rica by our commitment to the production and distribution of high-quality pharmaceuticals for the citizens of Costa Rica."

"Dr. Aron Millstone is the Executive Vice President of Research and Development."

"Dr. Millstone, could you please say a few words about our research."

"Thank you, Gregor, and a warm welcome to Mr. Lares Turncock. I hope you are enjoying our beautiful Costa Rica."

"We take pride in redistributing a portion of our profits to the ongoing effort in pharmaceutical research at our company. This takes the form of drug development, innovation in vaccine production, and translational clinical research on drug discovery."

"I have been with the company from the very beginning as a leader in the research team for Dr. Roster."

"Thank you and allow me to introduce our division chief of our research and development, Dr. Len Rachillas."

"Thank you, Dr. Millstone, and also a warm welcome to you, Mr. Turncock."

"Our primary focus is infectious disease and vaccine production."

"For obvious reasons, I cannot discuss details of our research efforts, but what I can mention is that we use state-of-the-art technology. We are proud to have attracted a dedicated team of exceptionally talented scientists."

"In particular, allow me to introduce our esteemed scientific team; Dr. Tedy Evans, M.D., Ph.D., Senior Scientist, R&D, Dr. Kuna Merman, Ph.D., Clinical Research Scientist, R&D, and Dr. Lille Garter, D.V.M., R&D, our in-house veterinarian in charge of the vivarium. They will join us shortly on the company tour."

"I am especially proud of our fellowship program. I would like to mention that our current fellow is Dr. Charro Belons. Unfortunately, he couldn't join us this morning due to overseeing a critical lab test."

"Unless there are questions, I will turn the meeting back over to Gregor."

Lares felt stonewalled by the generic approach of the teams' comments. Lares felt shocked that the scientists were not allowed to speak at the meeting. He could've easily found the information provided by the senior executives in a PR brochure of the company.

Deliberately appearing to be confused, Lares asked,

"My intent with this article is to summon interest from medical device and pharmaceutical companies to put down roots in the Greater New Orleans Biosciences Economic Development District. It is my hope, this article will instill interest in companies, such as yours, to join us. Do you think this would be possible soon?"

Gregor, appearing noticeably disturbed by the question, answered Lares,

"Establishing a manufacturing or distribution site in New Orleans was a topic of discussion at one of our board meetings. However, I'm not able to answer that question. Dr. Roster is your man."

Gregor was deliberate in his digression.

"Meanwhile, let's take you on a tour of our manufacturing and research areas."

Lares was used to this type of diversionary segue tactic by executives, who are trying to avoid a direct answer with rhetoric.

Having little choice in the matter, Lares replied,

"Excellent idea."

"Thank you, and it was a pleasure meeting everyone. I very much appreciate your valuable time and comments. I'm looking forward to the tour of your facilities."

In a hardy handshake, with kind words by some, and a hint of insincerity by others, the executives and scientists left the room.

Gregor was the last to leave. Turning to Lares, he said,

"Lares, please make yourself comfortable, and you are welcome to immerse yourself in some books from the library until I return. I will gather the team for the tour and return shortly."

Lares, noticing it was close to midday, did not expect the tour to happen for at least an hour. After all, it was Costa Rica time. That was fine with him because it gave him time to think about the group's comments. If nothing else, he could take in more of the beauty of the Costa Rica landscape from the darkly tinted windows. He could even peruse some books from the beautiful library.

He was a reporter. He couldn't sit idle while droves of thoughts were swirling in his head. Foremost was the appearance of the John Roster Centro de Investigation building. Five floors, and only windows surrounding the first and top floor. Why? It's different from other research facilities he has visited in the past.

"It could be the sensitive nature of the research and the need for added security. If you have fewer windows, you have less of a chance for unwanted intrusion." Lares thought to himself.

Then an epiphany came to him:

"I'm sitting here on the top floor with windows surrounding me on only two sides. The elevator and hallway entrance are in front, and this remarkable library is behind me. I noticed windows in the hallway by the elevator, but where are the windows behind me? Obviously, they were visible as I walked earlier toward entering this building. This room is also much smaller on the inside compared to the outside."

Lares investigative reporter skills told him there was something behind this impressive library collection in the back of the room. He walked to the library shelves and carefully perused the books. There were sections containing medical, legal, and even historical books that would challenge the most elite hospital library or successful attorneys' law-book collection.

He began looking for any clue on the bookshelves for a switch or lever hidden in the book arrangement.

"If I could only find the outlier, any book that doesn't belong in this library or is out of order." Lares thought to himself.

Lares carefully scanned the shelves he could make eye contact with across the width of the room. It was midway through his search, when he saw it, a 3-inch-wide book on the history of Costa Rica. It was oversized and had a simple cover with fake pages glued to each other. He pulled out the book and looked into the dark recess behind. He noticed a small button-like switch, and a tiny, red glowing LED light above the switch. He cautiously pressed the switch, and the light turned green.

Lares stood back as the bookshelves moved until he could see the outline of a door opening. Peering through the dimly lit doorway, he could faintly see outside trees in the distance. He carefully walked through the doorway and encountered a wide balcony with extended handrails. They stretched across the length of the room in front of him, only to be broken by a staircase. The stairs appeared to be leading downward to a lower floor in the building. This had to be the mysterious fourth floor.

He hesitated momentarily, not knowing what was awaiting him at the bottom of the staircase, but cautiously proceeded downward. Total silence surrounded the dimly lit stairs as Lares carefully walked down the winding staircase.

He reached the bottom of the stairs, where it brought him

into another short, but well-lit hallway, appearing to surround the entire fourth floor. The hallway had one side made of white concrete block. The opposite side contained heavy glass-enclosed windows. He was peering into some type of laboratory.

Two figures in the background were wearing white plastic suits, complete with headgear, and were attached to a coiled tube protruding from the ceiling. Lares had never witnessed this type of room firsthand. However, he knew it was a biocontainment facility, probably a BSL-4 level type as described and pictured in his CDC reference materials.

The scientists seemed to be examining some type of sample under a series of high-power microscopes. He also noticed a small cage in the room containing two white mice. One individual appeared to have a hypodermic syringe in-hand. The partner captured one mouse in the cage, held it, while the other appeared to inject the rodent.

"I'm gone!" Lares thought to himself as he quickly lurched back up the stairs, pressing an inside button that opened the library door, allowing him to re-enter the conference room.

He showed a sigh of relief when he didn't see Gregor standing on the other side of the entrance.

Lares was sweating, winded, and fearful at what he saw. All he could think about at the time was if he was under surveillance on the fourth floor. If so, someone would soon realize his fear.

His timing was perfect because Gregor returned to retrieve Lares for the tour 15 minutes later. There was no sign that Gregor was aware of his visit to the fourth-floor laboratory.

"Lares, I apologize for the delay, but I have the team together now and, if you will, please join us."

They both headed to the elevator in silence.

In the ground-floor vestibule, Lares noticed a small group gathered next to two heavily armed guards stationed at the entrance.

Gregor made the introductions.

"I believe you met Dr. Evans, Senior Scientist, Dr. Merman,

Clinical Research Scientist, and Dr. Garter, our in-house veterinarian. I would also like to introduce our research fellow, Dr. Charro Belons, M.D., Ph.D."

"Let's begin with the manufacturing buildings and then work our way back to the Centro de Investigation facility."

Entering the manufacturing areas, Lares noted the worn machinery and aged facilities. Each of the three manufacturing buildings revealed the same outdated equipment. The equipment in the manufacturing buildings was in stark contrast to the biocontainment lab, which boasted state-of-the-art equipment. Why?

Several possibilities exist, Lares thought to himself,

"The company spends more money on R&D rather than manufacturing? Of course, modernizing this area would cost jobs by introducing robotics."

The other possibility was more concerning to him.

"Maybe the manufacturing arm of the company is a cover-up for what's really going on in the Centro de Investigation facility?"

Gregor noticed Lares was not paying attention to the discussion and asked,

"Lares, do you have questions?"

As if suddenly awakened from a dream, Lares shook his head, and the group continued to the last building,

Gregor led the group into the remaining building. It was a massive, one-story structure, surrounded by a continuous exterior concrete platform leading to a truck loading area.

Gregor explained,

"This is the least exciting building, the product distribution center."

This was not the case for Lares. For him, it represented identities, addresses, and product types of evidence in his investigation. Lares felt a familiar knot in his stomach as they made their way through the distribution center's vast interior. They passed row after row of shelves stacked high with crates and boxes, each one holding secrets, waiting to be uncovered.

Boxes were trailing past him as the group walked through the area containing conveyor belts, leading to the outside concrete platforms, and ultimately into waiting trucks. Lares couldn't shake the sensation that he was in a maze, with each box a potential clue and each pathway a potential dead end.

The boxes were supposed to go to locations in Costa Rica. However, he noticed a substantial number of boxes had addresses to a single location in New Orleans, Roans Medical Supply, LLC.

Gregor noticed Lares interest in this cascade of boxes.

"You seem intrigued by those boxes," Gregor said, raising an eyebrow as he gestured toward the ones addressed to Roans Medical Supply, LLC.

Lares nodded, his mind working quickly.

"Please excuse me, and I don't mean any disrespect or intrusion, but I'm still wondering why you don't have a manufacturing facility in New Orleans. It would serve well to complement your medical supply distribution?"

"Lares, I have three words for you, 'follow the money'. No disrespect, but manufacturing cost is much less in Costa Rica."

Lares nodded, and the group headed back to the R&D facility. However, his thoughts lingered on the boxes addressed to Roans Medical Supply, LLC.

Gregor, Lares, and the team of scientists exchanged small talk on the way back to the Centro de Investigation facility. Once they arrived, Lares excused himself to a quiet corner of the reception area, pulling out his phone to search for information on Roans Medical Supply. After typing in the company name, Lares discovered something alarming. Not only was Roans Medical Supply, LLC under investigation for fraudulent medical supply practices, but the CEO, Jethro Roans, had been a suspect in illicit drug trafficking. If true, this information could have far-reaching implications for the involvement of Roster Pharmaceuticals.

Gregor, waiting in the elevator with his scientific team, waved Lares over to the open door.

"Lares, you look worried. Is everything alright?"

"Fine. Let's look at your research areas."

Gregor described the laboratory on their way to the second floor. Lares noticed that a keycard code secured the second and third floors, but the fourth floor required a tubular cam lock key for access. This type of key is very difficult to pick in any lock.

"Gregor, you mentioned that the second and third floors were laboratories. What about the fourth floor?"

Lares asked, curiosity clear in his expression. Gregor paused, choosing his words carefully.

"Storage. We're in Central America and supplies are not only difficult to get but will quickly disappear if not stored in a locked area. 'Secure them or lose them', is our motto."

Gregor's explanation made no sense. Lares couldn't discount the fact that he saw a biocontainment lab on the fourth floor.

"Why the coverup?"

The second floor opened into a bustling laboratory. Scientists in white coats moved about, focused on their tasks.

"This is where we conduct our microbiological research," Gregor explained, gesturing toward the rows of Petri plates being handled under carefully controlled conditions.

"Let's continue to the next floor, where our molecular testing is located."

The third floor housed the molecular testing area. Lares observed scientists analyzing genetic material and manipulating DNA with state-of-the-art instrumentation. Robotics facilitated the precise movements required for such delicate work.

They could only view the molecular testing behind a glass enclosed area. However, there was another spacious area that divided the room with access from the hallway. Peering through a small glass window with an embedded wire mesh, one could see that the entrance was an anti-room with a sink, lab coat area, and other supplies.

Dr. Garter, the in-house veterinarian, stepped to the front of the door.

"This is our animal facility, or more commonly referred to as a vivarium."

She frowned while preparing herself. "I have some bad news," she stated.

"You cannot go beyond this door. Unfortunately, we strictly control this area and only allow specially trained personnel to access it."

"However, I can assure you, we treat all animals humanely."

Lares nodded, feeling disappointed but understanding the necessity of the restrictions.

Gregor and the team escorted Lares back to the elevator.

Lares always considered himself a very astute investigative reporter. He had a talent for identifying people who will talk to him on a case. Dr. Charro Belons was such a person. He just knew by his eye contact and facial expressions that Dr. Belons wanted to talk to him.

Lares deliberately stood next to Dr. Belons at the back of the elevator. He even introduced himself again as a journalist.

"I'm pleased to meet you, Mr. Turncock. I heard about your work in New Orleans from Gregor."

The dialogue was brief, probably because Gregor gave a penetrating look to both Lares and Dr. Belons.

As the elevator door opened on the first floor, Dr. Belons discreetly slipped a small, white paper into Lares pocket.

Gregor and the group made their way out of the facility, leaving Lares to ponder over the unexpected slip of paper.

The taxi was waiting, so Lares quickly hailed it and jumped in. He settled into the back seat and pulled out the small white paper from his pocket.

"Urgent. Meet me at 7 PM tonight for dinner at Le Bistrot De Paris. CB."

# CHAPTER 16 –
# MALAS NOTICIAS

Tuesday, May 7, 3:57 P.M.
Grano de Oro Hotel
Calle 30, Aves, 2/4
San Jose, Costa Rica

U.S. Sky Marshal Edith Floral followed Lares taxi back to the Grano de Oro Hotel. The hotel's historical ambiance, with wood-laden arches and winding staircases, flourishing greenery, and well-placed artifacts, allowed Marshal Floral to blend into the background. As she kept her distance, Marshal Floral noticed Lares looking tense, scanning his surroundings for any sign of trouble. She was not aware of Lares dinner meeting, and Lares was careful to conceal the fact, in case he was being tailed.

Lares years of experience as an investigative reporter taught him some masterful tricks in evading surveillance. He was taking no chance to reveal his upcoming dinner with Dr. Belons to anyone. He strolled through the ornate hotel lobby, always glancing over his shoulder, and changing course several times to ensure he wasn't being followed.

The courtyard dining room was just ahead of him, around the grandiose, carved walnut reception desk. He continued past the reception area, entering the open-air terrace and covered spaces of the spacious courtyard. He paused, as if to take in the moment's beauty with a panoramic view. Anyone following him should have understood his intent. Tonight, will be a dinner in the courtyard dining room.

Lares backtracked to the reception area, and in a raised voice intended for the ears of a nearby bystander,

"Señor, I would like a dinner reservation for one at 8:30 this evening in this beautiful courtyard. The ambience is outstanding!"

The concierge nodded, placing the reservation in the system.

Marshal Floral, sitting next to the reception area perusing today's San Jose Times, heard the request. Noticing Lares was heading to his room on a nearby elevator, she made her way to the hotel bar for a drink. The open bar allowed her to have visual access to most of the lobby and the elevator area.

Lares did not go to his hotel room. Instead, he used the second-floor backstairs to exit the rear of the building. He was on his way for some sightseeing until his dinner meeting with Dr. Belons.

Tuesday, May 7, 5:36 P.M.

Roster Pharmaceuticals Instalacion

John Roster Centro de Investigation

Alajuela, Costa Rica

The goal of the fellowship program at Roster Pharmaceuticals was to train Dr. Belons in the use and application of molecular microbiology and infectious disease diagnostics. This experience contrasts with other scientists' positions at the facility. Their focus was on specific parts of a project as assigned by a senior scientist. As a security measure to protect sensitive research, they often employed this type of tunnel vision. Stating this differently, if you don't have knowledge of all the parts, the research aim will be difficult to determine.

However, Lares was not your 'typical researcher' because he had an exceptional talent for solving complex research questions. After all, he never lost a chess game in his life, and he could solve the Rubik's Cube in less than 10 minutes.

Dr. Belons had already undergone training in many areas of the research facility. Ironically, he wondered what type of pharmacological research would warrant the use of such sophisticated technology at this company. He trained in almost every part of the research facility, including the biocontainment laboratory. However, he was still unaware of the well-kept secret of the library/conference room entrance.

Since Dr. Belons knew Lares Turncock better from their conversations on the tour, he again reflected on these questions. The tour encounter made him think again and question the use of such sophisticated technology. His theory was that Roster Pharmaceuticals was not only involved with the genetic engineering of microbes, but for what end? Was there some kind of ulterior motive hidden behind the research?

He had a strong feeling that Mr. Turncock was not visiting only to gather background for a newspaper story, but to uncover incriminating evidence as an investigative reporter. His instincts were rarely mistaken, so he met with Mr. Turncock in secret to elicit some of his questions.

He often spent long hours in the night at the research facility, learning as much as he could about the testing at hand. However, tonight will be different. He will try to find clues on the type of research being performed. Since he had a scheduled testing slot in the molecular laboratory, that would be a good starting place.

As he made his way through the dimly lit corridors, a sense of anticipation gnawed at him. The soft hum of instrumentation seemed to echo his inner turmoil. He couldn't shake the feeling that something wasn't right about the research.

As he reached the entrance to the sprawling molecular laboratory, he paused. A door to the office was open. It was the office of the senior scientist; he made his presence known by slowly peeking inside the room. The scientist was not at his desk. He must've stepped out to either another lab or a meeting. Walking into the lab, he noticed it was vacant, with only the sounds of the liquid being pipetted by working robotics.

He walked about the lab, noting the various equipment and workstations. Pausing again at the senior scientist's doorway, he noticed a file on the desk titled.

'Project Nesting Dolls,'

"What a strange title for a research project," Dr. Belons

thought to himself.

Nervous and sweating, he was visibly anxious. He looked at some documents scattered about by the file. He deliberately did not want to touch or move any of the documents for fear of being discovered. Likewise, he perused some verbiage on those that were readily visible. Most of the papers were stacked on top of each other, but a few papers showed visible DNA base sequencing results. The most concerning document stated:

"Balamuthia mandrillaris, which was isolated from shower units in San Jose, Costa Rica, has been successfully cloned, sequenced, and genetically changed to possess virulence genes, giant viruses found in free-living amoeba, and select bacterial pathogens, according to researchers."

"The pathogenicity of the cyst form in a C57BL/6J strain of white mice was tested, and they discovered it to be highly effective in the LCD50 (i.e., lethal concentration dose that kills 50% of the test animal)."

Unfortunately, without disturbing the papers, Dr. Belons could not read further on the document, even though researchers have tested the cyst form in humans.

He heard footsteps approaching the office door. Dr. Belons quickly stepped into the main laboratory, stood in front of the sequencing instrumentation, and plucked a file from the lab bench.

Dr. Tedy Evans, senior scientist for the molecular R&D laboratory, walked into the room and stood behind Dr. Belons.

Opening the file, Dr. Belons quickly flipped through the pages, pretending to be engrossed in the contents. He was visibly shaking, trying to maintain his composure as Dr. Evans peered over his shoulder.

"Charro, don't you think you've had enough for one day? Please finish your work and go home."

Dr. Belons nodded and crammed the file back on the lab bench, feigning a casual composure. He was relieved to know that Dr. Evans did not suspect the true reason he was back in the lab.

Viewing the time, he had to leave or risk missing his dinner meeting with Mr. Turncock. The document discovery had to wait until later.

Little did he know, Dr. Evans had been onto him for quite some time.

Tuesday, May 7, 6:55 P.M.

Le Bistrot De Paris

Torres de Paseo Colón, Planta Baja, Restaurante Ubicado en Torres de Paseo Colón— Planta Baja

San Jose, Costa Rica

Le Bistrot De Paris offered the ambience of a French bistro in Costa Rica.

Dr. Belons met at Le Bistrot De Paris because they were less likely to be seen in public by his work colleagues, who frequented the local Costa Rican restaurants.

Dr. Belons made it to the restaurant just in time to see Mr. Turncock, already seated at a small table near the back.

"Isolated from eavesdropping ears," Charro thought to himself as he approached the well-hidden table.

"Mr. Turncock, I'm pleased that you could join me for dinner."

"Please, call me Lares."

Anton, the waiter, approached the table with a warm smile and took their drink orders. After he left, Dr. Belons paused in their small talk conversation and said,

"I'm not one for chance meetings and direct conversations with someone I don't know, but I sense we both have a mutual understanding of why we're here. My suspicion is that you are here under the pretense of a journalist seeking a story. You are here as an investigative journalist, seeking evidence for a recent incident worthy of your investigative skill."

Lares smiled, nodding as Dr. Belons spoke. He felt Dr. Belons was sincere. He chose his words cautiously, even though his gut told him he could trust him.

"Dr. Belons, let's say you are right, and I am here as an investigative reporter. What am I here to investigate?"

"You are here because you suspect that Roster Pharmaceuticals Instalacion may be hiding some type of research that is not aligned with the usual pharmacological stuff."

"Let me phrase this a little differently. Let's say that someone from the company shared information with an investigative reporter by inviting him to a dinner meeting. Do you know what the information may be about?"

"Mr. Turncock, can we stop with the innuendos? I believe we trust each other at this point."

"Absolutely! Tell me what you know, and I will keep you as a confidant, unless you decide otherwise."

"Agreed. I believe your reputation will proceed you on your word."

Both men paused in silence as the waiter, Anton, approached their table with a menu in hand and took their orders.

Dr. Belons spent the next 20 minutes before dinner relaying the details of what he knew about the research at Roster Pharmaceuticals so far. Likewise, Lares provided his findings to Dr. Belons on the New Orleans pneumonia deaths and the demise of Maia Revalue.

When he described the person allegedly responsible for the death of Maia Revalue, Dr. Belons realized that this investigation was even more sinister than he had expected.

"A highly respected individual within the company appears to be at the center of this web of deceit," Dr. Belons interjected into the ongoing conversation.

"You have just described Dr. Tod Firehall, an infectious disease physician on staff at our headquarters in New Orleans."

"Dr. Belons, I'm leaving early tomorrow morning, but I want to stay in touch with your findings. I have a secure VPN. Please consider using my email for any recent evidence. Please be safe and don't take any unwanted risks. I'll be in touch."
Tuesday, May 7:34 P.M.
Grano de Oro Hotel
Calle 30, Aves, 2/4

San Jose, Costa Rica

Lares arrived at his hotel just in time for his dinner reservation in the courtyard. He entered by the back staircase, and proceeded up to the third floor, and then down to the second floor, carefully viewing the hallway for any intruders. He walked up to his room door, scrutinizing the almost invisible hair he pasted on the door as a security measure. The Do Not Disturb sign was still intact, as well as the hair, so he proceeded down the elevator for his dinner reservation.

Lares, having an earlier dinner with Dr. Belons, now swirled and sipped a fine glass of cognac in the cozy courtyard. He couldn't shake off the unnerving feeling that someone was watching him. Trying not to gain too much attention, he summoned the waiter for his check. He glanced around, but no one seemed to focus on him.

Lares was wrong. Marshal Floral was sitting at a corner table, only a short distance from him, in the courtyard. The surveillance worked because she guessed Lares would expect a man to be tailing him. She also knew that he was not in his hotel room the entire afternoon. Marshal Floral, herself, often used the same tricks-of-the-trade, with the tiny hair on the door and the sign. He successfully evaded her, and now she was determined to find out what he was up to and who he was meeting with earlier.

The hour was late, and Lares had an early flight back home in the morning. He paid for his drink and left the courtyard, checking for any signs of surveillance as he made his way to his room.

Marshal Floral, being an air marshal, gained access to the flight manifests. He confirmed Lares was on Air Canada flight 958 departing at 8:10 AM tomorrow out of Juan Santamaria International Airport. His next call was to New Orleans, Gregor Osseo.

"Gregor, it's me. I'm still in Costa Rica but will be returning tomorrow on the same flight as our friend. We need to sever our relationship with our friend. I'll explain later in more detail."

Art Lifehold, alias Dr. Tod Firehall, alias Sky Marshal Edith Floral, is a CIA case officer, deeply embedded into the Costa Rica cartel, Jingoes New Reactional. Gregor Osseo is not aware of his identity. He only knows him as Dr. Todd Firehall, physician, and researcher for Roster Pharmaceuticals.

Thursday, May 9, 10:23 A.M.

Watkins & Swindon Medical Diagnostics, LLC (WSMD)

Mandeville, Louisiana

Despite feeling completely drained, Lares pushed himself to tackle the findings from Costa Rica. He headed straight to the WSMD lab, feeling the weight of the information he carried. Dr. Watkins and Dr. Swindon have been trusted friends for years. He knew they were working on the case. Now he needed to share this ground-breaking evidence with them, and fast.

Upon entering the lab, Lares went straight to the testing area, where he found Dr. Watkins and Dr. Swindon reviewing some test results.

"Lares, you're back!"

"How was your vacation?" said Dr. Swindon, with a smile and a friendly hug.

Appearing concerned about the question, Lares replied,

"It wasn't exactly time off; can we talk in private?"

"Of course," Dr. Watkins replied, leading Lares to a private meeting room next to the lab.

"Dr. Swindon, please join us. Of course, if that's OK with Lares?"

"Yes."

Lares took a deep breath, then reached into his shirt pocket and displayed a small Sony digital recorder.

"I know you have been looking into the mysterious pneumonia cases here in New Orleans."

"I've been following the events from the very beginning as an investigative reporter. I know you have an obligation to protect your case investigation."

"However, I would like to present my findings and hope that you will share your findings, or at least confirm the likelihood of what I am about to tell you."

"Lares, we have a long history, both professionally and socially, that allows us to trust your word. As always, this is in the strictness of confidence, and yes, please share your findings with us."

"I became very concerned when I first heard about the cluster of pneumonia deaths, especially CDC involvement. As a follow-up, I paid a visit to Dr. Catechin, our fine medical examiner. There I was eyewitness to some very unusual autopsies, and before I could follow up in the morgue, I fell unconscious and woke up in my car."

"Coincidentally, I was one of many reporters covering the death of Queen Maia Revalue. Because of the suspicious nature of the entire scene at her house, I interviewed several witnesses. I had a partial description of an individual fleeing from the scene. I thought nothing of this until I was talking to our Editor-in-Chief, Shepard Althorn. He was acting very suspicious lately, so in one of our discussions, I noticed a business card on his desk for a local company, Roster Pharmaceuticals. I took a chance and staked out the place for a few hours, hoping to see someone matching the description of the suspicious individual at Queen Maia's crime scene."

"To get straight to the point ..." I found this suspicious man at Roster Pharmaceuticals headquarters, 1515 Poydras. I discovered that their manufacturing and research facilities are in Costa Rica.

"My vacation was a trip to Costa Rica as an investigative reporter. I disguised the real reason as a front for a special piece on a New Orleans medical device venture. My instincts tell me that this company was involved in some kind of nefarious scheme. I believe I was right."

"All of my articles and investigations comprise notes, documents, recordings, and, of course, the trustworthy mental notes in my head."

Lares placed the small Sony recorder on the table and pressed the play button.

The threesome listened intently to Dr. Belons recorded testimony for close to an hour. Dr. Belons detailed the suspicious activities and documentation he had witnessed at Roster Pharmaceuticals.

"Lares, I can tell you this aligns with our findings in the case. You need to know that we are working with the FBI, among others, in this case. Let me make a digital copy of your recording for our records and for the FBI. For now, my concern is your safety," Dr. Watkins said with a look of concern.

"Let's meet again this afternoon. I'll call you with a time."

Lares gathered his notes and recorder, mentally preparing himself for the next crucial steps in exposing Roster Pharmaceuticals.

Lunch at his favorite restaurant, Acme Oyster House, and a po-boy fried oyster sandwich with a cup of seafood gumbo would take his mind off this concern for his safety.

Thursday, May 9, 1:44 P.M.

Acme Oyster House

724 Iberville Street

New Orleans

Where y'at? The iconic Acme Oyster House, in the French Quarter, is often the answer at lunchtime in New Orleans. That's what Lares told his boss, Shepard, when he texted him to see when he was coming to the office.

"In about an hour," texted Lares.

Dr. Tod Firehall contacted Shepard. He wanted to arrange a meeting this afternoon with him and Mr. Turncock about some interesting news.

Lares finished his last bite of the savory oyster po-boy and wiped his lips with a napkin. Just as he reached for his cup of seafood gumbo, Lares phone buzzed again with a text from Shepard.

"Meet me in my office within the hour."

Confused but intrigued, Lares wondered what exciting news was in store for him at the office.

Lares usually found walking to lunch was an exercise that

would justify the po-boy and seafood gumbo caloric intake. Aside from that, it made him feel good.

He had worked out the perfect route from his New Orleans Tribune office to Acme Oyster House over the years.

Go from Royal to St. Charles, then make your way through Common St., Elk and Basin Streets, and N. Claiborne Ave. to Esplanade Ave. and the Tribune. He rarely deviated from his route, the weather being the only outlier.

Unbeknown to Lares, Art Lifehold was planning to ambush him as he turned on N. Claiborne Ave. to Esplanade Ave.

Lifehold cleared the intersection and forcefully pushed Lares down to distract him from the pinprick in his neck. Before Lars could even look up to see what happened, Lifehold was out of sight.

Rubbing his neck, and feeling a little drowsy from the fall, Lares stood up and continued walking to the office.

"I'll give him less than half an hour, before the poison takes his life," Lifehold said to himself.

Thursday, May 9, 2:39 P.M.
New Orleans Tribune, Office of Lares Turncock
2317 Esplanade Avenue

Lares was sluggish in his walking, and he had attributed this feeling to the unfortunate incident. He could barely make it up the staircase to his office, where he had to sit at his desk, gasping for air.

Shepard swung open his office door and said,

"Lares, in my office, please!"

It was just then he noticed Lares was unresponsive. His eyes were wide open, and his pupils appeared to be fixed. He also appeared to be very rigid in his chair, as if posing as a statue.

Shepard immediately checked his pulse. There was none. He dialed 911.

"I have a person in my office that, I believe, is dead. Please send an ambulance to 2317 Esplanade Avenue. I'm on the second floor of the New Orleans Tribune. I'm the Editor-in-Chief, Shepard Althorn."

# CHAPTER 17 - WHISTLEBLOWER

Thursday, May 9, 3:09 P.M.
New Orleans Tribune
2317 Esplanade Avenue
Medical personnel, local law enforcement, and federal officers overcame the office of Lares Turncock. The media pressed against the police barricades at the Tribune building, clamoring for a glimpse of the developing scene.

Special Agent Lawins took charge of coordinating the investigation, his sharp gaze surveying the chaotic scene and keeping the media at bay, at least for now.

Special Agent Lawins directed Dr. Watkins and Dr. Swindon to join him at the crime scene. This order came shortly after their debriefing to the FBI on the evidence uncovered by Lares in Costa Rica.

Detective Ottovino was puzzled by the FBI's involvement in a case that stemmed from a single death reported on a 911 call. If someone had informed him about Lares visit to Costa Rica, he would have known the reason.

Special Agent Lawins could now see a pattern emerging in Lares Turncock's death, a thread that connected recent events to Lares Turncock's mysterious trip to Costa Rica. He would reveal his thoughts after the autopsy.

Detective Ottovino was at the scene because he suspected it was a homicide. He assumed Special Agent Lawins showed up for the same reason.

After seeing the FBI team in full force and taking charge of his crime scene, he became visibly disturbed. He confronted the special agent.

"Lawins! Let me guess, you have information that you need to share, which indicates that my crime scene falls under your jurisdiction because it is linked to the pneumonia cases?"

"Detective Ottovino, thank you for asking."

"The answer is yes, and it is fresh evidence I will share with you when we secure the body for autopsy at the morgue."

Ottovino scowled, then composed himself before replying, "Fine, but I expect a full briefing as soon as we arrive at the morgue."

Special Agent Lawins nodded, and the two men walked away in opposite directions, knowing what they had to do to secure the crime scene.

Dr. Watkins and Dr. Swindon followed close behind, their expressions mirroring Detective Ottovino's mix of frustration and concern.

Shepard was still in disbelief about Lares death. He appeared pale, distraught, and speechless when approached for questioning by the FBI. He just sat motionless on the plush chair in his office, wondering what he got himself into.

Special Agent Lawins approached him.

"Mr. Althorn, you are the one who found Mr. Turncock in his office. I need to take your statement. Please outline the details leading up to finding Mr. Turncock and any other details that occurred before medical and law enforcement personnel arrived."

Shepard remained motionless and speechless.

"Mr. Althorn, I'll allow you a few minutes to collect your thoughts, but I'm not leaving until I have your statement."

Shepard spoke softly but gave a brief statement.

Special Agent Lawins knew there was much more to the story and decided a 24/7 surveillance was the best approach for uncooperative witnesses.

Thursday, May 9, 6:36 P.M.

New Orleans Medical Examiner Office

## 3001 Earhart Boulevard

Dr. Catechin was examining the body of Lares Turncock, when the team arrived in the city morgue. They watched as Dr. Catechin carefully examined every detail of Lares Turncock's body surface. He spoke slowly, with exact medical details for the recorded notes.

"Most prominent is the intense rigor of the body, which does not appear to be rigor mortis in the time of death. The extent of the rigor appears to be more consistent with pre-mortem paralysis, possibly the result of a toxin or poison. At this time, my preliminary cause of death would be asphyxiation."

Dr. Catechin's meticulous examination revealed crucial evidence that hinted at foul play. He continued the physical examination and discovered a source for the delivery of the toxicant.

"I am noticing a small, recent puncture wound on the back of the neck, which resembles a needle-stick. This could be the entry point for the toxicant."

Dr. Catechin carefully collected trace evidence around the puncture wound, preserving it for further analysis. He included a blood specimen for toxicology and other testing.

Special Agent Lawins viewed enough of the autopsy. He was suspicious that Lares Turnock died in a manner like Maia Revalue, a deadly poison. "Lares knew too much." He thought to himself.

He signaled to the others; Detective Ottovino, Dr. Watkins, and Dr. Swindon to follow him into the nearby conference room.

They briefed Detective Ottovino on the evidence provided by Lares trip to Costa Rica. He cross-referenced it with the information he got during the investigation, and a pattern emerged.

"We have a deadly virus hiding inside a parasite, a free-living amoeba, that can quickly cause pneumonia and death in humans. According to our fine doctors, the two hospitals involved used the most potent antimicrobials without success. Now, we have evidence from a dead man, Mr. Turncock, that a research facility in Costa Rica may be genetically modifying such an agent." Said Special Agent Lawins.

He continued, "Maia Revalue may have been a distracter from the actual murderer. A poison caused her death found only in South America. I don't believe in coincidence, Costa Rica is next door to South America, and this may be evidence linked to a cartel and drugs, cocaine."

Dr. Swindon abruptly stood up and proclaimed,

"That's it, the answer for the delivery of the Balamuthia mandrillaris cyst. How is cocaine introduced into the body of the addicted person? The usual way is by forceful 'snorting' through a tiny straw. What can be simpler than that?"

"All victims showed evidence of cocaine in their hair samples. The presence of cocaine in the hair samples of the ten victims explains why more people did not contract the deadly pneumonia. The million-dollar question is, why only a handful of people?"

Special Agent Lawins, nodding his head, spoke up and said, "Using a special blend of the deadly agent and cocaine, someone specifically targeted the victims."

Friday, May 10, 8:08 A.M.

Roster Pharmaceuticals, Inc.

1515 Poydras, Suite 1906

New Orleans

Dr. Tod Firehall was strategizing with Dr. Roster in his office. Dr. Roster was the only one who knew his identity, Art Lifehold. They were the perfect team; Dr. John, Roster, physician and retired military special forces, and CIA Case Officer Art Lifehold. They were the masterminds behind the project, 'Nesting Dolls'.

"Nice work, Dr. Firehall."

"Lares Turncock will no longer be a problem for us."

"However, what about our other issue in Costa Rica? I have it from a credible source that Dr. Belons met with Mr. Turncock the night before he left San Jose."

There was an obvious look of surprise on Art Lifehold's face, "Somehow, he eluded me. I guarantee that will never happen again!"

"I will hold you to it, and you know I'm always good at my word."

"Understood."

"Devon will book you on an early flight tomorrow morning to San Jose. Find out what Dr. Belons knows and take care of it."

"Not a problem."

"On another topic, was there any issue with Nacket and the swap of the cocaine packet?"

"It all went smoothly."

"Art, call me on a burner and keep me updated. I'll make sure everything else is in place for our 'Nesting Dolls'. project"
Sunday, May 12, 10:45 A.M.
Roster Pharmaceuticals Instalacion
Alajuela, Costa Rica
Dr. Roster hired as an infectious disease consultant Dr. Tod Firehall. He is not a physician, but he has medical field training from his military days. He was Dr. Roster's partner in the 'Nesting Dolls' project, a secret operation to gather and research biological warfare agents for military purposes.

The Roster Pharmaceuticals research staff received instructions to solely focus on their research and were strictly prohibited from discussing any details with other staff researchers. This insured no one except for Dr. Roster and Dr. Firehall would know the exact sequence of steps leading to the project's final product. The consequences of breaching this directive were severe, as Dr. Firehall made it ever so clear to the staff.

After losing almost a day because of travel time, Dr. Firehall scrambled to catch up to his original schedule for the 'Nesting Dolls' project. The tight timeline demanded an unwavering adherence to the schedule. Any delay might jeopardize the entire project.

There were four phases to the 'Nesting Dolls' project.

First, find a suitable vector that could protect the infectious microbe from the most severe environmental conditions. A free-living amoeba cyst is that type of vector. It can withstand severe conditions of temperature, pressure, ultraviolet radiation, and dehydration.

Second, genetically engineer one of the large viruses recently found to infect free-living amoeba to be highly virulent. This includes extreme multi-drug resistance, allowing it to cause death from respiratory failure within one to two days.

Art Lifehold (alias Dr. Tod Firehall) and Dr. Roster felt delighted as they reached the end of the third phase. This phase comprised two parts. The first was to test the engineered, infectious agent in laboratory animals. This was successful, and the second part was to test the lethality in human subjects. Here, they mixed the biological agent with cocaine and distributed it to unsuspecting users in New Orleans.

The third phase received high praise for its success, but now federal agents may uncover evidence that could put the project at risk. The success of Project 'Nesting Dolls', Phase 4, is in jeopardy if the federal investigation prevails.

Lifehold tried to divert attention away from Roster Pharmaceuticals by poisoning Maia Revalue and Lares Turncock, but it had a minor effect on slowing the investigation. Especially concerning for Dr. Roster and Dr. Firehall, was Dr. Belons knowledge of the project, and who he might have shared that knowledge with over the past few days.

Dr. Firehall did not waste any time tracking down Dr. Belons in the molecular lab. "Belons, we need to have a little chat," Firehall said with a stiff smile, blocking the exit.

Dr. Belons was at a crucial part in preparing a sample for sequencing analysis.

"Dr. Firehall, I need to finish this step, and then we can talk."

He was usually good at withholding facial emotions, but not this time. He just heard about Lares death and knew about the likelihood of Dr. Firehall's involvement in Maia Revalue's death. The sweat dripping down his forehead and the frantic look in his eyes showed his fear.

Dr. Firehall always considered himself a top-notch

interrogator. His words, rather than torture, would often elicit wanted information from the subject.

"Since you were on the tour with Mr. Turncock a few days ago, I wanted to share with you they found him dead in his office."

"How unfortunate. I am sure there will be an investigation concerning the cause of his death."

"Somebody also told me you had dinner with him before he left. Did he discuss anything that might be of interest?"

"I don't think I can help you because I had worked late in the lab the other night. Dinner was a sandwich and a cup of coffee at the lab."

"Interesting. My friend must have mistaken you for someone else. Keep up the good work, and if you hear anything, please come find me."

Dr. Belons tried to keep his composure as he finished the sample preparation. He knew that Dr. Firehall was on to him, and now he had to act quickly to gain as much evidence as possible.

He put the sample into the testing instrument and started the analysis. He could hear the liquid siphoning by the pipettes and the green check marks appearing sequentially on the computer screen in front of him. The results were coming in as expected, but Dr. Belons couldn't shake the feeling that he was being watched. Indeed, Dr. Evans was keeping a close eye on his every move.

It should take at least several hours to complete testing, and now it's almost noon, so Dr. Belons finished the day in the forth-floor biocontainment laboratory. Once there, he intended to gather data, or at best to get a sample to prove the existence of project 'Nesting Dolls'.

As he navigated the security protocols, Dr. Belons reached the biocontainment laboratory and suited up. He suited up in a solid white, water impermeable laboratory suit from head to toe, seamlessly enclosing himself. He attached his life-support hose to the spiral tubing hose overhead, and crossed the room, heading towards the large, liquid nitrogen sample storage unit. Just then, he noticed a smaller box labeled desiccated samples, 'Restricted', showing a keypad on the right side of the storage unit.

With cautious curiosity, Dr. Belons approached the smaller 'Restricted' box, feeling a sense of intrigue mingled with apprehension. Without hesitating, he punched in the code he had discreetly got from Dr. Evans office. It worked. The lid opened, revealing an arranged row of labeled, vacuum sealed packets containing what appeared to be dust. The packets, each measuring 1/2 inch by 1/2 inch, displayed a date and a lot number on their labels. There must've been at least 100 packets, carefully arranged in ascending date order.

"This packet must contain the free-living amoeba cysts. There must be millions in each of these small packets. Well, this all makes sense now because a cyst, like a bacterial spore, can withstand extreme dryness, and this is the perfect preservation method." He thought to himself.

He carefully removed a single packet and rushed to the anti-room inner door. Now, inside the anti-room, he removed his bodysuit in strict compliance with the biocontainment de-gowning procedure.

Peering into the lab area, he noticed a dark figure moving alongside the outside hallway, windowed viewing area. It appeared to be Dr. Evans. He walked back-and-forth as if he were trying to see who was in the room.

Dr. Belons was not aware that Dr. Evans was tracking his every move in the research building. The required radioactive monitoring badge attached to every staff scientist in lab coats contained a GPS tracking device. This was a security measure installed by Dr. Roster to ensure that every scientist followed their assigned task.

At that moment, Dr. Belons realized that he would be in danger of getting caught with the stolen packet if he couldn't escape from the area. So, he sprinted towards the elevator and found that someone had shut it down. Then, he rushed to the emergency stairway, but discovered the door was locked. He pulled out his key card, waved it over the door sensor, and was relieved that the door opened. Only when he looked back towards the hallway did he notice the silent alarm had been activated. There it was, a small, flashing red light embedded in the ceiling.

He descended to the third-floor molecular laboratory. The faint sound of approaching footsteps echoed in the corridor. Dr. Belons frantically entered the lab and stood by a sequencing instrument, pretending to wait for test results. Just then, Dr. Evans entered the doorway and walked over to him, saying,

"Dr. Belons, please join me in my office. Now."

Dr. Belons appeared visibly shaken, slightly red in the face, and a hint of sweat on his forehead. He was in the 'fight or flight' mode as he approached Dr. Evans office.

The small packet was in his lab coat pocket, but he had to find a way of concealing it on his person. Looking at the hallway entrance to the offices, he noticed a first aid kit. He took a Band-Aid from the kit and embedded the small packet onto the underside of the gauze padding. He then placed the Band-Aid on the underside of his left forearm.

"Dr. Belons, I am very pleased with your work in the Molecular Sequencing Lab. In fact, I know you've been here often, working late hours into the night. I'm at a critical point in one of our projects, where I would need to complete the sequencing analysis for my report tomorrow morning. I want you to help me to complete the sequencing analysis tonight, so I can incorporate it into my morning report."

"Absolutely, Dr. Evans. I'll catch an early dinner and meet you here later this evening."

In his discussion with Dr. Evans, he noticed several times keystrokes involving numbers, most likely passwords, to access of his computer and to store files on his computer. Fortunately, Dr. Belons had a photographic memory and could remember these numbers. He was hoping they would allow him access to the computer and to open crucial evidence files for his investigation.

Dr. Belons continued his laboratory work into the early afternoon, waiting for a chance to access Dr. Evans office computer. He knew Dr. Evans would leave his office unlocked for at least a half an hour. During that time, he would join the administrative staff in the fifth-floor conference room for their daily summary reports.

It was 3:55 PM when he had the chance to slip into Dr. Evans's office. Facing a dark computer screen, he typed in a computer access password. It worked. He quickly navigated through the files, and noticed one of particular interest, entitled 'ND'. He tapped on it and found it to be encrypted. In his mind, he experienced a flashback to various number sets, and on his third try, the file opened. It appeared to have a multitude of separate sequencing files. No matter, he copied the 'ND' master file to a tiny 64 GB USB retrieved from his lab coat pocket, shut down the computer, and left the office.

Dr. Belons knew he was not safe. Even worse, his life was most assuredly in danger. Dr. Evans made this real clear when he wanted to meet him, a training fellow, later in the evening at the lab.

It was now approaching 4:30 PM, so he left Roster Pharmaceuticals Instalacion. He had no intention of ever returning.

# CHAPTER 18 – CONFRONTING THE CHINGO

Sunday, May 12, 6:18 P.M.
Juan Santamaria International Airport (SJO)
San Jose, Costa Rica

Dr. Belons left Roster Pharmaceuticals Instalacion campus in Alajuela and drove straight to Juan Santamaria International Airport. He felt his life was in imminent danger and decided to leave Costa Rica on the next flight out of the country. Unfortunately, the earliest flight was in the morning at 8:10 AM, with a 24-hour flight time to New Orleans. However, it would not arrive until Tuesday morning. That was a problem. He was sure Dr. Evans or Dr. Firehall would track him down before he could even board the plane.

He always felt he was a resourceful man, so he devised another plan of action. Likewise, he would still purchase a round-trip ticket, but his intent would be to use this flight as a diversion. He could then fly out of a smaller airport after staying overnight at a nearby hotel.

The closest international airport was Tobias Bolanos International Airport, San Jose. However, this posed another concern, double booking under the same name. He didn't have an alias, so he couldn't use another name.

"Think, Charro, think. What can you do?" He whispered to himself.

Then it came to him. He thought about what Lares Turncock

told him at dinner,

"I have a secure VPN. Please consider using my email for any additional evidence."

Sitting in his car at the airport parking lot, he pulled out his computer and took a chance, sending an urgent email to Lares Turncock. His hope was: Law-enforcement would monitor the late Mr. Turncock's computer text messages and would respond.

He was in luck because within 20 minutes; he received a reply to his text message. It read,

"Dr. Belons, this is FBI Special Agent Lawins. We expected a text from you once you received the word of Lares Turncock death. I understand your concern, and I want you to remain calm. I will arrange immediate air transport for you out of Tobias Bolanos International Airport, San Jose. You were wise to arrange the flight out of Juan Santamaria International Airport. This gives us a little more time to ensure that we can extract you by midnight. Check your email again within the hour. I'll be sending you the exact time and tarmac location for the flight. Be safe and take no chances and don't talk to anyone."

He replied,

"Thank you, Special Agent Lawins. I will await your instructions."

Sunday, May 12, 11:48 P.M.

Tobias Bolanos International Airport (SYQ)

Tarmac outside of Gate 4

San Jose, Costa Rica

Dr. Belons anxiously awaited by the dim glow of the tarmac as his extraction flight loomed closer. Suddenly, the sound of an approaching aircraft pierced the quiet night, signaling the fulfillment of Special Agent Lawins promise.

He slowly, but cautiously, walked towards the open door, approaching the short staircase on the Citation (CE-750) aircraft. Out stepped a tall, balding, slim man in his early fifties,

"Dr. Belons, I am FBI Special Agent Jock Lawins. I'm glad to meet you, but we have little time. Please board the aircraft, and I'll brief you on the way."

As soon as Dr. Belons took another step, he heard gunshots in the distance and saw shadows of figures approaching fast. Two other FBI agents quickly ran out of the jet, wielding their 9 mm Glock 17 in return fire.

Special Agent Lawins was already on the plane with Dr. Belons.

"Agent, what is happening outside? I thought we were safe!"

"My guess, the gunfire, is coming from gang members belonging to the dominant Costa Rica cartel, Jingoes New Reactional. They keep a close watch on the smaller airports in the area because of competitive drug trafficking. They view this type of jet as a threat, either believing it is a rival cartel or law enforcement. My agents will contain the gun battle, then we will be off and flying."

As quick as it started, the gun shots ceased, as the agents ran back to the jet. Special Agent Lawins closed the door and gestured for the pilot to take off. The engines roared to life as the aircraft taxied down the runway, leaving the chaos behind.

Two men took hold of the rusty fence surrounding the runway and rocked it. One of the other men on the runway angrily shouted,

"Los gringos se escaparon. El Señor Tod no sera feliz." (The gringos got away. Señor Tod will not be happy.)

These men were members of the Jingoes New Reactional, sent by Dr. Firehall to track down and capture Dr. Belons alive for interrogation.

Miguel pulled out his cellphone in one hand, while waving his pistol in the other, he forcefully hit a speed dial number.

"Señor Todd. This is Miguel. FBI agents outnumbered us at the airport. We tried to stop them, but the Citation (CE-750) jet took off with Dr. Belons."

There was a long silence before the voice of Dr. Firehall angrily shouted,

"Failure is not acceptable, Miguel! I'll deal with you later," and he hung up.

A few minutes later, someone fired another gunshot from

the area behind the rusty fence. Miguel fell to the ground with blood dripping from his forehead, and a chunk of bone and brain tissue clinging to the hairs on the back of his head. He fell to the ground, dead, and his compadres walked away in the opposite direction as if to condone the punishment for his failure.

Art Lifehold, alias Dr. Tod Firehall, placed his 9 mm Walther back in his holster and shook his head with a smirk on his face. He thought to himself,

"Belons, you just made everything much worse for yourself. You have no idea of what you have gotten yourself into by becoming an FBI informant."

Monday, May 13, 2:37 A.M.

Citation (CE-750) aircraft cabin

The Gulf of Mexico

The violent action he encountered at the airport disturbed Dr. Belons. At takeoff, he slumped into a nearby comfy chair, locked his seatbelt, and closed his eyes.

After a few hours, he relaxed while listening to the soothing background whisper of the jet engines and coasting over fluffy clouds at 30,000 feet. He opened his eyes slowly and noticed Special Agent Lawins sitting directly across from him, typing on his laptop.

"Thank you, Special Agent Lawins, for saving my life. I don't even want to think about what could've happened if you hadn't shown up in time."

"Dr. Belons, as trained professionals, we are always prepared for unforeseen events. However, I must admit, I didn't expect that welcoming committee last night."

"We have eyes on the ground in Costa Rica, but there was no forewarning of the ambush at the airport. Your rescue was successful, but maybe next time the outcome may not be so good. Believe me, I'm not trying to scare you, but if the Jingoes New Reactional cartel was responsible for the ambush, they won't stop until the job is done."

"So, if I understand you correctly, my life will always be at risk?"

Special Agent Lawins nodded his head in confirmation as Dr. Belons closed his eyes and shook his head in disbelief.

"The FBI will protect me. Right? I have valuable evidence that will incriminate Roster Pharmaceuticals. Are you telling me that the Jingoes New Reactional cartel is also connected to them?"

"Dr. Belons, the FBI believes this Costa Rica cartel is widespread in the Americas and somehow involved with Roster Pharmaceuticals. How and in what capacity is being investigated. I can tell you; this is a very dangerous, well-funded, global cartel with members as far-reaching as New Orleans."

"So, now I'm a target anywhere I go in the world?"

"I can't answer that question, but I can answer your question about FBI protection. If your evidence is credible and incriminating enough for prosecuting Roster Pharmaceuticals, we can place you in a witness protection program. If you agree to the program, I want you to understand that you will also be obligated to testify as an FBI informant."

"Is that my only choice? There must be other options for a whistleblower, such as me?"

"I wish I could offer you other viable options, but I can't think of any right now. This case is what we call a 'RICO case'. RICO stands for the 'Racketeer Influenced and Corrupt Organizations Act'. It is a United States federal law designed to punish individuals, as well as the leaders, associated with criminal organizations. If we don't bring down the leader, you may never be safe. Likewise, it would be impossible for the FBI to protect you from every attempt on your life. These organizations have hundreds, even thousands, of members. Honestly, your best option is going into a witness protection program."

"Dr. Belons, we are only about an hour away from landing in New Orleans. Let's continue this conversation at our FBI headquarters."

Swallowing hard, Dr. Belons nodded, the weight of his decision settling in as the plane descended towards New

Orleans.

Monday, May 13, 6:37 A.M.

Federal Bureau of Investigation Headquarters

2901 Leon C Simon Drive

New Orleans

They brought Dr. Belons into a dimly lit room, which contained only a table surrounded by three chairs. One side of the room contained a one-way viewing mirror, where Special Agent Lawins and Agent Starters were watching and listening. Dr. Starters was an exceptional forensic psychologist. Her specialty was criminal profiling. She wanted the good doctor to acclimate to the new surroundings, while she watched for any signs of emotional stress before starting the questioning.

The agents entered the interrogation room, sat down across from Dr. Belons, their expressions serious and focused.

"Dr. Belons, I am Agent Starters. I am a Forensic Pathologist for the FBI. Special Agent Lawins and I will ask you a fair number of questions today. I will also record our session."

The agents exchanged a quick glance before Special Agent Lawins spoke up.

"Dr. Belons, I understand you've been with Roster Pharmaceuticals for over a year under a two-year research fellowship."

"That is correct, Special Agent Lawins."

"I'm curious. Why suspect nefarious research activity now, after a year?"

"That is an interesting question. My suspicion started the very first month, because of the advanced instrumentation, and their coveted secrecy among the staff and research scientists. It was not on my mind until Mr. Turncock showed up last week. I followed some of his stories in the past, when he was an investigative reporter. I sensed he had a purpose that went beyond just a story about a research park in New Orleans."

"He didn't have to say a word to me when we were on the site visit. Our eye contact said it all."

"Please continue."

"Agents, I pride myself on character assessment, and I took a chance with Mr. Turncock, asking him to meet me for dinner that night. I took every precaution to make sure nobody from Roster Pharmaceuticals knew about the meeting. I gave Mr. Turncock, to the best of my knowledge, incriminating evidence on the questionable research activity at the company. Now, it's my belief that Mr. Lares Turncock died because of that information."

"Is that true?"

"The FBI suspects that may have something to do with his sudden death."

"Dr. Belons, you mentioned you have other evidence for us. What is this other evidence?"

"Actually, there's much more to this," Dr. Belons said, with a sense of urgency clear in his voice.

"I have acquired a sample of the alleged infectious agent, the one possibly involved in the cases you are investigating here in New Orleans."

Dr. Belons paused for a moment, the weight of his findings becoming palpable in the air.

"I not only have the agent, but I also have DNA sequencing files that will support this mysterious research project."

Special Agent Lawins nodded and made eye contact with Agent Starters, saying,

"Let's take a brief break."

The agents returned to the viewing room, and Special Agent Lawins asked,

"Starters, what do you think?"

"He's showing no sign of falsehood in anything he said so far."

"Look at him in that room. He appears relieved that he is safe and wants to cooperate with us in any way possible."

Meanwhile, Agent Starters gave a quick call to the U.S. Marshals Service in New Orleans, to enrol Dr. Belons in the Witness Protection Program.

They returned to the interrogation room, where Dr. Belons

gave them the packet containing the dried cysts and the USB thumb drive.

Lawins examined the evidence, looked up at Dr. Belons with a steely gaze, and declared, "This is a breakthrough."

He then turned to Agent Starters and instructed, "Get a team to analyze this evidence immediately, and also make sure Dr. Watkins Lab is involved."

"Dr. Belons, we just started the witness protection process. It won't take long, but we need your 100% cooperation with the instructions that US Marshal Eliza Sparkly will give you."

Dr. Belons appeared tired and worried but squeaked out a meek smile of relief.

"Understood. Thank you, agents."

Monday, May 13, 9:48 A.M.

Watkins & Swindon Medical Diagnostics, LLC (WSMD)

Mandeville, LA

Special Agent Lawins arrived at the WSMD lab carrying a small cardboard box with a biohazard emblem, marked with a warning, 'UN2814 INFECTIOUS SUBSTANCE AFFECTING HUMANS'. The box contained instructions to contact CDC in case of damage or leakage. Inside, there was a small aliquot of the dried cyst agent, enclosed in two double-walled, screw-cap glass and metal tubes.

"Dr. Watkins is expecting me," he declared to the receptionist, as he walked past the front desk, ignoring her instructions to sign the visitor log.

"Tell the doctors to meet me in the lab, now," he shouted, heading to an open elevator with slowly closing doors.

Dr. Watkins and Dr. Swindon met him in front of the BSL-3 containment room. Inside the containment area, an Assistant Research Scientist (ARS) had already gowned up and was waiting. Dr. Swindon placed the box inside the pass-through compartment. The ARS retrieved the package and began the unpacking process, followed by sample preparation comprising inactivation and sequencing.

Special Agent Lawins followed the doctors to a nearby

conference room. Everyone was eager to view the digital contents of the USB from Dr. Belons. Wasting no time, Dr. Watkins inserted the USB into the conference room's computer.

A single folder appeared on the screen titled 'ND'. Special Agent Lawins, not one for patience, reached for the mouse and clicked on the folder. The screen literally exploded, revealing hundreds of individual sub-folders. The doctors perused the folder titles, noticing a sequential order according to the file origin date. Dr. Watkins clicked on the most recent folder entitled GO. TE.0510.04. It flashed opened, displaying a short DNA sequence of several hundred bases.

"ATG-TCC-CAA-TGCTAT-AAC-TAT-TGG-GTC...."

Dr. Swindon quickly interrupted,

"Let's plug this sequence into our nucleic acid decoding software and see what it displays."

Dr. Watkins nodded and transferred the DNA sequence into the software. The program displayed the following results:

"No Match. This DNA appears to consist of a random base pair sequence with multiple stop codons. Multiple frame-shift or base deletions may be present."

Dr. Watkins tested several other files and found the same results.

"This is strange! I can see one file displaying this type of result, but multiple files. These file name extensions are not any of the standard types used by sequencing software."

"Dr. Swindon, what are your thoughts?"

Dr. Swindon leaned back in her chair; brows furrowed in concentration.

Closing her eyes for a couple of minutes, she shrugged her shoulders.

"It's probably a code. Heck, they encrypted everything else. Why not their emails?"

Special Agent Lawins just shook his head in disagreement.

However, Dr. Watkins appeared to be very excited by the idea of a code, and spoke up,

"Actually, that's a great idea, Dr. Swindon."

"Just give me a moment to explain. What if they modified the triplicate genetic code to encrypt their emails?"

"That would be sheer genius!"

"This 'ND' folder is a massive file. It would make sense to embed decryption software somewhere in this 'ND' file. Let's see if there is a software program somewhere among these sub-folders."

Dr. Watkins searched through the contents of the massive 'ND' folder for a file ending with a recognizable program extension, such as, '.exe'.

"I Believe I found it, 'AAtoProtein.exe'."

Dr. Swindon nodded in agreement and leaned forward to inspect the contents of the "AAtoProtein" program.

"Now, let's execute the program and see what happens." Hopefully, the program won't contain a Trojan horse virus because we have already screened for that by opening the file.

A blue screen popped up containing an outlined rectangular box. Dr. Watkins did a cut and paste of the DNA sequence from the first file. A tab appeared at the bottom of the box with the word 'decrypt'. He tapped the button, another screen appeared with the words,

"Tedy, I'm delighted to hear our Project Nesting Dolls is so successful. I believe we are now at the point where we can start stage four. I'll keep you posted. GO."

A stunned silence engulfed Special Agent Lawins.

"Doctors, I must congratulate you on your amazing ingenuity in this case. Unfortunately, we now reached the toughest part, figuring out the plan for the agent. Since this is the most recent email, it tells me we have no time to waste."

"Keep this USB thumb drive safe."

"It contains a copy of the original that we sent to Quantico."

Special Agent Lawins arose, turning as he approached the conference room door, said in a loud tone of voice,

"I have a terrible feeling about this one!"

# CHAPTER 19 - DEADLY REVELATION

Tuesday, May 14, 9:02 A.M.

Roster Pharmaceuticals, Inc.

1515 Poydras, Suite 1906

New Orleans

The illicit drug trade has invaded Costa Rica with cocaine distribution. Jingoes New Reactional is currently the dominating cartel. This illicit drug trade, accompanied by money laundering and violent crimes, threatens the very stability of the region. It poses a significant burden on law enforcement efforts. This notorious Columbian cartel challenges the DEA, CIA, and other federal agencies.

Jingoes New Reactional has also aligned with several industries around San Jose, including Roster Pharmaceuticals. A chilling realization sinks in as the connection between the cartel and Roster Pharmaceuticals unfolds. Dr. Tod Firehall has been paying the cartel in return for special services, such as eliminating anyone that may jeopardize the success of his 'Nesting Dolls' project.

Dr. John Roster, founder, and owner of Roster Pharmaceuticals has known CIA Case Officer Art Lifehold, alias Dr. Tod Firehall, from his special forces days in the military. They kept in touch over the years, but it wasn't until Lifehold directed lucrative military contracts to him that their deadly partnership took form.

Neither man was trustworthy to the other, and they both knew it. It didn't matter because their mutual goal was all that counted. It was to accumulate wealth no matter what it took. John Roster wanted the lucrative military contracts, and Lifehold always made that possible with his connections. However, Case Officer Lifehold had an ulterior motive, and we will soon discover what it is.

Dr. Roster sat in his office chair, quiet and visibly troubled. He pondered the implications of his partnership with Case Officer Lifehold and the dangerous revelations that were surfacing.

"Art, what were you thinking when you shot Mateo? We pay Jingoes New Reactional handsomely for special services, and you react by killing someone when they fail the mission. Don't you think we will see consequences for that irrational act?"

"No, and you will never question me again about my actions. You understand what I'm saying to you?"

"I am always a few steps ahead of anybody else, and they know it."

Dr. Roster was about to speak up, but something in Case Officer Lifehold's tone made him pause.

"Yes, but I damn well hope you're right!"

The stoic expressions of the two men towards each other were classic.

After a moment of deafening silence, Dr. Roster asked,

"So, what is the next step with Dr. Belons?"

"Next, we need to make sure that Dr. Belons understands the consequences of attempting to double-cross us."

"I know exactly how the FBI works, and I will take care of that part."

"We have more important things to worry about. Just make sure we're on track for our project deadline."

Dr. Roster nodded in agreement, realizing that they were walking a dangerous path with high stakes.

Tuesday, May 14, 10:13 A.M.

Central Intelligence Agency (CIA)

Langley, Virginia

Four other top-level CIA officials summoned CIA Case Officer

Leonid Wascott into the conference room for a special meeting. Wascott was Case Officer Lifehold's back-up for the cartel infiltration in Costa Rica.

Wascott entered the room and closed the door behind him. He took a seat and listened intently, curious to hear about the latest developments on the mission.

"Case Officer Wascott, we are sending you to Costa Rica."

"We need more eyes on the ground. You'll be following Case Officer Lifehold."

"Yes, sir."

"Our friends have informed us at the DEA, one of their field agents, Mojos Mariners, is missing. The DEA had him deeply embedded in the Jingoes New Reactional cartel. Only the DEA and CIA were aware of his undercover work."

"Find out what's going on."

"Yes, sir."

"You also need to know the last communication received by DEA Field Agent Mariners."

"He mentioned that someone had embedded a Chinese agent in the cartel network."

"Shortly after this communication, he disappeared."

"Approach Case Officer Lifehold cautiously. We must rule him out as a double agent. His alias with Roster Pharmaceuticals and Jingoes New Reactional cartel is Dr. Tod Firehall,"

"Understood" and Case Officer Wascott was now on his way to San Jose, Costa Rica.

Meanwhile, Case Officer Lifehold's office at Langley buzzed with tension as investigators swarmed the area, seizing documents and computer equipment for analysis.

Wednesday, May 15, 9:00 A.M.

U.S. Department of Defense (DoD)

Office of the Secretary of Defense (OSD), Pentagon

1400 Defense Pentagon

Washington, DC

The Pentagon is the world's largest low-rise office building, comprising 6,500,000 square feet (0.6 square kilometers) of office space. The Secretary of Defense heads the DoD, and reports to the Commander-in-Chief, the President of the United States (POTUS). Housed within the Pentagon, is the Joint Chiefs of Staff (JCS), comprising senior military leaders from each of the service branches. The Joint Staff advises the POTUS, the Secretary of Defense, the Homeland Security Council, and the National Security Council on military matters.

Four-Star General Goren Pottage, Chief of Space Operations, and member of the JCS, headed investigating the 'Nesting Dolls' project reported in Costa Rica.

The debriefing for 4-Star General Pottage, and other senior staff from various government agencies, revealed shocking evidence. There was incriminating evidence revealing that CIA Case Officer Lifehold was colluding with the Chinese on the 'Nesting Dolls' project in Costa Rica.

General Pottage reviewed the evidence, poring over every detail for a clue that might reveal the true nature of Case Officer Lifehold's involvement in the alleged collusion. He spoke to the group,

"One of our own, a high-level officer, is possibly working with the Chinese. Hmmm."

"We are to prepare for the worst-case scenario, a terrorist, or bioterrorism attack. You are to cover all intrusion points; air, land, and sea."

The stern-faced commanders encircling the large, oval table stared back at him, absorbing the gravity of the situation.

The meeting was over, but now the logistical and, most assuredly, tactical challenges have begun.

General Pottage knew that uncovering the truth behind Case Officer Lifehold's actions was crucial to preventing a potential catastrophic event. He wasted no time in debriefing the JCS Chairman on the proceedings. Likewise, the Secretary of Defense will debrief the POTUS.

Thursday, May 16, 1:35 P.M.
Roster Pharmaceuticals Instalacion
Alajuela, Costa Rica

Dr. Evans oversaw the genetically engineered cyst development and production for the 'Nesting Dolls' project. It was an arduous task. Millions of the free-living amoeba, Balamuthia mandrillaris needed to be cultured, infected with the genetically modified megavirus, converted into cysts, and then dehydrated. The process of scaling up enough of the final product would take at least a month, depending on the number of vessels used in the amoeba culture.

The biocontainment laboratory was the ideal location for this process since the virus-infected amoeba were even more infectious than the amoeba itself. However, once the amoeba reached the dried cyst stage, they could package them with desiccants, making them safer for storage and future use.

Dr. Evans was a clever researcher. He knew how to produce the cysts rapidly, from culture to final product. He even designed a special culture area in the biocontainment laboratory, hidden behind some supply shelves. Only Dr. Evans and a few others directly involved with the 'Nesting Dolls' project had access to this area.

The organization gave Dr. Evans, as senior scientist, full control over the biocontainment laboratory. He made out the schedule, who could use the lab, and at what time. It was up to his discretion alone.

He maintained a rigid schedule for culturing the amoeba. He would always check the cultures in the morning, afternoon, and evening, ensuring there were no problems. His careful attention to detail paid off and producing the virus-infected amoeba proceeded with no issues.

The biocontainment lab was vacant, it was scheduled for the afternoon inspection. He put on a gown and suit with a mobile oxygen device instead of the overhead retractable tubing. He carefully walked to the supply shelving area in the back of the room and waved his key card over a decoy wall plate. The wall slowly opened, forming a door that harbored the supply shelves.

He carefully walked into the dark room. It lit up, dimly, as he entered. The warmth of the room engulfed his body, even with the protective biocontainment suit. The room was a spacious walk-in incubator containing hundreds of tissue culture vessels.

Dr. Evans examined row after row of rotating, liter sized bottles containing a red tissue culture media. Each of these vessels contains living cells that were infected by the free-living amoeba. It was a simple process that produced massive quantities of reproducing amoeba. The color-coded vessels showed that the bottles with green caps contained Balamuthia mandrillaris infected with a virus.

A small laboratory table was at the back of the room. It was here that he used the stereoscope to view some bottles randomly and estimate amoeba density and cyst production. During this stage, the bottles underwent dehydration, which is a critical step in preserving the amoeba for packaging.

On the side of the table was a 2 by 5-foot safe that contained a key card entry pad. Dr. Evans waved his card over the pad, swung the latch upward to his right, and opened the safe. Large plastic containers lined the inside of the safe, five times the size of the carbon dioxide propellants used in air guns. Each of these vessels contained millions of dehydrated cysts and a propellant gas under pressure. This vessel was the final, deadly product to be used in the 'Nesting Dolls' project.

A contented smile spread across Dr. Evans face as he gazed upon the multitude of vessels in the safe. Closing the safe, he thought to himself,

"Everything is on schedule, as planned. It won't be long now."

Thursday, May 16, 2:05 P.M.

National University of Costa Rica

Heredia, Costa Rica

Heredia is approximately 10 kilometers to the north of San José, the capital of Costa Rica. It is home to the main campus of The National University of Costa Rica, one of five public universities in Central America. Approximately 12,000 national and international students attend the main campus.

CIA Case Officer Leonid Wascott, alias Dr. Delo Wainscott, is posing as a visiting professor on the Faculty of Social Sciences, the School of International Relations. The President of the University was told Dr. Wainscott was an undercover journalist. He was there to gather background information on an upcoming book. He was to keep his identity in strict confidence.

Alias, Dr. Wainscott's mission was to infiltrate the Jingoes New Reactional cartel and investigate Case Officer Lifehold's involvement in the cartel and the 'Nesting Dolls' project.

Heredia was the ideal location since it was between San Jose and Alajuela. It was also the ideal cover for a visiting professor.

Dr. Wainscott's plan was to familiarize himself with the area, especially the Roster Pharmaceuticals campus. He would then visit the research facility, presenting himself as Dr. Wainscott, a visiting professor at the National University of Costa Rica. He would explain that he was gathering information from many of the local industries for analysis and critique of international relations, as it relates to the biotechnology and pharmaceutical industries.

His direct superior only knew the undercover mission of Case Officer Wascott. Likewise, Case Officer Lifehold, alias Dr. Firehall, had never met him and knew nothing about his history with the CIA.

Dr. Wainscott's immediate task at hand was to find Dr. Firehall and learn as much as possible about his involvement with Roster Pharmaceuticals and Jingoes New Reactional.

# CHAPTER 20 - PRESSURE POINT

Thursday, May 16, 7:30 P.M.
Roster Pharmaceuticals Instalacion
Alajuela, Costa Rica

Dr. Wainscott was careful not to reveal his presence in the dense jungle surrounding the Roster Pharmaceuticals campus. He made his way through the thick foliage, following the narrow trail that only those familiar with the area would notice. The satellite map he'd studied the night before guided him, confirming each turn and landmark. His night vision goggles enhanced his view, allowing him to navigate the shadowy terrain without a misstep.

He set up his surveillance on a strategic point in the terrain, allowing him visual access to most of the buildings, especially the research facility. Taking out his night vision binoculars, Dr. Wainscott scanned the area, noting the activity around the research facility. It was clearly Dr. Firehall, with two other men entering the building.

It was a long night, but the melody of the insects and other creatures in the surrounding jungle was comforting to Dr. Wainscott. This served as a reminder that he was not alone in this foreign environment.

Dr. Wainscott saw two men exiting the research facility around midnight. This time, the men wielded handcarts with what appeared to be wooden crates about the size of a standard suitcase. Dr. Firehall led the men to another building, which appeared to be a shipping area with a loading dock and trucks alongside.

Dr. Wainscott captured a facial image of the two men as they exited the building. After captioning clear facial images, he sent them directly to Langley for identification. He also saw the license plate on the vehicle the two men were driving as they pulled away from the loading dock and sent it to Langley as well.

Then, Dr. Wainscott focused on Dr. Firehall. He noticed the expressions on his face when he was talking on his cellphone. The severity of Dr. Firehall's expressions hinted at the urgency of the conversation. He rushed to his car and sped off in the distance. Something was up.

Dr. Wainscott emerged from his secluded position in the heavy jungle covering and headed down towards the Roster Pharmaceuticals campus. He retrieved a thermal imaging device from his backpack and scanned the area as he proceeded towards the shipping building.

He detected three images on his device, one at the far end of the dock area and the other two in the research facility. Not only that, but he couldn't take the chance that they were armed guards, so he had to be very cautious in his approach to the area.

Tracking their movements, Dr. Wainscott discreetly made his way toward the shipping dock. The dense foliage kept him hidden as he cautiously neared the area, his senses on high alert for any signs of danger or surveillance equipment. He easily gained access to the entrance because of his locksmith expertise.

He cautiously opened the door and, as he approached the end of the building, he noticed the stacked crates by the dock area door. The shipping labels were mostly in Chinese, but the destination was legible and revealed,

"Wanning, China,"

Taking a mental note of the destination, he turned his attention back to the task at hand. Raising the thermal imaging device once more, he scanned the crates. What he could see was an aligned arrangement of many rows of small canisters.

Suddenly, he caught a glint of something reflective from the corner of his eye. In the distance, but coming towards him, was an armed guard waving a brightly lit flashlight. He quickly ducked behind a stack of boxes, heart pounding in his chest as he assessed his options. Peering around some crates, Dr. Wainscott was relieved that the guard passed without noticing him hiding among the boxes.

He quickly headed towards the exit of the shipping area, keeping close to the wall to avoid detection. He made it back to his car and sped away from the campus, keeping an eye out for anyone in pursuit.

Friday, May 17, 8:00 A.M.
Federal Bureau of Investigation Headquarters
2901 Leon C Simon Drive
New Orleans
Files and notes cluttered Special Agent Lawins desk as he pored over the evidence from the pneumonia death cases. The phone rang, jolting him from his concentration.

"Lawins, this is Mortlake. We need to talk."

"I'll meet you at your office in an hour." With that, the line went dead, leaving Lawins with a sense of urgency.

Slogger Mortlake is the Regional Director for the US Department of Homeland Security (DHS), New Orleans. The communication between Special Agent Lawins and Director Mortlake was always tenuous, mostly because of turf defense.

This time, Lawins knew Mortlake had information that he needed, and time was running out. Today would be different. It was a day Lawins and Mortlake would have to find common ground to solve the case.

With a deep breath, Lawins gathered his files and prepared for Mortlake's arrival. Over the next hour, he organized the evidence, arranging it to best present his findings to Mortlake. Lawins deliberately kept DHS out of his case investigation. He knew Mortlake would be more likely to share information if he could prove the investigative skills of the Bureau's work on the case.

The DEA was involved and Lawins felt the FBI was more than capable of handling the narcotics trade in greater New Orleans.

The burning question for Special Agent Lawins was why DHS had this sudden interest in the case? To him, it still seemed like a cocaine-related investigation, involving multiple deaths, and somehow connected to a Costa Rica cartel supplier.

DHS knew the FBI was handling the case, so why was DHS interested? Lawins thought to himself.

His desk phone buzzed, interrupting his thoughts. It was Lawins office assistant, informing him that Director Mortlake had arrived and was heading to his office.

A gentle knock sounded on the door, and Lawins straightened in his seat, mentally preparing himself for the challenging negotiation that lay ahead. He arose from be-hind his desk and met Director Mortlake with a firm handshake at his office door.

"Director, it's always a pleasure. Please, have a seat."

Director Mortlake simply nodded his head and spoke in an abrupt, sarcastic tone of voice.

"Special Agent Lawins, do you remember September 11th?"

"I know you are aware of the communication problems between the agencies."

"The FBI has been defending this nation for a long time, and I respect that dedication. You know they created DHS because of 9/11, with the purpose of avoiding any such deadly event in the future."

"Believe me, I will not lecture you further on this issue. I just want to hear it directly from you."

"Why didn't the FBI bring DHS into this investigation earlier?"

Special Agent Lawins appeared taken back by his directness but maintained his composure as he explained,

"Director, we initially believed that the case fell within the jurisdiction of the FBI."

"It was not until recently that we found out from a whistleblower out of Costa Rica, there was much more involved than cocaine distribution throughout greater New Orleans. The company headquarters for the whistleblower is also located here in New Orleans."

"Right, and when did you find this out?"

A moment of silence occurred before Special Agent Lawins answered.

"We brought the whistleblower back to FBI headquarters this past Monday."

"Almost five days, Special Agent Lawins! Five days! You know, a lot can happen within a couple of hours, let alone five days."

"Director, I understand your concern, but we were verifying the whistleblower's claims and gathering evidence to corroborate the information."

"Here, this is a detailed report on the investigation."

Director Mortlake shook his head in disapproval as he took the report from Special Agent Lawins outstretched hand.

"You realize we have plenty of information from other agencies at this point. I'm sure yours will fill in the gaps and possibly bring new information to the case."

"Special Agent Lawins."

"I am the one in charge, and here is how we will proceed."

"DHS, with the help of the DEA and FBI, will find the evidence so that we can interrogate the local head of the cocaine network."

"Understood." As Special Agent Lawins escorted Director Mortlake to his office door.

Friday, May 17, 1:38 P.M.

Deep in the Louisiana Bayou

Ascension Parish

Gonzalez, Louisiana

Special Agent Lawins used one of his confidential informants to locate the stash house of Rafael Nacket. Rafael was a key figure in the local cocaine network that had been under investigation by the FBI and DEA for months. Together with the team, they fully planned the raid on the stash house, aware of the heightened security surrounding Rafael's operations.

The Louisiana Bayou was a challenging territory for the team of agents approaching the stash house. The thick, tangled underbrush muffled their steps, and the air was heavy with the scent of damp earth and decaying leaves. Alligators lazed in the murky waters; their eyes fixed on the approaching group.

The lead agent's thermal detector had at least a dozen figures surrounding and inside the heavily guarded house. They observed Rafael Nacket inside the building. He needed to be captured alive for interrogation.

Taking a deep breath, Special Agent Lawins signaled to his team to spread out and prepare for the raid. The agents moved in silently, their training guiding their every step as they closed in on the stash house.

The FBI fired a barrage of shots, causing several bodyguards to fall to the ground. Bullets zipped past as the team returned fire, taking down the remaining guards. Rafael Nacket, being defenseless, surrendered without resistance, and the authorities took him into custody.

Friday, May 17, 6:38 P.M.
Federal Bureau of Investigation Headquarters
2901 Leon C Simon Drive
New Orleans

Rafael Nacket, local drug lord for the greater New Orleans illicit drug trade, sat emotionless on the uncomfortable metal chair in the FBI interrogation room. It was now close to an hour, sitting in the warm room, staring at the walls with the large one-way mirror in front of the table.

An agent finally entered the room, and Rafael Nacket's gaze remained fixed on the mirror. With a stoic expression, he studied the agent's every move, his eyes betraying nothing as the agent took a seat across from him.

"Rafael, you have some serious charges. You could face a death sentence, or at least enough prison time to put you away for life. Would you like to make a statement in your defense?"

He just stared at the agent for a long, tense moment, as if considering his options.

"I had no weapon, and you wounded and killed my bodyguards."

"Why would I get the death sentence for that massacre at the hands of the FBI?"

"Mr. Nacket, we found many kilos of uncut cocaine at your residence. That finding, alone, can send you away for 15 to 20 years."

The FBI agent then placed a photograph of undercover DEA Field Agent Mojos Mariners on the table in front of Rafael.

"That is the least of your worries."

"Do you recognize this person?"

Nacket was silent, but replied in a gruff voice,

"He looks familiar. I know plenty of people, and many people know me. I'm not good at names. Who is this guy?"

The agent placed three other pictures in front of Nacket. Each scene in the picture revealed Nacket talking to the DEA field agent.

"OK, it's one of my guys. So, what, I talked to plenty of people all the time?"

The agent replied,

"Nacket, this person is missing, and we want to know where we can find him."

"I can't help you with that because I don't stalk people I know."

"Mr. Nacket, our FBI team, discovered his body parts spread among the gators at your Bayou stash house, which is why we are charging you with homicide."

Rafael was silent for a moment, then nodded slowly before replying in a calm voice,

"I would like to make a deal."

The agent leaned in, his eyes narrowing.

"What kind of deal?"

"His death is not my doing. I can tell you who was involved and even give you a lot more info, depending on the deal."

The agent, abruptly, arose from his chair without saying a word and left the room.

In the adjacent room behind the one-way mirror, Special Agent Lawins and Director Mortlake watched the exchange.

Special Agent Lawins leaned in and whispered.

"What is your opinion of that, Director Mortlake?"

"Time for you and me to have a little chat with Mr. Nacket."

Rafael Nacket slowly stood up from his seat and turned to face the one-way mirror, a confident smirk on his face. He knew he held a key piece of information that would change everything.

The two men entered the interrogation room, and Director Mortlake spoke.

"Mr. Nacket, this may seem like a game to you, but it's nothing like, let's make a deal."

"Not only will we charge you for the death of your guy, but we will also charge you for the deaths of 12 other people."

"I am the Regional Director for the US Department of Homeland Security, DHS. This case is well beyond homicide. It's considered a threat to US security. It's now classified as a homeland terrorism. Do you understand what I'm saying to you?"

"Hey, look, I'll admit to distributing cocaine in New Orleans, but I'm not responsible for killing these people. I'll tell you everything I know, but I want a deal."

The terrorist implication visibly shook Nacket. He repeated in a whimpering tone of voice,

"I didn't kill these people. Any deal we make can't include these homicides!"

"So, start talking, and we will see how it goes. No guarantee at this point."

"Alright, I'll tell you what I know, but I want protection, or I'm a dead man."

"Keep talking."

"I am good at selling a sought-after product."

"Stop! Give us facts and something useful, or we're out of here."

Nacket appeared reluctant, but understood he had little choice in the matter.

"We work closely with a company based in New Orleans

on Poydras, Roster Pharmaceuticals. Their manufacturing operations are based in Costa Rica. Another local company, Roans Medical Supply, also serves as our distributor."

"So, these two companies are part of the cocaine distribution chain. Correct?"

"Yes."

"We need names."

"I have only one direct contact, Tod Firehall. Any orders come through him. Basically, the system runs itself."

"Firehall interrupted our usual business dealings over the past month twice with unusual orders."

"Explain."

"Well, we carefully count and distribute our product to our dealers."

"On two occasions, Firehall gave me 10 packs of products, the first time, and then only 2 about a week later. I was told to give them to our best dealers. I felt threatened by him."

"Why were these packets special?"

"Honestly, I do not know. It was an order, and you never question or refuse any order."

"Who is the cocaine supplier?"

"Costa Rica is run by the Jingoes New Reactional cartel."

"This is what I know, and now I need protection and a deal."

"You will be under protective custody until your information checks out. We're talk deal after that."

The two agents left the room and returned to the observation room.

"Lawins, I think they deliberately withheld information from him about the role of Roster Pharmaceuticals."

"My gut feeling is the same."

"I'll call the US Marshal office here in New Orleans and arrange a temporary, protective custody."

"Lawins. Understand, DHS is now in charge, and I'll keep you updated."

"Understood, Director."

# CHAPTER 21 - DIABOLICAL GENOME

Saturday, May 18, 5:30 A.M.
Federal Bureau of Investigation Headquarters
2901 Leon C Simon Drive
New Orleans

A black SUV with tinted windows pulls up in front of the FBI headquarters. A woman steps out, her suit impeccably tailored, and her cold, dark eyes scanning the surroundings with eerie precision. She is a US Marshal that has orders to place Rafael Nacket in protective custody.

She presents the paperwork to the FBI agents, and they hand over Mr. Nacket, handcuffed, to the Marshal. As she escorts Rafael Nacket towards the waiting SUV, her every move radiates a resolve that unnerves even the seasoned FBI agents.

Once inside the vehicle, she restrained Nacket. He is now secure in a bulletproof vehicle, including a heavy, polycarbonate window separating the driver from the back seat, handcuffed prisoner.

"Sit back and relax, Nacket. You'll be right at home in your new place. You're under my protection now, and I will guarantee that no one will ever find you."

The US Marshal's voice held a note of finality, leaving no room for argument as the SUV merged into the early morning traffic, carrying Rafael Nacket.

Rafael dozed off, his mind still reeling from the events that had led to this moment. He woke up and experienced a probing pain in the back of his neck, as though someone had stabbed him with a needle. He was still in handcuffs but couldn't even raise his arms. As Rafael struggled to stay conscious, the US Marshal glanced at him through the rearview mirror, her eyes calculating. His breathing became exceedingly difficult until he struggled to take a final breath.

Art Lifehold, alias U.S. Marshal Edith Floral, succeeded in his mission. He knew Rafael was not aware of the details of project 'Nesting Dolls' but could not take the chance of any more disclosure to government officials. Again, his trusted golden frog poison was dependable and quick.

He predetermined the perfect dumpsite for the body, a desolate site in the Louisiana Bayou, where no human ever ventured. The rest was up to nature and the alligators.

As the SUV slowed to a stop in the eerie, mist-laden landscape, the sun rose over the Louisiana Bayou. As Lifehold stepped out of the vehicle and opened the rear door, the lifeless body of Rafael Nacket was in the back seat. Struggling, he managed to drag the body into the swamp water, where he secured weights. The tumbling splash of Rafael's body echoed through the wetlands as Lifehold watched, his expression a mask of grim determination. Lifehold gazed at the sinking figure of Rafael and muttered,

"No loose ends."

Saturday, May 18, 7:06 A.M.

Watkins & Swindon Medical Diagnostics, LLC (WSMD)

Mandeville, Louisiana

Dr. Watkins office exhibited a spectacular view overlooking Lake Pontchartrain. Across the lake, the morning mist was just dissipating, revealing the vibrant greenery of cypress trees lining the water's edge. His gaze lingered on the peaceful scenery before he turned back to his desk, where the decoded 'ND' file reports using the AAtoProtein.exe software program lay open.

Dr. Watkins leaned in close, his brow furrowed in concentration as he analyzed the encoded data. He still marveled at the genius involved in using the modified triplicate genetic code to encrypt emails and other documents. After hours of dissecting the encoded data, a sudden realization hit him like a lightning bolt. The encoded data wasn't just random gibberish; it held the key to unraveling a conspiracy that went deeper than he could have ever imagined.

The string of encoded emails revealed a sinister web of political manipulation and corporate corruption, reaching into the highest echelons of power. Department of Defense contracts, requiring high-level security clearance, unravel in the string of emails. These contracts laid the foundation for a classified project known only by its code name, project 'Nesting Dolls'."

Watkins knew he now held the key to a Pandora's box of secrets, but with knowledge came great danger. Embedded in the data were actual sequences for the dangerous free-living amoeba, Balamuthia mandrillaris. The implications of this discovery sent a shiver down his spine. He spent valuable time and effort securing his findings. Realizing that exposing this information to the wrong people could make him a prime target for those who have a vested interest in "Project Nesting Dolls".

Dr. Swindon bolted towards his office, her footsteps hurried and filled with urgency.

"Tombak, Special Agent Lawins just informed me they transferred the key witness in our case, Rafael Nacket, to a US marshal under protective custody."

"Unfortunately, no one knows the identity of the US marshal. Lawins has no lead on their whereabouts and is assuming that someone may have kidnapped or eliminated him."

"Elise, this sounds like a calculated move to thwart our investigation. We need to act fast and step up our security measures," Tombak replied, the urgency clear in his voice.

"I am discovering more evidence, which is very disturbing, that suggests involving the highest level of government agencies and possibly high-ranking political figures."

"I'm also carefully teasing out the encoded data on the genetic manipulation of the free-living amoeba Balamuthia mandrillaris. Someone knows what they're doing, and it is a diabolical approach."

"This is far beyond our expertise. We need to consult our colleagues at NIH now! I'll text Dr. Smithcraft and Dr. Dhyana. If we hurry, we can catch a United flight and be there by 4 PM."
Saturday, May 18, 4:48 P.M.
National Institutes of Health (NIH)
National Institute of Allergy and Infectious Disease (NIAID)
9000 Rockville Pike
Bethesda, Maryland
Together, Tombak and Elise hurried through the bustling NIH campus, exchanging worried glances as they made their way to the NIAID building. The late afternoon sun cast long shadows across the paved pathway as they approached the imposing building, their thoughts consumed by the urgent need to unravel the sinister mysteries.

Dr. Smithcraft met them at the building entrance, and they made their way to Dr. Dhyana's office. As they entered the office, Dr. Dhyana greeted them with a concerned look.

"Greetings, Tombak and Elise. This recent development is quite alarming."

"I've investigated our database, and I noticed a $360 million dollar NIH RFP awarded to Dr. John Roster, M.D., Roster Pharmaceuticals Instalacion, New Orleans, Louisiana. It's been active for about a year. What makes it interesting is that the subcontractor list includes the Department of Defense."

"SN485888D6579 is a hybrid contract, describing the research and development of parasitic agents to serve as vectors for genetically engineered viruses. The researchers would selectively modify the genetically manipulated virus with genes to infect a specific target host, such as Homo sapiens/human."

"This is select agent development for gain-of-function (GOF) research."

"Biowarfare agent development."

"You now have two of the foremost experts in this area at your disposal, me and Dr. Smithcraft."

"What have you discovered?"

"Dr. Dhyana, we are on the same page as you. I have a timeline of genetic sequence information leading from a relatively noninfectious, amoebic megavirus to a highly infectious, respiratory agent, or more specifically, bioterrorism agent," said Dr. Watkins.

The team studied the genetic mutations and their implications. As they delved deeper, a chilling realization dawned upon them. The amoebic megavirus was not only capable of destroying lung tissue, but it also harbored a built-in defense system.

Dr. Swindon turned to the team with a grave and solemn expression. Slowly, shaking her head, she spoke,

"This is so remarkable! So diabolical! It's one of the most ingenious approaches I've ever seen."

"It's all because we discovered a 'missing link,' masquerading as a giant virus in these small, unicellular amoebae."

"Compare this virus to those infecting humans. They require living cells because they are not large enough to carry life-sustaining genes. Recently, we have discovered giant viruses in amoeba, carrying some of their own life-sustaining genes."

"Using a technology called CASPR Cas-9, you can genetically engineer a virus genome. The beauty of this is that you can replace some of these genes with those that have pathogenic potential. Hence, we can build our own bioterrorism agent."

"This giant virus also has a built-in defense system. Now, we can't even use our limited number of antiviral agents, such as acyclovir or cidofovir, because of resistance genes."

"The amoeba's protection of the megavirus until its release would make it challenging to develop vaccines. Ironically, even if you kill the amoeba with antiparasitic drugs, you will still release the megavirus."

The team faced an unprecedented challenge, one that might change the course of biological warfare. The implications were chilling, as the potential consequences of such a weapon could be devastating.

Dr. Smithcraft sighed heavily, his mind racing with the implications of what Dr. Swindon discussed.

"Allow me to summarize our findings. I first want to say, hope, and pray we can prevent the use of such a dangerous biological agent."

"Someone introduces Balamuthia mandrillaris, containing the modified megavirus, into a human host. The route is most likely respiratory because the amoeba is in the cyst form."

"Once introduced into the host respiratory system, the cyst develops into the trophozoite form. In this form, the amoeba is mobile and eats its way throughout the lungs."

"The immune system then attempts to attack the invading amoeba and releases the protected megavirus. It's this megavirus that does the most damage and kills the person quickly, within a day or two."

"As we observed with the patients who recently served as guinea pigs, all antibiotics, antivirals, antifungals, and even the immune system itself proved ineffective against the megavirus."

"Now, we have credible evidence to support this deadly cycle."

"It's a true diabolical genome," Dr. Swindon concluded, her voice heavy with concern.

Dr. Smithcraft nodded gravely, absorbing the harrowing details. Distracted in his thoughts, he glanced at the clock and realized they were running out of time because Dr. Watkins and Dr. Swindon could not miss their return flight.

Dr. Smithcraft concluded the meeting with a dire closing statement.

"We have defined what, but now we have to determine who will disperse this biological agent, when, where, and how it will be done."

# CHAPTER 22 - LOOK TO THE SKY

Monday, May 20, 6:20 P.M.
Roster Pharmaceuticals
Alajuela, Costa Rica

Tod Firehall met three men, Alberto, Fernando, and Leonardo on the loading dock of the Roster Pharmaceuticals shipping and distribution building. They were locals, but not the friendly type. Their tattoos displayed a story of violence and telltale numbers signifying incarceration in the past.

"Good morning, gentlemen," Dr. Firehall said, addressing the group with a firm nod, as he authoritatively tapped a stack of crates beneath his hand.

"This is precious cargo, so guard it with your life." He mumbled with a sinister smile. He handed Fernando, the obvious leader, with his hand extended, a bulky white envelope.

Inside the sealed envelope was a bundle of crisp $100 bills, $5,000 in total. Alberto and Leonardo exchanged wary glances as Fernando pocketed the envelope, his fingers flipping over the crisp bills to check the contents. None of them spoke a word. Their expressions confirmed the silent agreement. As they turned, a helicopter descended from the sky, bearing the distinctive logo of Roster Pharmaceuticals painted on its side.

The three men scurried off to load the crates into the back of a dust ridden Jeep, haphazardly painted with green and black military style camouflage. The dusty terrain crunched beneath the Jeep's tires as they drove off towards a secure airfield hidden deep within the Costa Rican jungle.

Firehall, covering his eyes from the setting sun, watched as the helicopter touched down with a gust of wind. The door opened and Dr. John Roster stepped out, his authoritative presence filling the air as the sun glinted off his silver-streaked hair.

The two men exchanged meaningful glances as they made their way toward each other. Firehall nodded, as a signal of assurance that the project was in its final stage and nearing completion.

"John, welcome back home," exclaimed Firehall, extending his hand in greeting as they clasped in a firm handshake.

Unaware by both men, Wainscott was observing the entire scene from a nearby hidden garden area. They were being photographed by the undercover CIA special agent. Using his 1000 mm telescopic lens, he captured the license plate of the departing jeep. The agent quickly sent the intelligence back to headquarters, realizing the stakes were much higher than initially thought.

Langley was quick to respond in identifying the owner of the vehicle. It belonged to a known member of the Jingoes New Reactional Cartel.

Wainscott believed that the mysterious crates were heading towards only one destination: Wanning, China. With this vital information at his disposal, Wainscott knew he had to act quickly. He radioed for backup and set out to intercept the Jeep before it could reach the airstrip.

Unfortunately, satellite tracking would not be an option because of the dense jungle canopy. However, it provided him with GPS access to nearby runway locations often used by drug runners. Wainscott knew he had to act fast to intercept the Jeep before it vanished into the sunset.

He ran through the thick jungle foliage, locating his SUV, and maneuvered it to a vantage point near the only clear runway in the area. There it was in the distance, the camouflaged Jeep, speeding towards a Citation (CE-750) jet, engines roaring, and ready for flight.

Wainscott gripped the steering wheel with determination, knowing that he had to stop the illicit cargo from leaving the country. The dark silhouette of the jet loomed larger as Wainscott hit the gas, barreling down the rough jungle terrain towards the tarmac.

Suddenly, gunshots rang out, shattering the stillness of the jungle evening. Two black Humvees were on his tail and closing in fast. Wainscott swerved to avoid the gunfire, his heart pounding as he steered the SUV towards cover.

The impending darkness and swirling dust clouds from the chase saved him. The vehicles raced past, their thundering engines drowning out the sounds of the jungle.

Within a couple of minutes, the noise of roaring jet engines reached his ears from above. A sense of security enveloped him, but he couldn't shake the feeling of failure. A sense of failure and frustration weighed heavily on Wainscott's shoulders.

He peered up at the night sky, watching the jet disappear into the setting sun and piercing the evening cloud cover. The shipment was on its way to China, and somehow, he had to stop it.

He retrieved his satellite phone from his backpack, and punched in the activation code for Langley,

"Cobra 36547. Package was not retrieved. CE-750 is now airborne."

"Copy, Cobra 36547."

"Wainscott, focus," he murmured to himself, punching in a second number to connect with his backup team.

"Cobra 36547. Abort."

He knew the mission had taken an unexpected turn, but he had to regroup and reassess the situation. The amber glow of the moon highlighted the silhouette of the jungle canopy as Wainscott headed back to the safe house.

Tuesday, May 21, 7:34 A.M.
Roster Pharmaceuticals Instalacion, Boardroom
Alajuela, Costa Rica
Firehall appeared pleased with himself as he confronted John

Roster, Gregor Osseo, and Tedy Evans as the morning sun broke through the windows. Their project was now in the last phase and near completion.

"I warned you that Wainscott was trouble," Firehall sneered, as he directed his attention to Dr. Roster.

"We've been compromised," John Roster said grimly, cutting through the tension in the room with his voice.

The other two men appeared lost in the conversation, exchanging worried glances as they waited for Roster's response.

"Gentlemen, Dr. Delo Wainscott, a visiting professor from the National University of Costa Rica, has been asking for an appointment with me. The president of the university is a good friend of mine, so I called him. He was sketchy about this Dr. Wainscott, his background, and his intent for the visit."

"Let me cut to the chase. I understand from our new friends in Costa Rica, Dr. Firehall and our facility have been under surveillance by Dr. Wainscott. My take, he's a ghost. Probably, CIA or some other government agency. Let me enlighten you with another fact: he was also tracking our shipment last night on the way to the airstrip. Our friends averted the attack but lost the target and failed to neutralize the attacker."

"Dr. Firehall, please enlighten our team on the progress of the 'Nesting Dolls' project."

Firehall shifted in his seat, casting a wary glance at Dr. Roster.

"The progress has been steady, but with this new revelation, we may need to change our timetable," Firehall said, his eyes narrowing with determination.

"The packages are well on their way to China. We instructed the pilot to deviate from the original flight plan and refueling schedule. This will cause confusion for anyone tracking the jet. Unfortunately, the schedule change will probably add another half-day onto the original 26-hour delivery."

"There is some flexibility in our schedule, but the project will have a successful outcome."

Dr. Firehall. "Let's not underestimate our adversary," said Dr. Roster.

Wednesday, May 22, 6:38 A.M.

Central Intelligence Agency (CIA)

Langley, Virginia

The failed attempt to stop the cargo shipment out of Costa Rica caused immense concern by the DoD and multiple government agencies involved in the case.

The White House received a briefing on the situation, and POTUS issued a directive to allocate additional resources for tracking and intercepting the cargo.

General Pottage, Director Mortlake, and other high-level officials received an NSA briefing on the Citation CE-750 flight from Costa Rica.

"Satellite reconnaissance recorded multiple refueling stops along a random flight path."

"The zigzag flight pattern, captured by satellite reconnaissance, demonstrates that the plane is headed for China."

"The brevity and remote location for each refueling event made it impossible to carry out a successful interception." Reported Special Agent Matrioshka.

"SIGINT (Signals Intelligence) is reporting heightened chatter regarding a potential bioterrorism attack."

"We have already briefed Director Mortlake on the matter."

The briefing room fell silent as everyone absorbed the gravity of the situation. Realtime satellite imagery provided by the NSA appeared on the large screen at the front of the room, showing the Citation CE-750 on a course to China.

"We have every reason to believe the specific destination is Wanning, China. As you can see on the screen, the jet is in Chinese airspace. The two dots on each side of the Citation CE-750 represent Chinese J-20 stealth jets."

"There has to be some precious cargo on-board for such high-level protection by four of the Chinese finest fighter jets."

"Allow me to make a critical point. Even if we knew the exact flight plan of the aircraft, we would not neutralize the target. The risk of attempting to destroy this bioterrorism agent in the air or on the ground could have drastic consequences on local or even global exposure."

"We have already provided a detailed briefing on the specifics of the genetically engineered biological agent to everyone. If you recall, it is the cyst form of a free-living amoeba, Balamuthia mandrillaris, infected with a deadly megavirus."

"SIGINT, with data support from NIH, in collaboration with Dr. Watkins and Dr. Swindon at WSMD, New Orleans contends the vehicle of dispersion is atmospheric."

"This begs the question, what do we know about Wanning, China? All of you know the answer, because of the recent gigantic weather balloon incident in the United States."

"Intelligence predicts that they will load this agent onto one of these giant, maneuverable balloons and disperse it somewhere in the USA."

"Allow me to conclude our briefing with a last point intercepted from the SIGINT chatter."

"Somehow, the massive Sahara dust storm currently affecting the eastern seaboard is also being discussed. Why? The answer is unknown, but we suspect the bioterrorism agent may be seeded into the dust storm by these giant weather balloons."

"Thank you for your attention."

"The briefing is now concluded, and we will provide you with any further updates by text as they become available."

# CHAPTER 23 - FOR THE GREATER GOOD

Wednesday, May 22, 11:18 A.M.

Roster Pharmaceuticals

Alajuela, Costa Rica

Dr. Roster sat in his office chair, agonizing over the heated discussion at yesterday's meeting. His eyes fixated on the encrypted email displayed on the computer screen. He knew the message contained sensitive information that could change everything. He opened the text message. It stated,

"The time has come to take action."

"Meet me at the usual place tonight at 8 PM."

Dr. Roster's heart raced as he read the message, recognizing the sender's code name. He quickly composed a response, acknowledging the instructions and confirming his presence at the rendezvous point.

Dr. Firehall entered the office, raising an eyebrow as he noticed the urgency in Dr. Roster's facial expression.

"Is everything going as planned, John?"

"You appear preoccupied."

"Yes, everything is fine," Dr. Roster replied, forcing a composed expression as he minimized the email window.

Both men kept secrets from one another, and they knew their limit to the level of trust toward each other over the years.

Dr. Firehall glanced at the closed email window, a hint of suspicion lingering in his eyes. Unsure of how much to reveal, he chose his words carefully.

"What's with the sudden urgency, John? You seem more

distracted than usual," he inquired, his demeanor conveying a sense of caution.

Dr. Roster hesitated, weighing his options. The weight of his decision hung heavy in the air, but he knew the time for secrecy was over. He took a deep breath and met Dr. Firehall's gaze, knowing it was time to confide in his longtime colleague or face the consequences. He witnessed firsthand the immense power that Dr. Firehall possessed, particularly when it came to punishing disloyalty.

"We have a problem!"

"The email I just received is from Marietla Corrion. It has a high level of encryption and uses a codename, so there is no need to worry about other eyes on the text message."

Marietla Corrion is an attractive, 48-year-old Costa Rica woman, intimately involved with John Roster. She proudly claims responsibility for facilitating the introduction between Dr. Roster, his company, Roster Pharmaceuticals, and Mool Ceros.

Ms. Corrion is a falcon for the Costa Rica Jingoes New Reactional Cartel. Mr. Ceros is the Costa Rica drug lord for the cartel.

"It's Marietla. She wants a meeting tonight at 8 PM."

Without hesitation, Dr. Roster continued, "She mentioned a pressing matter that involves our recent dealings with the cartel."

"John, we need to handle this carefully. We can't afford any missteps with our connections to the cartel. We need their protection, and we need to fortify Roster Pharmaceuticals."

"What if this is an ambush?"

"No, the stakes are too big for that outcome. We need each other at this point."

"Agreed, but we have to be prepared for any contingency."

"Trust me, I have it under control."

Wednesday, May 22, 8:00 P.M.

Xandari Resort & Spa Village

Tacacori, Costa Rica

This contemporary boutique hotel and resort is only 3 miles (ca. 5 km) north of Alajuela. It is located atop a ridge, overseeing coffee fields and the Central Valley. Plush and secluded, it provides a perfect meeting place for the wealthy and those who desire exceptional privacy.

Dr. Roster strolled into the dining terrace and glanced around, checking for any signs of potential danger. Mr. Ceros had already taken a seat at a table in the corner, with Marietla beside him. Strategically, cartel bodyguards had hidden in each corner of the dining area.

Dr. Roster feigned nonchalance as he took a seat across from Mr. Ceros.

"Mr. Ceros, it's a pleasure, as always. What can I do for you and your beautiful associate?"

Mr. Ceros smirked, his eyes gleaming with a mix of cunning and authority. He leaned forward, his voice low and deliberate.

"Dr. Roster, I understand that there have been some recent distribution problems."

"They need attention."

"I am sure that you will rectify them immediately. Our clients are getting restless, and we can't afford any more delays. Understand."

Dr. Roster nodded, maintaining his façade of complacency.

"It's under control, but I will have a need for more specialized staff to deal with the current distribution shortfall."

Mr. Ceros gave a curt nod, a silent signal for Marietla to step forward.

"John, you remember you promised me dinner tonight, right?" said Marietla as she gave a playful smile, her eyes challenging Dr. Roster. He felt a familiar chill run down his spine as Marietla's playful smile held a hint of impending danger.

Dr. Roster forced a smile, his mind racing to defuse the tension while keeping up appearances.

"Of course, Marietla. I never forget my promises," he replied, determined to keep the situation from escalating.

Mr. Ceros raised an eyebrow, observing the interaction with

keen interest. He made a mental note to keep a closer eye on the dynamics at play within his organization.

With a brief nod to Mr. Ceros, Dr. Roster escorted Marietla to a nearby table for dinner. Mr. Ceros left the restaurant, but two of his bodyguards took their seats at a separate table, strategically positioning themselves for an uninterrupted view of the couple.

Settling into their seats, Dr. Roster and Marietla engaged in light conversation, masking the tension simmering beneath the surface.

"John," said Marietla, "Mool is sending you and me an obvious message."

Dr. Roster's composure remained unwavering as he leaned in, responding with a reassuring tone, "I know, Marietla."

He glanced towards the bodyguards, strategizing on how to handle the increasing complexity of the situation while ensuring Marietla's trust remained unbroken.

"John, I trust you."

Her words resonated with him, igniting a determination to navigate the treacherous waters ahead with care and precision. He reached for her hand, giving it a reassuring squeeze.

"Let's enjoy dinner and this beautiful view of the Central Valley."

Meanwhile, hidden within the lush jungle terrain, Dr. Firehall strategically positioned himself to neutralize any impending ambush of his friend, Dr. Roster. As a master marksman, he never disappointed his contractor. He was steadfast in positioning the crosshairs on his MK-18 rifle scope, dead on, to any threat at the terrace restaurant.

He noticed Ceros leaving the restaurant with his bodyguard, but no sign of Dr. Roster or Marietla. There was no evidence of gunshots, so he perused the terrace with his rifle scope and recognized the couple was enjoying dinner. With steady hands, he kept his aim focused around the couple, ready to act instantly if danger presented itself.

He stood guard for hours, ensuring the safety and well-being of his partner. As the evening wore on, the tranquility of the setting sun enveloped the restaurant. At sunset, the couple went their separate ways, without incident.

Dr. Roster prearranged a meeting point with Dr. Firehall at the foothill of the Central Valley. They met as planned and exchanged a simple nod to confirm each other's safety. They have now gained the heavily armed cartel security from drug lord Mool Ceros.

Dr. Firehall uttered an inaudible sigh of relief. The mission had been a success, and Ceros was now fortifying the protection of his investment.

"There is the obvious, loose-end, Dr. Belons," Dr. Firehall thought to himself, but he knew exactly how to deal with him.

Thursday, May 23, 5:30 A.M.

Weather Forecast Center

Wanning, China

Wanning is a city in the southeast region of the Hainan Province, in the People's Republic of China (PRC). It is the southernmost province of China, bordering on the South China Sea. Tourism is the major source of the economy, with tropical scenery, 5-star hotels, resorts, and beach access.

Hainan Island is home to the People's Liberation Army (PLA) Navy Hainan Submarine Base and the strategic nuclear submarine naval harbor at Yalong Bay. Hainan is also the location of GhostNet, a cyber spying operation that goes undetected. The U.S. is aware of Hainan being the launch site for the infamous, high-altitude balloons (HABs) detected in U.S. airspace at various times. The Chinese have claimed that the prevailing winds blew them off course, but they are highly suspicious of maneuverable, airborne surveillance or reconnaissance vehicles.

Worldwide, forecasters launch over 2,000 weather balloons daily. Both use balloons in the United States and China to monitor atmospheric conditions.

The typical balloon is about 20 feet (ca. 6 m) wide when it reaches 20 miles (ca. 32 km) and explodes because of the increasing atmospheric pressure. Onboard are instruments to measure the weather, along with a radio transmitter to relay the information to a ground station.

In contrast, the HAB is approximately 200 feet (ca. 61 m) wide, contains a technology bay, antennas, and 16 solar arrays mounted on the 65-foot bay. It is also capable of self-propulsion by rudders and propellers for maneuverability.

The high-altitude balloons are difficult to detect by radar and can easily evade anti-aircraft weapons. They fly at an altitude of 60,000 feet (ca. 18 km). This is well above the ceiling for business jets at 51,000 feet (ca. 16 km), or commercial airliners at 45,000 feet (ca. 14 km).

HABs are the perfect airborne vehicles for delivery of a biowarfare agent. They are stealthy in design, capable of carrying a massive payload in the technology bay and exhibit remote maneuverability with bio-agent delivery control.

China recently launched a couple of decoy HABs and one carrying the 'real deal', two dozen canisters containing the Balamuthia mandrillaris cysts. The canisters, composed of heavy-duty plastic, can withstand the high-altitude pressure. A rotating, Ferris wheel-like arrangement secures each canister. A small motor rotates the wheel. This would allow precise control over volume delivery to the desired target. What nobody knew was the content of the payload on the decoys.

The HABs would eventually ascend to hyperspace, where they will remain undetectable until they reach Canada and Northwest Alaska.

China expects that the US military will not intercept or destroy the balloons until they pass into the Atlantic over the East Coast of the United States. The intended target was Washington, DC.

Monday, May 27, 7:30 A.M.
NORAD and USNORTHCOM
Peterson Space Force Base
Colorado Springs, Colorado
NORAD (North American Aerospace Defense Command) and the NORAD/United States Northern Command (USNORTHCOM)

serve as a central collection and coordination facility. They provide the commander, the U.S., and the leadership of Canada with any information on aerospace or maritime threats.

General Robin Rosinol, the commander in charge of USNORTHCOM/NORAD, studied the latest satellite images with furrowed brows. An unknown location near Wanning, China released three high-altitude balloons into the atmosphere about a week ago, and now they appear on satellite surveillance heading towards Canada. They are, off course, and not influenced by the prevailing winds.

"This is déjà vu for these high-altitude balloons (HABs), reminiscing of our recent Chinese incident." Remarked General Rosinol.

"The last time we encountered a similar balloon, it had a payload suggestive of surveillance equipment, and not meteorological."

General Rosinol continued, "We need to consider the possibility that these HABs could carry a payload that poses a threat to our national security."

"We can't afford to take any chances, especially with the recent tensions in the region," General Rosinol continued, pointing at the satellite images.

"You are to stand down for now, and track and report until further notice. F-22 Raptors are to be on 24/7 alert."

General Rosinol issued her orders with a firm and decisive tone, her gaze fixed on the images of the HABs.

Canadian command, being patched into the entire discussion, acknowledged,

"Copy that, General Rosinol."

She thought to herself, "This is a volatile situation. I know that my orders are 'for the greater good' of our country and the world as well."

# CHAPTER 24 - THE WITNESS

Tuesday, May 28, 8:00 A.M.
FBI Headquarters
2901 Leon C Simon Drive
New Orleans

Special Agent Lawins stepped into the bustling FBI headquarters, a cacophony of ringing phones and hurried footsteps filling the air. The conference room door swung open, and every conversation ceased as all eyes turned to the figure standing in the doorway.

He began the morning briefing on the project 'Nesting Dolls' case. Clearing his throat, Special Agent Lawins addressed the room filled with agents,

"Over the past couple of weeks, we placed Dr. Belons in a safe house."

"He is the key witness in the case."

"This case is unprecedented in its complexity, internationally connected, and has the involvement of many agencies, including the military."

"As of now, our top priority is to ensure Dr. Belon's safety."

"We already started the witness protection process. As quickly as possible, we will transport him to a remote, undisclosed location. We will orchestrate this process through the U.S. Marshals Service, Eastern District of Louisiana. U.S. Marshal Eliza Sparkly will be in charge."

"I have orders from the highest level to ensure that we take every security measure to protect him."

"As you know, an unsub (i.e., unidentified subject) posing as a US Marshal took Rafael Nacket ten days ago. There is no information on his whereabouts, but we believe our ghost, alias Dr. Firehall, is involved and may be our unsub."

"Study and commit to memory the pictures, names, and aliases in your briefing folders."

"We need to find out what happened to Mr. Nacket," said Lawins, his voice firm with determination.

"It's time to squeeze your confidential informants (CIs). I want tough pressure!"

"We need concrete leads, and we need them now," Lawins declared, a sense of urgency in his voice.

"Agents. Our surveillance hot spots will be Roster Pharmaceuticals and Roans Medical Supply."

"Start working on the field, the clock is ticking," Lawins commanded. As agents prepared to disperse to the designated locations, their mission was clear.

Tuesday, May 28, 1:18 P.M.
Tulane-Gravier Neighborhood
University Hospital Vicinity
New Orleans

New Orleans has, historically, witnessed one of the highest murder rates in the nation, which has surged since hurricane Katrina. Compounding the homicide problem is the exponential rise in drug trafficking. The NOPD and federal agencies struggle to contain the evolving drug trade in greater New Orleans. The use of CIs is absolutely vital to their law enforcement efforts.

Special Agent Lawins met Detective Ottavino at the outside entrance of the University Hospital Emergency Department.

"Special Agent Lawins, I appreciate the debriefing, but why are we meeting?"

"Rafael Nacket,"

"I understand you lost him to a person posing as a U.S. Marshal. Any leads on that individual?"

"No helpful leads. However, what I didn't tell you in our debriefing was that we suspect our elusive Dr. Firehall as the prime suspect."

"Interesting! Again, why am I here? What do you need from NOPD?"

"The FBI has a CI in new Orleans that may be useful. I want you to bring her in for questioning. Charge her in any way you see fit, but we need to have a discussion. She is the most credible source we know currently."

"This case is top priority. Protect her identity the best you can and keep her safe."

"Yes sir. I will assume this is a joint interrogation. Correct?"

Special Agent Lawins nodded his head and presented a brief smirk in his facial expression to Detective Ottovino.

"Correct," replied Special Agent Lawins.

"This is a joint interrogation, and we need to handle this with extreme caution, under my authority."

Detective Ottavino nodded, understanding that the agency was calling the shots.

Tuesday, May 28, 4:35 P.M.

NOPD 8th Police District

300 Royal St.

New Orleans

Detective Ottavino, escorted by a couple of detectives, led the CI, Ms. Corpalia Bitok, into the interrogation room. The room was small, with a single table and two chairs. The fluorescent lights hummed overhead, casting a pale glow over the room.

Ms. Bitok, a tall, attractive 29-year-old redhead, appeared visibly nervous. Ms. Bitok worked as a cocktail waitress in the high roller rooms at Harrah's New Orleans Casino.

Detective Ottavino pulled out a chair for Ms. Bitok, motioning for her to sit. As she sat down, Detective Ottavino placed a comforting hand on her shoulder.

"We brought you in for your protection. No charges, we only want information."

Ms. Bitok glanced around the room, taking in the sterile surroundings before meeting Detective Ottavino's gaze.

Suddenly, Special Agent Lawins in the doorway disrupted

the soothing humming from the overhead fluorescent lighting.

Corpalia flinched in surprise at the unexpected appearance of the special agent.

Detective Ottavino stood up, acknowledging Special Agent Lawins with a polite nod. Standing, he took his position in the corner of the small room, next to the outsized, one-way viewing mirror.

"Corpalia, it's been awhile. How are you?" said Lawins.

"Special Agent Lawins. Why am I not surprised that you were behind this NOPD visit? I'm fine until now. This must be important for you to appear in-person and with such pizazz."

"It is, Corpalia. I have always told you that you have the best 'ear' in New Orleans. You know how valuable our relationship has been over the years."

"We need to know the whereabouts of Rafael Nacket?"

"Rafael Nacket? I heard he went missing about a week ago. I also heard that he was last seen being escorted by a U.S. Marshal and driven off in a black SUV before sunrise around the FBI headquarters."

"It appears to me that you might've lost him. True?"

Corpalia hesitated for a moment, her brow furrowing in thought. "I might know a thing or two, but what I can say is that he has not frequented the casino since he has disappeared."

"Corpalia, you are always honest with me."

"Anything you might've seen or heard would be helpful."

"The FBI and DEA raided Rafael's stash house in the Gonzalez bayou. I would assume that was successful, or you would not have brought him into custody."

"What you don't know is that Rafael knew someone was coming for him, and he knew it was out of his control. It was the first time in his life he experienced fear. He was always so confident, so untouchable. The 'Fifolet' probably has him, unless someone even more dangerous has gotten to him first."

"Corpalia, the Fifolet is nothing more than sheer folklore; you, before anyone else, should not believe in such nonsense."

"The Fifolet is hard-wired into the Louisiana culture and, for what it's worth, I don't know what's truth or folklore. People believe the Fifolet is the spirits of the dead, seeking revenge on the living for some type of unresolved business from the past."

"I've been told that Rafael Nacket encountered a glowing and flickering object in the swamp water at his stash house. He even screamed aloud to his bodyguards, but quickly disregarded the call for help when it disappeared as quickly as it appeared."

"The locals believe the Fifolet have taken him, never to be found."

"Other rumors state the CIA is involved and one of their ghosts has eliminated the man. That's all I know about Rafael Nacket."

"Appreciate the information, Corpalia. Anything new, you know how to find me."

Lawins and Ottavino stepped outside the room, glancing down the dimly lit hallway as Lawins spoke in a low, urgent voice.

"I believe we have our answer. The CIA has taken care of our witness and now Dr. Belons has to be protected at all costs."

Wednesday, May 29, 5:30 A.M.

U.S. Marshals Service

Eastern District of Louisiana

Hale Boggs Federal Complex

500 Poydras Street, Suite 724

New Orleans

A black Cadillac Escalade with dark-tinted windows entered the security parking lot of the iconic federal skyscraper. U.S. Marshal Eliza Sparkly, from the Witness Security Division, opened the rear passenger door and joined the two deputy marshals escorting Dr. Belons to the airport.

The Escalade pulled away from the federal complex, its tires humming on the pavement.

"Dr. Belons, I have set everything up," U.S. Marshal Sparkly said.

"We have a secure route to the airport, and we have also established your new identity."

"I'll provide more detailed information when we are airborne."

"I know you are tense, but I need you to stay calm and follow my instructions."

"Your safety is our top priority," she added, her gaze steady and reassuring.

Traffic gradually became denser as they neared the airport, but the marshals remained alert, ensuring strict adherence to the tightly coordinated security measures.

The secure federal hangar lay straight ahead on the dimly lit tarmac. As the Escalade turned into the brightly lit hanger, the Citation (CE-750) jet, engines roaring, appeared ready for taxiing.

As the Marshals guided the vehicle to a stop, the hatch of the jet opened. A team of marshals escorted Dr. Belons on board the aircraft.

Dr. Belons was surrounded by tension, which made the sleek and modern interior of the jet a stark contrast. A 42-year old retired U.S. Air Force captain piloted the jet. The air force fighter pilot greeted Dr. Belons. U.S. Marshal Sparkly escorted him to a comfortable seat and ensured his safety before takeoff.

Wednesday, May 29, 7:19 A.M.

Airborne — 38,000 feet (ca. 12 km)

Albuquerque, New Mexico

Dr. Belons glanced out the window at the stunning view of the New Mexico landscape far below. He felt a sense of relief as the jet ascended into the clear blue sky.

"Dr. Belons, it's time to talk."

A calm but serious expression on U.S. Marshal Sparkly's face made it clear that the conversation was about to become earthshaking.

She handed the apprehensive looking doctor a bulky, letter sized manila envelope.

Dr. Belons sighed as he took the envelope from U.S. Marshal Sparkly's outstretched hand. Breaking the seal, he poured the contents on the small serving table in front of both of them.

Directly in front of him lay his new identity and home.

Dr. Carlo Bretons was his alias, showing his picture on the official US passport. In addition, there were documents detailing his cover story, professional credentials, and undercover agents he would be required to contact in case of an emergency.

The marshal began the briefing for the doctor,

"You are now, officially, Dr. Carlo Bretons, a medical doctor from 'Doctors Without Borders'. You have a love of travel, and your favorite pastime is collecting seashells, snorkeling, and scuba diving."

"I tried my best to customize your new identity with your past."

"Marshal," said Dr. Belons,

"Yes, Carlo."

"I appreciate all the effort you've put into setting up my new identity. It fits my character and life activities, but now I must get use to my new name, Carlo Bretons."

"Sit back and try to relax. We have a long trip ahead of us. I'll continue our briefing later."

Wednesday, May 29, 3:47 P.M.

The Pacific Ocean

As the plane hummed through the sky, heading west towards the Hawaiian islands, Dr. Charro Belons, alias Dr. Carlo Bretons, awoke from his sporadic catnaps.

"Marshal, where are we?"

"I'm glad you caught some sleep. A short time ago we refilled in LA, and now we're heading towards Honolulu, Hawaii for a final refueling."

"Where are you placing me? Australia?"

"No, we must keep you within the jurisdiction of the United States. Your new home will be Palau."

"Palau? Is that a part of the United States?"

"Yes, and no. Allow me to explain."

"Palau, or I should say, the Republic of Palau, is an island in Micronesia, in the western Pacific. The republic comprises the Federated States of Micronesia (FSM) and includes about 330 other islands."

"The islands have full sovereignty and are a presidential republic in free association with the United States. This means we provide defense, funding, and access to social services and the republic uses the United States dollar as its official currency."

"Palau is paradise and the ideal place for your security and your new life."

"So, for now, that's where you will live," the marshal assured him.

Carlo nodded solemnly, taking in the information as the reality of his situation sank in.

"Relax. We still have a way to go, but I can assure you it's for the best."

# CHAPTER 25 - PALAU

Wednesday, May 29, 6:06 P.M. (HST UTC -10)

Daniel K. Inouye International Airport (HNL)

FBI secured aircraft hangar

Honolulu, Hawaii

Two Marshals and flight crew members waited in anticipation as the Citation (CE-750) jet carrying Dr. Carlo Bretons taxied into the secure hanger. The Marshals Service took a different approach in handling the protocol for this high-risk witness protection target compared to others. The deputy marshals and flight crew were to be replaced halfway through the relocation. This would provide an additional level of security for the distant, hidden location.

The two replacement marshals and flight crew prepared to take over the responsibility of escorting Dr. Carlo Bretons to his final secure location. Their expressions stern, they stepped forward and exchanged nods with the departing team. As the departing team passed by, one of the replacement marshals made eye contact with Dr. Carlo Bretons, giving him a slight nod with a quivering smile.

U.S. Marshal Sparkly noticed the rather odd gesture and made a mental note to keep a closer watch on the marshal during the rest of the journey.

The door lifted and sealed itself. With the security checks completed, the Citation (CE-750) was now in route to its final destination.

Thursday, May 30, 4:30 A.M. (Friday, 6:30 A.M., UTC +9)

Palau International (ROR)

Koror City, Palau

Following a brief refueling stopover at A.B. Won Pat

International (GUM) in Guam, the final destination was now in plain sight, Koror City, Palau. The view from the jet approaching the island paradise was nothing short of breathtaking. Azure waters stretched as far as the eye could see, with green landscapes dotting the horizon.

The natural beauty mesmerized Dr. Bretons spreading out below, a moment of calm washing over him as he watched the stunning scenery unfold. The sun was just beginning to rise, casting a warm and ethereal glow over the landscape.

Koror City is the commercial center of Palau, on Koror Island (i.e., Oreor Island). The city has many resorts, nightclubs, restaurants, and hotels, serving as a popular tourist location. It is also the largest city among the hundreds of islands, occupied by half of the country's population.

Palau is also part of "The US-Affiliated Pacific Islands (USAPIs)". Palau is one of the three freely associated states in the Pacific region.

The three freely associated states have a Compact of Free Association agreement with the United States, making them independent countries rather than US territories.

Tourism is an essential part of Palau's economy. The people are friendly and especially welcoming to their visitors. The island's vibrant culture and rich history create an atmosphere of warmth and hospitality that enchants visitors from around the world.

Foremost, Palau is one of the seven underwater wonders of the world. Their infamous reefs are breathtaking, surrounding the hundreds of islands. The exquisite beauty of the landscape and encompassing ocean pathways are world renowned for unprecedented geological and biological diversity. Palau's crystal-clear waters and diverse marine life attract visitors from far and wide.

Dr. Bretons could not have imagined a better place to start a new life. The peaceful allure of Palau's natural wonders filled the good doctor with a sense of contentment. He felt it was all worth the pain and effort. It took his mind off the upcoming testimony, allowing him to find solace in the tranquil embrace of the island.

The landing was rough, with the small jet fluttering as it touched down on the tarmac of the remote runway. The aircraft gradually came to a stop, and U.S. Marshal Sparkly continued her final briefing before she could release him into his new surroundings.

"Dr. Bretons, I am sure that you understand it is paramount for you to always use your alias name."

"Any breach of your name or new identity could compromise your witness protection agreement. Do you understand?"

"Yes, I understand, U.S. Marshal Sparkly."

"Now, let's review the details of your new identity. Please interrupt me if you have questions."

"You are, Dr. Carlo Bretons, with medical doctor training at St. George's University, School of Medicine, Grenada, West Indies. Your residency training in 'Family & Community Medicine' was at Tulane in New Orleans. Your credentials are in the document package I gave you earlier on the flight."

"You will volunteer at a local hospital as a part of humanitarian medical care, representing 'Doctors Without Borders' (i.e., Médecins Sans Frontières, or MSF). General medicine, vaccination, and tuberculosis control are your official areas of expertise. If asked how long you will support healthcare in Palau, state, about a month. You will join the medical staff at Belau National Hospital and the clinics."

"Your cover story is solid, but you must be prepared to keep it up."

"Any confirmation of background inquiries and credentialing should not be a problem."

"Are you good so far? Questions?"

"Will I have any contact with family or friends?"

"Unfortunately, it will be as if you disappeared without a trace. It is possible, after the testimony, for some of this to change, but I expect you to be under witness protection until we are sure of your continued safety."

"If there is ever any doubt that your identity would be at risk, we would also need to move you to a new location and give you a unique identity."

U.S. Marshal Sparkly handed Dr. Bretons a vacuum-sealed plastic bag containing a cell phone.

"You are to always keep this cell phone on you. Access it by your fingerprint or by using face recognition. You cannot call outside Palau, but you will have web access."

"The address app contains a single phone number. This number is only to be used in case of a life-threatening emergency or anything you deem as a high-risk event, including a breach in your identity."

"You are to identify yourself by using the code words, 'diving buddy'."

"I repeat, only call this number if you are in danger. It will trigger an evacuation plan with an irreversible cascade of actions."

Dr. Bretons nodded, taking in the situation's gravity, the weight of the responsibility settling heavily on his shoulders.

The marshal continued,

"Now for the fun part, Dr. Bretons."

"You will stay at the Palau Carolines Resort. It is 1.8 miles (ca. 3 km) from the center of Koror and 8.3 miles (ca. 13 km) from Rock Islands Southern Lagoon. The lagoon is a great place for much water activity, including snorkeling and scuba diving."

"I'm sure you can take full-time advantage of this on your off time from the hospital clinics."

The doctor's excitement was palpable as he imagined exploring the stunning marine life and the stunning underwater beauty waiting just outside his front door.

"Dr. Bretons, as you disembark from this aircraft, an older model white GMC SUV will be waiting for you at spot-6 in the Hertz rental parking lot."

"Take care. Your continued safety is our highest priority."

The doctor checked his surroundings as he stepped off the aircraft, feeling the warm breeze and hearing distant waves.

He made his way to spot-6 and found the parked GMC SUV.

Opening the door, he could already smell the salty air and feel the anticipation building inside him.

He was on his way to a new life adventure.

Friday, May 31, 1:52 P.M. (UTC +9)

Belau National Hospital

Koror, Palau

Dr. Bretons felt energized at the opportunity to once again practice hands-on primary healthcare. As he strode through the hospital doors, smelling antiseptic and the hum of patient activity welcomed him back to the rhythm of life as he once knew it.

The Chief of the Division of Medical Services, Dr. Alisha Vycors, DChMS, welcomed him with open arms. She placed an ornate, handmade, wooden bead lei around his neck. This was the traditional welcome ceremony for visitors helping the Palauan people.

"Ungil sueleb. Good afternoon, Dr. Bretons, and welcome to Palau."

Dr. Bretons heart swelled with gratitude as he embraced the warm welcome, feeling an instant sense of belonging.

"Come, let me introduce you to our hospital staff."

Dr. Vycors led the way into the winding hospital corridors. Dr. Bretons followed, eager to meet the dedicated individuals he would work alongside. The hospital staff greeted him along the way, with wide smiles and eager handshakes, giving him a sense of camaraderie.

The hospital examination rooms were small, it appeared nothing like those in US cities. They were minimally stocked with medical supplies and equipped with only the most essential medical devices.

Upon reaching the end of one of the short hallways, Dr. Vycors directed attention to a small room where a group of doctors and nurses had gathered for a case discussion.

"Please, Dr. Bretons, join the group. We value your input on this tough case," said Dr. Vycors.

As Chief of the Division of Medical Services, it was her

responsibility to assess the medical expertise of any new physicians.

She listened intently, absorbing Dr. Bretons thoughtful analysis and compassionate approach. The fresh perspective that Dr. Breton brought to the case earned him newfound respect from the hospital staff.

"Dr. Bretons, we are fortunate to have you providing healthcare to our community," she said as they approached a small office area and pointed to a vacant desk.

Dr. Bretons smiled, feeling grateful for the warm welcome as he settled into his new workspace.

Suddenly, nurse Leilani appeared in the doorway and made deliberate, almost compassionate, eye contact with Dr. Bretons.

There was a prolonged moment of silence before she said,

"We need you in the emergency room, Doctor."

Nurse Leilani is a member of a recent medical consortium sent to Palau. She joined the group, 'Nursing Beyond Borders', as her affiliation.

She was a tall, slender figured Polynesian woman with a gentle but commanding presence. Her dark eyes held the weight of experience, and her voice carried an air of quiet authority.

Dr. Bretons quickly rose from his desk, ready to offer his expertise in this time of need. As they hurriedly made their way to the emergency room area, he noticed her name on the identification card swaying about her neck.

"Leilani."

"What a beautiful name."

"I've always felt a deep connection to the meaning of my name," she replied with a soft smile, glancing at Dr. Bretons.

"It means 'heavenly flowers' in our language," she said, keeping her gaze on the floor as they stepped into the emergency room.

Their eyes met again with laser precision, only to be disrupted by the call overhead,

"Code blue, code blue, code blue, emergency room area."

Dr. Bretons and Nurse Leilani sprang into action, their years of training revealing precision and focus. They quickly assessed the situation and worked seamlessly as a team, their movements coordinated and purposeful. The tranquil energy exuded by Leilani provided comfort to both the patient and the entire medical team.

Through their heroic efforts, the hospital team saved the patient's life.

Dr. Bretons and nurse Leilani left the emergency department, walking in opposite directions. However, they managed to, once again, make direct eye contact with each other before departing.

As he left the hospital and headed to his new home on the island, the good doctor couldn't shake the image of Nurse Leilani imprinted in his brain.

He couldn't shake off the image of her serene strength and the echo of her mother's translation: "heavenly flowers always bloom after the storm."

# CHAPTER 26 - LOVE IN PARADISE

Saturday, June 1, 6:30 A.M. (UTC +9)

Palau Carolines Resort

Koror, Palau

Nestled in a jungle-like setting, at the top of the village hamlet of Ngerkebesang, the Palau Carolines Resort is in the western expanse of Koror State. Unlike the energetic ambience of downtown Koror, it provides a peaceful hideaway.

The landscape reveals the rolling hills of Engoll and the beauty of Ketund Hill. It is the ideal location, with only eight bungalows, for Dr. Carlo Bretons escape from his previous life.

Carlo woke up from the best night of sleep since all the chaos began. There he laid in his plush king-size bed, staring at the magnificent mahogany, mangrove, and bamboo decor in his rustic bungalow. This was his home, at least for now.

He knew he was dreaming, "everyone dreams," thinking to himself. "It's a matter of waking up at the right time during your sleep cycle to remember your dreams."

Today, he was thankful he couldn't remember his dreams because he knew they would be nothing less than haunting nightmares. However, yesterday was different, but why?

Suddenly, the reality of the past day hit him like a ton of bricks. After taking a deep breath, Carlo reached for the mahogany table by the bed to grab his legal pad. Ever since his exhausting days as a medical student and resident, he jotted down notes, just in case his sleepless days in training played tricks on his memory.

Carlo perused the pages of yesterday's notes. True to his profession, he developed his own cryptic shorthand over the years. Carlo would even challenge his peers to decrypt his handwritten notes, and they failed every time. Doodling was also a part of his note-taking. The pictures served well as a memory hook over the years.

Yesterday's notes detailed the unexpected encounter with the mysterious, attractive nurse at the hospital. The intricate details of his own doodling mesmerized him for her. She appeared as a "Polynesian goddess" with a streaming waterfall and smoking volcano in the background. He had sketched her with a warm smile and an aura that drew him in, as if she held the secrets of paradise within her.

"This had to be a manifestation of some underlying attraction to the woman." Carlo thought to himself. He had to see her again.

Saturday, June 1, 4:38 P.M. (UTC +9)

Rock Islands Southern Lagoon

Koror, Palau

Carlo spent most of the early afternoon exploring the lush, vibrant flora and fauna of the Rock Islands Southern Lagoon. He was hoping to clear his mind and gain some clarity on his lingering desire to see nurse Leilani.

As he ventured through the trails, a gentle breeze carried the sweet scent of tropical flowers and led him to a secluded beach. He sat down on the warm sand, his mind still wandering back to Leilani's captivating presence in his office.

Looking out at the crystal-clear turquoise water, Carlo decided he would take a chance and ask her out for dinner. Hopefully, he would encounter nurse Leilani once more.

Sunset was rapidly approaching the lagoon, making the trails difficult to see. Just as he pondered his next move, he heard a faint voice calling out to him from behind the winding path.

"Dr. Bretons, it's nurse Leilani. I thought that was you back at the trailhead. We must think alike."

Instantly, a smile formed on Carlo's face. He turned to face

Leilani once again, their eyes meeting in the dimming sunlight.

"Nurse Leilani. You're right, we must think alike."

"Rock Islands is incredibly beautiful. I hope you enjoyed your day. This is a great way to relax after a hectic hospital shift."

"Yes, we seem to be very much alike in our love of work and nature,"

"Leilani."

"Would you like to join me for dinner tonight?"

"Please, I'm not trying to be forward or anything, but I was just heading out and would love to have some company."

"I would be delighted to join you for dinner. Where would you like to meet?"

"I read stellar reviews about a restaurant in Koror City, Elilai Seaside Restaurant and Bar. Want to try it?"

"Sounds marvelous. I need to freshen up, so how about if I meet you there at around 8 o'clock?"

"Great. I'll make the reservation and meet you in the bar."

Saturday, June 1, 7:34 P.M. (UTC +9)

Elilai Seaside Restaurant and Bar

Medalaii, Koror, Palau

The restaurant was the perfect romantic setting, along the seaside of Koror, with the waves gently lapping at the shoreline. It was as if time had come to a standstill, leaving tonight as the escape from reality. Carlo could not believe he was having dinner with Leilani. Maybe his new life was in some existential fashion.

He arrived early and sat at the bar, sipping a Manhattan, admiring the spectacular shimmering moon over the ocean.

Then he noticed Leilani stepping into the restaurant, her captivating smile lighting up the room. Her radiance took him aback, as she walked towards him with an alluring smile.

"Good evening, Dr. Bretons. Your choice of restaurants is impeccable."

"Good evening, Leilani, and please call me Carlo.", he said as he offered Leilani a seat next to him at the crowded bar.

Leilani ordered a Mai Tai, and the couple enjoyed a casual conversation until the waiter interrupted,

"Doctor, your table is ready. Please follow me.", said the waiter as he led them to the most scenic spot in the restaurant.

The soft glow of the candlelit table seemed to make her even more radiant than before.

"Carlo, thank you for inviting me to dinner. Like you, I'm new in town, and here for the month as a volunteer from 'Nursing Beyond Borders'. It's nice to meet someone so quickly, and especially a fellow humanitarian in healthcare."

Carlo found it interesting that she knew about his humanitarian connection, 'Doctors without Borders'.

"Why?" He had to ask,

"So, you know, I'm here with the group, 'Doctors without Borders', and it's also my first adventure with the organization."

"I know, Dr. Vycors was kind enough to tell me about you yesterday when I arrived at the hospital."

Carlo was relieved because he's been so paranoid since his extraction from Costa Rica. Leilani is the real deal, he thought to himself.

As they toasted to the Hippocratic oath and a pleasant evening, Carlo couldn't help but feel a sense of warmth, captivated by Leilani's infectious laughter and genuine demeanor.

The waiter approached the couple, and they ordered more drinks. Then, Leilani asked Carlo to place the same order for them both,

"Let's start with the appetizer, sesame seared catch of the day, followed by the coastal fish chowder, and the main course, the grilled catch of the day."

"Excellent selection, doctor."

"Leilani, I am impressed that you trust my culinary taste."

"Carlo, I almost feel as if we're soulmates. Bon appétit."

They had a delightful dinner with conversation that flowed effortlessly. Laughter and the sound of waves crashing in the distance filled the night air. Carlo took a moment to admire Leilani's smile, knowing that she was the one he wanted to share this paradise with tonight.

Leilani's eyes sparkled in the dim light, and Carlo knew that this was the beginning of something beautiful.

It was late when they finished their dessert and after dinner cocktails, but Carlo had to ask,

"Would you like to join me for a nightcap at my place? I'm staying at the Palau Carolines Resort."

Leilani nodded with a mischievous twinkle in her eyes. They both felt the attraction, acknowledging the undeniable chemistry between them as they left the restaurant and made their way to the resort in the moonlit night.

Sunday, June 2, 8:28 A.M. (UTC +9)

Palau Carolines Resort

Koror, Palau

The whisper of the ocean just outside his window, the sunlight filtering through the bamboo slatted shutters, awakened Carlo.

He stretched, savoring the tranquility of the morning, before turning to find Leilani still fast asleep. It was a moment of pure contentment after last night. He knew that he'd found someone who understood the beauty of this paradise.

He reached over and softly caressed her naked, slender, brown body. She slowly turned in his direction, her firm, voluptuous breasts rising and falling with each peaceful breath, and a delicate smile tugging at the corners of her lips.

"Good morning, my love," she murmured, her heart swelling with affection.

"Good morning, my love," he replied, pulling her close. She climbed over his naked body, placing her shapely legs on each side of his hip.

Inseparable, she slowly elevated, and they pressed each of their naked bodies together until exhaustion overcame them. They separated and rolled onto opposite sides of the massive king-sized bed, dripping with sweat.

"Oh, my love, you are wonderful!" Leilani spoke softly, passionately, and breathless.

"And you are a goddess in this paradise."

Carlo firmly believed that he had found his true soulmate.

Thoughts of the passionate night and morning lovemaking Carlo spent with Leilani consumed him. With every moment, he felt a deeper connection with her.

Breakfast was a private affair, with Leilani serving exotic fruits and freshly baked pastries while sharing memories of her childhood with Carlo. He couldn't help but smile at her infectious laughter and the sparkle in her eyes.

The day was young, so Carlo and Leilani headed to the white sand beach near the resort, sharing thoughts about their romantic encounter. As they reached the edge of the water, Carlo turned to Leilani and said,

"Let's explore the underwater life of beautiful Blue Corner on our own; it'll be just you and me."

"What a wonderful idea. It will be our special day. How heavenly, just us, the magical sea, and all its secrets."

Sunday, June 2, 12:38 P.M. (UTC +9)

Blue Corner

Ngerukewid and German Channel, Palau

Blue Corner is on Palau's barrier reef to the southeast of Koror, at the northwest end of Ngemelis Island. It is one of the best dive sites in the world, including such marvels as the large underwater cavern, Blue Holes, and Palau's famous Napoleon Wrasse.

Strong underwater currents are the hallmark of Blue Corner. These strong currents arise because of the limited number of channels that allow water to flow inward and outward from the lagoon during tide changes. This creates the forceful, turbulent, and unpredictable currents encountered in the Blue Corner waters.

There are hundreds of islands that are surrounded by a barrier reef, with a bountiful variety of schooling fish, feeding upon plankton. Likewise, the larger predators, such as sharks, tuna, giant grouper, and even barracuda, feast upon the smaller ones. It's no wonder Palau is home to the largest schools of fish in the world.

It took about an hour by speedboat to arrive at Blue Corner, but the beauty of the islands and the picturesque lagoon were breathtaking along the way. The turquoise waters, gently lapping against the boat, held a promise of adventure and beauty just waiting to be explored.

Arriving at Blue Corner, Leilani smiled and nodded, feeling a rush of excitement at the thought of diving with Carlo. They hurried to retrieve their scuba gear. Leilani also brought along a spear gun and strapped a diver's knife on her slender, long leg.

"I love scuba diving. We can even catch our fish for our dinner tonight." She said, slipping into her wetsuit with a joyful gleam in her eye.

"Can you hunt your fish here in Blue Corner?"

"I'm not sure, but look around. There's no one as far as the eye can see. What's the harm? The fish are everywhere, and this could be one of our most cherished memories."

Carlo agreed and admired Leilani's adventurous spirit. He slipped on his diving gear, eager to explore the vibrant underwater world with his soulmate.

As they entered the water, a sense of adventure overwhelmed them, diving into the crystal-clear ocean. The vibrant coral reef stretched out before them, a kaleidoscope of color and life. Their first encounter was a wall of about 30 feet (ca. 9 m). It seemed endless, looking down at hundreds of feet of giant Gorgonian sea fans and corals. They encountered large schools of snappers, Chevron barracudas, and triggerfish everywhere.

The current was overwhelming, and he lost sight of Leilani.

"There is no need to panic." He said to himself.

Carlos surveyed the underwater landscape. He dove to the 40-foot level, and did a 360° turn, thinking she might've followed some schools of fish to greater depth. Still no sign of Leilani.

He looked up towards the surface, but he couldn't see her anywhere. The panic rose inside him. Where could she have gone? Had she encountered some trouble? For a moment, a deep sense of dread consumed him.

As he turned to look in a different direction, nothing more than a vanishing shadow sideswiped him. He knew what that meant, shark! He knew he had to stay calm or risk the chance of not finding his love.

Again, he tried a 360° swirl and noticed a diver in the distance. It had to be Leilani,

"Thank God!" He thought to himself.

He quickly swam towards the figure in the distance. It was Leilani, but she just fired her speargun at him.

The spear pierced his right shoulder, causing excruciating pain and a dense cloud of blood in the water.

"Why?" he said through his regulator, his voice muffled.

It was Leilani, and she was swimming towards him swiftly with a knife in hand.

Carlo could only think to himself, "What the hell is going on?"

Painful as it was with the spear in his arm, the adrenaline rush gave him enough energy to fight off the attacker, Leilani.

They tumbled forcefully in the water, with clouds of blood escaping from his wound. Finally, Carlo grabbed the knife from Leilani's hand and stabbed her in the lower abdomen. The wound must've punctured the spleen because the sudden cloudburst of blood blocked his view of the surrounding landscape.

The sharks were now on full alert. They were gathering in force, and nothing could stop the frenzy attack that was about to occur.

He checked Leilani for signs of life, but he became convinced that she had passed. He knew he had to leave the area and fast, or he would be next on the menu.

He grabbed the dive knife and made his way towards the surface, hoping to escape the impending danger. As he surfaced, the sky darkened, and a storm brewed, adding to the urgency of his escape. The rough waves made it nearly impossible to see the boat, but he had to keep swimming, desperately hoping to find safety.

He miraculously made it to the boat. Looking out over the spot where he reached the surface water, he could see the ominous presence of the sharks lurking, their dorsal fins darting through the churning waters.

There is no doubt in his mind that Leilani was gone, and with her, his chance of a happy life. It was a bitter realization, but he knew he had to focus on survival now.

He was lucky; the spear did not penetrate any major arteries, as he painfully pulled it from his shoulder. He quickly retrieved the first aid kit from the boat's sleeping compartment, storage area, and applied a compress to the wound. Pulling the fabric tightly around his shoulder, he winced in pain but forced himself to stay composed, knowing that his survival depended on it.

After tending to his wound, he focused on navigating the stormy seas, determined to find a safe harbor. He guided the direction of the boat's bow by maneuvering it with the elbow of his uninjured arm, while holding his cellphone in his hand.

Struggling with his cell phone in trying to enter the emergency number, he said, in an exhaustive tone of voice, "This is 'diving buddy'. I need help. Fast!"

# CHAPTER 27 - ALASKA

Monday, June 3, 07:10 MDT
NORAD and USNORTHCOM
Peterson Space Force Base
Colorado Springs, Colorado

General Robin Rosinol stood at attention in the dimly lit command post, studying the wide, illuminated computer screen spanning the length of the wall. The data streaming in from satellite feeds painted a vivid picture of activity along the Aleutian Islands. General Rosinol was monitoring the status of the command she gave days earlier, a scale-up of the military presence in the area.

The commander took decisive action because of the concern about another high-altitude balloon incident with the Chinese. The military scale-up was to appear as a military training operation, rather than a defensive action for the United States.

Reconnaissance units were now reporting unusual movement within Russian airspace close to Alaskan territory. In addition, intelligence reports showed Chinese, as well as Russian warships, were being tracked in international waters near the Aleutian Islands. This activity is far from typical for this region and is most assuredly because of the recent U.S. military scale-up along the Aleutian Islands.

The tension in the room was palpable, as the General considered the potential implications of the heightened activity.

NORAD has been tracking the three high-altitude balloons traveling over the Pacific Ocean. They have now breached the U.S., Canada, and territorial waters airspace at 70,000 feet (ca. 21 km). They are heading toward the continental United States.

"This is clearly an airspace violation. Why are they here?"

stated General Rosinol.

"We must assume they're collecting data. We need to act now before they reach critical areas," replied the Chief of Air Operations.

General Rosinol agreed and replied,

"Yes, and we can't afford the worst-case scenario, one or all three balloons might carry a weapon of mass destruction (WMD). No matter if it's biological, chemical, or nuclear, the safest place to down them is in shallow U.S. territorial waters in an unpopulated area along the Alaskan shoreline."

The commander contacted the Secretary of State, who received the go-ahead from the Commander-in-Chief, President Aaron Legrand, to execute the plan.

General Rosinol then began issuing orders to strategize an interception plan.

The Air Force prepped several squadrons of F-22 Raptor fighter jets for deployment and briefed their pilots on the critical mission at hand. General Rosinol gave the orders,

"We already have the Federal Aviation Administration (FAA) onboard with closing the airspace over a large perimeter with temporary flight restrictions. This should clear the area for you and allow a seamless approach to the balloons."

"Your mission comprises three parts."

"You are to locate the targets, neutralize any incoming or outgoing communication from the target using your onboard blocking technology, and disable the balloon using your AIM-9 Sidewinder."

"I repeat, disable the balloon and try to minimize damage to the payload. The U-2S's will also support you at ceiling altitudes with photo surveillance and communication blocking using their electronic warfare suite."

"We will alert you when the balloons reach the appropriate, unpopulated U.S. territorial waters along the Alaskan shoreline."

"Understand that time is of the essence. You have your orders."

General Rosinol stood silent, riveting her attention on the satellite picture appearing on the massive screen in front of her. She was patiently waiting for the Chief of Air Operations to select the drop-dead point to execute the plan.

"General Rosinol, it's a go for execution now."

She nodded sharply, issuing a swift command without hesitation.

A satellite followed the entire operation on the massive screen at the front of the command headquarters. The F-22 Raptor fighter jets real-time camera footage, and images from U-2S flybys supplemented close-up details the satellite or F-22's could not accurately detect.

All three high-altitude balloons were successfully downed over U.S. territorial waters along the Aleutian Islands. Several F-15Cs were on site, and already employing Sniper targeting pods to record the location of debris.

"That was the simple part," thought General Rosinol, "now that it's a diplomatic incident, the actual game begins, with the grueling politics, outrageous rhetoric, and finger pointing."

"General Rosinol, the Secretary of State, is online and wants a status update."

General Rosinol turned to her communication officer. "Patch the Secretary through," she commanded with poise.

"Secretary, what you are seeing right now on the monitors is the retrieval phase of the mission. The Overlord Unmanned Surface Vessel Vanguard (OUSV3) out of San Diego will secure the area, and the Navy SEALs will deploy to respond."

"Great job, General Rosinol," replied the Secretary of State.

"You and your team handled the situation with impressive precision. What's the next step in retrieving the remnants?"

"The seal team will assess the location, account for as much of the payload as physically possible for a diver. Alongside the team, we are deploying the Orca Extra-Large Unmanned Undersea Vehicle (XLUUV)."

"Sir, I understand the XLUUV is still in the trial phase, but this is the perfect time to test its limit in a real-life naval operation. This autonomous undersea vehicle has a large payload capacity. The best part of this vehicle is that it can operate independently, hopefully easing safety issues for our troops."

"General Rosinol, I agree. Your plan is sound."

"I need frequent updates and any sign or even suspicion of hostile forces brought to my immediate attention."

"Yes, sir."

The Secretary of State, finishing the call with General Rosinol, nodded and leaned back in his chair. Feeling a mix of anticipation and concern as he pondered the complex recovery mission.

He turned to the President sitting directly across from him in the Situation Room in the West Wing of the White House.

"Mr. President, we have a problem."

Monday, June 3, 13:10

Situation Room

Washington, D.C.

In the West Wing of the White House, the Situation Room is on the first floor. National Security Council (NSC) staff meet in this 5,000 square foot (ca. 465 m²) operations center in time of national or international crises. The President of the United States (POTUS), Chief-of-Staff, National Security Advisor, Homeland Security Advisor, and other senior advisors are often present or briefed on the intelligence and crisis support discussions.

His face stern, the president leaned closer to the Secretary of State. "What's the problem?"

"We are in the payload recovery phase from the downed balloons. We have our 'military best' retrieving the debris. That's not the problem. My concern is what we find and how we handle the global fallout from the discovery."

"I understand your concern, but that's ultimately a decision for POTUS. Me, the Commander-in-Chief."

"Now, what's the current status on the ground?" said the president.

"General Rosinol is exceptional in her leadership of the recovery operation in Alaska."

"Preliminary reports confirm some debris is inconsistent with meteorological equipment."

"The balloon material itself is very similar to what NASA uses for their designs."

"We also recovered solar arrays and various intelligence collection sensors."

The president nodded, processing the information.

"What do we know about the origin of this equipment?"

"A guided-missile destroyer and a guided-missile cruiser are securing the sites. Coast Guard cutters and helicopters, and FBI counterintelligence agents are also assisting in the recovery effort."

"We know the origin of the balloons, China. The word from FBI counterintelligence is that none of the debris or equipment recovered so far has any country-of-origin identifiable labels."

President Legrand sighed heavily.

"We need a coherent policy response, and we need it immediately."

"Yes sir. It's already in the works. We are crafting the response for the public as we speak, for your approval," said the Chief-of-Staff.

The President peered authoritatively at the NSC members and the senior advisors surrounding the table as the room fell silent.

"Make sure that all communication aligns with our intelligence findings."

"There's not a lot of leeway here. Today, most of what will happen will be highly classified."

The communication line from NORAD remained open, but muted. A voice suddenly interrupted the president's comments.

"This is General Rosinol. We have just retrieved dozens of small, self-contained plastic vessels from one of the three balloon debris."

"They are cylindrical and approximately 10 inches (about 25

cm) long by 2 inches wide (about 5 cm) in size."

"The unlabeled vessels also appear to be quite buoyant."

"All retrieved vessels are already in transit to the FBI Laboratory at Quantico, for forensic analysis."

The Secretary-of-State made direct eye contact with the CIA Chief, sitting directly across from him. He appeared to be nodding his head upon hearing the update, and spoke,

"Earlier, we briefed all of you in this room about the likelihood of a bio-engineered infectious agent possibly falling into the hands of the Chinese."

"These vessels, most likely, contain that agent. We won't know for sure until Quantico confirms it."

"If this is true, we need to spin this story for the media, maintain security, and avoid public panic at all costs. We don't need another COVID-19 disaster." stated President Legrand as he left the Situation Room for the Oval Office.

Monday, June 3, 16:00

White House, Press Briefing Room

1600 Pennsylvania Avenue NW

Washington, DC

The Press Secretary opened the afternoon briefing by escorting the National Security Communications Advisor to the podium.

"Greetings."

"Earlier this morning, our naval and military forces were conducting a planned military operation in Alaska, around the coastal area of the Aleutian Islands."

"Even though Russia received a warning about the exercise, they still believed it necessary to assert their presence in international airspace."

"Our military also observed Chinese and Russian warships in international waters near the Aleutian Islands."

"A formal response from the Russian Ministry of Defense stated it was this year's joint exercise with the Chinese military, similar to last years, Northern/Interaction-joint exercises."

"It is our understanding, the Russian/Chinese activity is benign."

"It represents China's and Russia's global ambitions to flex their 'freedom of navigation' operations."

"I can only take one question," as he pointed to the reporter in the small press corp.

"I heard from an unnamed source there were also Chinese meteorological balloons involved this morning. Can you confirm or deny this? Can you give us more detail on these balloons?"

"David, this is obviously a developing story. Keep in mind that the activity is benign."

"We will keep you briefed on the situation."

"Thank you all for attending the briefing." Stated the Press Secretary as they both exited the Press Briefing Room, with a sense of urgency.

Reporters murmured among themselves, chasing leads and piecing their stories together. As season reporters, they all knew there was much more to this developing story than a simple military exercise.

# CHAPTER 28 – TIME FOR THE TRUTH

Sunday, June 2, 4:35 P.M. (UTC +9)
Blue Corner
Ngerukewid and German Channel, Palau

Carlo lay motionless on the ice-cold floor of the anchored speed boat, still tossing and turning in the perilous storm along the narrow shoreline. His wound continued to bleed profusely, because of his struggle with the powerful tide and the stiffness of the boat's steering wheel in navigating through the treacherous waters.

Blood soaked the tight compress, creating a large puddle on the floor of the vessel. The assault probably caused damage to an artery. The need for suturing the wound was obvious, as he could bleed out.

It has been over two hours since he placed the emergency call. He felt completely drained and had no energy left in his body.

The storm showed little sign of letting up soon, and sunset was approaching fast. Desperation set in as he wondered if help would arrive in time.

The torrential rain and thunder even muffled the sounds of the splashing waves. However, above all this background noise, he could faintly hear something in the distance. His eyes were burning from the constant saltwater spray, but he focused on an object barely above the skyline, approaching him in the distance.

He pushed himself up from the boat floor, using his free arm, and noticed a military style helicopter hovering near the shoreline. It was one of the new military rescue choppers, a twin-engine UH-60M Black Hawk. This modern aircraft could withstand extreme conditions on the battlefield or in rescue operations.

Relief overwhelmed him as he realized help had finally arrived. His struggle for survival was over for today, but he realized he may have won this battle, but could he win the war?

Sunday, June 2, 8:43 P.M. (UTC +10)

A.B. Won Pat International (GUM)

FBI, Security Restricted Hangar

Guam, Guam

The Black Hawk helicopter, transporting Dr. Carlo Bretons, landed safely in Guam after a turbulent flight. The trained medical officer, on-board, cleaned and sutured his wound, and administered a unit of blood and broad-spectrum antibiotics. He appeared coherent and in good spirits at the time of landing.

The medical team transported him by gurney to the secure FBI Hangar, where U.S. Marshal Sparkly greeted him.

Dr. Bretons attempted a weak smile as the marshal peered at him with a deeply concerning expression,

"You've lost some blood, Dr. Belons, but you're out of the woods now and in stable condition."

"Your cover has been compromised, so I will address you as Dr. Charro Belons."

"I know it's not what you want to hear, but we need to give you a new identity and relocation."

"We have a long trip ahead of us, but when you feel up to it along the way, I need exact details in your debriefing."

The Citation (CE-750) engines were roaring, and the jet was prepared for taxiing and takeoff. U.S. Marshal Sparkly helped Dr. Belons climb the short flight of stairs and secured him in one of the plush aircraft seats.

The door shut, the engines roared with a deep humming, and the jet taxied onto the tarmac for takeoff.

Minutes later, the jet was airborne and climbing to 39,000 feet (ca. 12 km). The destination was Honolulu, Hawaii, where they would refuel before continuing to the United States mainland.

It was about halfway through the flight when U.S. Marshal Sparkly debriefed the doctor. She turned on a nearby recording device,

"Dr. Charro Belons, do I have your permission to record this debriefing session?"

"Yes, I suppose, as long as it will not be used to incriminate me."

"It will not, unless you are dishonest in the questioning or discussion."

"I understand."

"You had a serious wound when we found you. How did this happen?"

"I met a nurse at the hospital. Her name was Leilani. She was part of an outreach unit representing 'Nursing Beyond Borders'. Her professional skills impressed me, and there seemed to be a chemistry between us. We had dinner, and I became intimately involved with her. We spent some time together scuba diving."

"There we were, scuba diving in the most beautiful spot in the world. That's when it happened. She turned on me underwater, and shot me with a spear gun. I guess it was lucky it didn't hit more mid-body, or I would be dead. She knew it didn't kill me, so she grabbed her diver's knife and tried to finish me. I overpowered her and stabbed with the knife. I killed her! There was no other option."

"The pain was unbearable with the spear in my shoulder. Almost immediately, a frenzied group of sharks surrounded the area and began closing in on us. I couldn't help her, so I swam, as best I could, back to the boat."

"Marshal, can we continue this discussion later? Suddenly, I feel very exhausted. I should probably get some rest."

"Absolutely, doctor, but allow me to give you your new alias. You need to practice committing your new name to memory."

"Dr. Belons, we now assign you the identity of Dr. Cesar Holborn, a renowned zoologist specializing in exotic reptiles. We will brief you on your new location later in the flight."

U.S. Marshal Sparkly placed the familiar manila envelope containing his new alias credentials on the table in front of the good doctor.

"Here are your new credentials. Study them carefully. We will talk after you get some rest."

U.S. Marshal Sparkly left the good doctor for his rehabilitation time on the flight.

She signaled to the two deputy U.S. marshals on the flight to meet her in the rear compartment. They hurried; the sound of their footsteps muffled by the drone of the airplane's engines. Quietly closing the cabin door, U.S. Marshal Sparkly spoke,

"Marshals, we found a mole among us who joined our team during the flight from Honolulu to Palau while transporting Dr. Belons."

"This is a top priority, witness. The information is being shared on a 'need-to-know' basis."

"I suspect the aggressive attack on Dr. Belons resulted from leaking information from this mole on his Palau relocation, which is why I am briefing you. Despite taking extreme measures to ensure the witness's protection, the service experienced a breach."

"You know the top priority of the mission and the irreplaceable value of this witness. Any unusual activity, no matter how trivial you feel it is in your eyes, is to be brought to my immediate attention."

"Understood!"

"Yes, Marshal Sparkly. Understood." Replied each Deputy U.S. Marshal.

Hours later, after a brief refueling in Los Angeles, the plane was now destined to the final location, Washington, DC.

Dr. Belons felt rejuvenated after his long-awaited sleep, but someone lightheaded because of the time zone differences imposed by the arduous flight. He knew he had to stay alert. He couldn't shake the feeling that danger was imminent.

In the back of the compartment, U.S. Marshal Sparkly stared

at the laptop screen, typing her reports, being surrounded by stacks of open file folders. With a final plop of her delicate fingers on the keyboard, she closed the laptop and addressed Dr. Belons.

"Doctor, let's continue our briefing on your new life in the Washington, D.C. area."

"Washington, DC?" Dr. Belons appeared surprised and confused at the mention of the new relocation.

"Actually, your residence will be in Virginia, but you will be on staff at the Smithsonian's National Zoo in Washington, D.C."

"Your closed-door testimony, before the Senate Subcommittee on Emerging Threats and Capabilities, is less than a week away. This will give you some time to acclimate to your residence and your position with the Smithsonian's National Zoo."

"I'm a medical doctor and not a veterinarian. Won't I stand out as unknowledgeable, being a reptile specialist?"

"No. You will represent the staff physician at the zoo. They have a need for a physician, specializing in life-threatening events that may occur in the Reptile House. You will be in training and shadowing the head zookeeper responsible for the reptiles."

"OK. I think I can get used to this role. However, how safe is this area? This is the same area for which I will provide testimony."

"You require a new relocation within the continental United States. The Washington, D.C. Metro Area is one of the most highly protected regions in the country."

"I hope you're right." This was Dr. Belons only thought as the Citation (CE-750) prepared for landing at Dulles International Airport, Washington, D.C.

Wednesday, June 5, 11:30 A.M.
National Zoological Park
3001 Connecticut Avenue, NW
Rock Creek Park
Washington, DC

One of the oldest zoos in the United States and part of the Smithsonian Institution is the National Zoological Park, also known as the National Zoo. With two facilities, the zoo houses 2,700 animals and 390 different species, approximately 20% of which are endangered.

Dr. Cesar Holborn, a renowned zoologist specializing in exotic reptiles, received a gracious welcome from the zoo director, head pathologist, and staff veterinarians the day before. They were excited to welcome a physician into the group at the Reptile Discovery Center (RDC).

Dr. Holborn was eagerly awaiting his training and shadowing the RDC head zookeeper. The celebrated collection of reptiles fascinated him, including some of the most elusive species he has ever seen. He realized he lacked training in veterinary medicine but had extensive experience from his home country of South America in the care and management of deadly snake bites.

Likewise, he spent the day familiarizing himself with the different reptile species, gaining intricate details about their care and management in captivity. It was an exhausting day, but he was used to long hours supporting his thirst for knowledge in fresh adventures.

It was nighttime and the zoo grounds grew quiet. Dr. Holborn, pleased with his new relocation, spent additional hours familiarizing himself with the policies and procedures manual assigned to him as a new staff member.

Suddenly, an unusual rustle from the darkened corridor near his office drew his attention. Curiosity peaked, Dr. Holborn stood up and cautiously walked towards the source of the sound. A thin, swaying shadow appeared on the wall of the room, quickly retracting as he felt liquid flowing from his forehead and eyes.

Within minutes, he lost his eyesight and felt a painful stabbing sensation on his forearm. Panic welled up inside him as he fumbled for his phone. Another painful feeling overwhelmed his left leg as he dropped to the ground and recoiled into a motionless heap. Desperately, he gasped for breath, feeling the cold floor against his cheek. His only feeling was that of a slithering, cold object sliding over his back and retreating into the darkness of the room.

Dr. Holborn feels his chest tighten with extreme anguish, ultimately leading to his suffocation and death.

On the floor of his office, a 4-foot, light-brown snake slithered towards the open doorway, heading directly towards the outside zoo area. As the venomous reptile moved away into the shadows, an eerie silence blanketed the office.

However, there was another movement within the shadows. It was a male figure holding a burlap bag and a metal rod with a hook on the end.

Just as the snake attempted to slither into a nearby bed of grass, he snatched the snake's diamond shaped head with the hook, grabbed its tail, and placed it into the burlap bag.

The man in the shadow, Art Lifehold, successfully neutralized the mark and completed his mission.

The snake was a Philippine spitting cobra, Naja philippinensis. This venomous snake possesses one of the more toxic venoms among the cobra species. This is a potent postsynaptic neurotoxin, affecting respiratory function, and causing neurotoxicity and respiratory paralysis. The cobra can spit the venom at a target up about 10-feet away.

Thursday, June 6, 9:00 A.M.

U.S. Senate Committee on Armed Services

Senate Subcommittee on Emerging Threats and Capabilities

Russell Senate Building, Room 228

Washington, D.C.

The Senate Subcommittee on Emerging Threats and Capabilities handles policies and programs related to special operations, intelligence, counterterrorism, homeland defense, among other areas. The subcommittee has oversight of budget accounts, DoD offices, and DoD commands and agencies. Homeland defense was the area of interest for today's subcommittee testimonies, focusing on the 'Nesting Dolls' project.

It was the big day for the closed-door, senate subcommittee

hearing involving a special inquiry into the use of federal funds to support the 'Nesting Dolls' project. Six majority and five minority senators chosen along party lines were present to hear the sworn testimonies related to biological agent research.

The panel heard testimonies from Dr. Watkins, Dr. Swindon, FBI Special Agent Lawins, CIA Case Officer Leonid Wascott, and other high-level government and military officials regarding their investigation into the 'Nesting Dolls' project.

Each official explained their investigation to the senators and answered their questions.

However, the key witness and whistleblower, Dr. Charro Belons, was noticeably absent and his current whereabouts, unknown. Extensive efforts were underway to locate him, but Dr. Belons appeared to have vanished without a trace. His absence left the subcommittee without their critical eyewitness.

The goal of the hearing was to determine any misuse of federal funds and assess potential implications of national security. The military already briefed the senators on the Alaska encounter with the Chinese balloons. They did not mention this at the hearing.

It was clear to the subcommittee members by the testimonies that federal funds supporting this gain-of-function research were used successfully in developing a novel biological agent.

Unfortunately, the worst-case scenario has already occurred. The biological agent was missing and known to be in the hands of the Chinese. This treasonous action was the handiwork of the CIA Case Officer Art Lifehold.

Lifehold is a seasoned and resourceful CIA case officer who knows the system well. He even left a trail of bodies as an effective cover-up.

It wasn't until Dr. Watkins, Dr. Swindon, and FBI Special Agent Lawins started investigating the mysterious pneumonia deaths in New Orleans that the actual story unraveled. Lifehold was smart. He used the voodoo-hoodoo religion and the illicit cocaine drug trade as diversionary tactics to mask the actual plan and develop an effective biological agent for a bioterrorism event.

Lifehold and his lifelong partner, Dr. John Roster, devised a near perfect plan. Using his position as a high-level CIA case officer, Art Lifehold exploited the nation's vulnerabilities for his gain. His partner, Dr. Roster, possessed the medical knowledge and molecular expertise to develop such a deadly agent. The two conspirators were almost successful with their plan until the US military thwarted completing the last phase in Alaska.

The subcommittee meeting was over, and Dr. Belons body was eventually found at the National Zoo. However, Lifehold and Roster were still at-large, but concerted efforts of multiple government agencies were confident in their capture.

# CHAPTER 29 -
# CONSPIRACY THEORY

Friday, June 7, 10:00 A.M.
The U.S. Capitol Building
Washington, DC

The U.S. House Armed Services Committee (HASC) is a standing committee of the U.S. House of Representatives. HASC has oversight and funding power over the Department of Defense, the United States Armed Forces, and part of the Department of Energy. Law specifies the HASC budget in the National Defense Authorization Act (NDAA), providing monetary control when deemed necessary.

The Senate Subcommittee on Emerging Threats and Capabilities briefed the HASC Chair on the funding concerns resulting from the recent testimonies in the 'Nesting Dolls' project. The HASC has power over funding under NDDA, but it was too late for budget modifications on this compromised project. However, the committee took immediate action to increase oversight on the status and funding of similar projects.

Another congressional activity, today, included The United States House Permanent Select Committee on Intelligence (HPSCI). The HPSCI has oversight of the U.S. Intelligence Community. This involves eighteen agencies, departments, and offices, including the Military Intelligence Program. The CIA and DHS were of particular interest in these proceedings, as recent testimonies suggested they were more deeply involved in 'Nesting Dolls' than previously disclosed.

Today, a closed hearing special session was to convene in

HVC-304, entitled: 'People's Republic of China (PRC) Threats to the Homeland'. A frequent topic of discussion on the HPSCI agenda was the Chinese military and intelligence threats posed by high-altitude balloon (HAB) incidents. Recent alarming revelations regarding Chinese espionage tactics fueled this hearing, sparking intense debate among the committee members.

The session had special significance, since there was indisputable evidence of sped up HAB sightings over the United States and other countries. Unlike past incursions, the recent Alaskan incident was especially concerning because it involved a cluster of several HABs. Alarming was the payload on one of the HABs harboring an alleged biological agent. The current working theory from military intelligence was this HAB could have been targeting the continental United States with a bioterrorism event. Likewise, the other HABs could serve as decoys.

It was clear to both the Senate and House committee members that immediate measures had to be taken to fortify national defenses against these high-altitude threats. The discussions urged the necessity for advanced surveillance and counter-measure systems. Specifically, the discussions stressed the importance of incorporating next-generation satellite monitoring and AI-driven defense mechanisms.

It was now up to the POTUS, the Joint Chiefs of Staff, and senior military leaders to take action as deemed necessary to secure the country.

Friday, June 7, 2:30 P.M.
The White House, West Wing, Situation Room
1600 Pennsylvania Ave NW
Washington, DC

President Aaron Legrand sat at the head of the long conference table; his face set in a grim expression. He looked around the room at his closest advisors and military leaders.

"Let me make this clear. I don't want another high-altitude balloon debacle with the Chinese, again."

"We will use Article 8 of the convention states in our defense. The Chinese did not get permission from us for three HABs: aircraft flown without pilots before their incursion into the state of Alaska."

"We were performing military drills in the Aleutian Islands at the time of the incursion. In our earlier press briefing, we already informed the public about this military exercise. It is my understanding, from our intelligence people, that only military personnel had visual evidence of the HABs. Obviously, the Chinese are aware of their missing balloons, and will await our Press briefing on the topic."

"Again, let me make this clear. All information on this balloon incident is to be considered, classified, at the highest level."

President Legrand gave a stern look to the Secretary of Defense and continued,

"We can't afford any leaks."

"The consequences of even the slightest misstep could be catastrophic for our country and the world."

The Secretary of Defense nodded in agreement, feeling the weight of the responsibility settle on his shoulders.

"Understood, Mr. President," he replied, his voice resolute.

"Sir, allow me to debrief everyone with a summation of our investigation, and speculation on the intent behind the Chinese incursion."

President Legrand leaned back in his chair, nodding for him to proceed.

"Our extensive intel sources have gathered a wealth of information on a project called 'Nesting Dolls'."

"HASC approved a grant to a pharmaceutical company based in New Orleans, which funded this research. However, the actual research took place on their research campus laboratory facility in Costa Rica."

"The highly classified research involved gain-of-function, genetic manipulation of infectious agents."

"They awarded the grant to a renowned infectious disease

physician and molecular biologist, Dr. John Roster."

"Dr. Roster, received this grant, which was one of many he had previously received from NIH and the Department of Defense."

"Since this type of research is highly sensitive and requires extreme oversight, we placed a CIA case officer, working as an alias, on-site to monitor the progress of the project. This CIA case officer had worked undercover with Dr. Roster on several missions in the past."

"We since discovered, Dr. John Roster and CIA Case Officer, Art Lifehold, have conspired with the Chinese to develop and hand over a biological agent to the People's Republic of China (PRC)."

"Both Roster and Lifehold are on the "most wanted" lists of everyone, including the CIA, FBI, and Scotland Yard."

"Their involvement with foreign operatives has far-reaching implications for national security."

"They will be found and captured."

"The name for the project describes the biological agent of concern. I'm sure all of you know about the Russian, 'Nesting Dolls'."

"These collectors' pieces are detailed wooden dolls, usually six or seven, with decreasing size contained within the outermost, largest doll."

"Similarly, the biological agent developed by Dr. Roster is a free-living amoeba that harbors an infectious bacterium and virus. The amoeba is protecting the microbes inside from the immune system of the host. Once the immune system destroys the amoeba, the deadly microbes escape and kill the host."

"This divisive tactic is like the ancient story of the Trojan horse."

"The virus we're referring to is just not an ordinary virus, but it is a megavirus. Scientists can manipulate the genome of the virus with virulence and anti-microbial resistance genes. This makes it an effective bioterrorism agent."

"The burning question remains; how do you deliver this

biological agent to its target population?"

"I will simplify this by saying, a free-living amoeba has a highly resistant lifecycle stage, called a cyst. One can dry this cyst and place it into containers for dispersal."

"The HABs can carry these containers and disperse the agent into the Sahara dust cloud currently encroaching upon the US. Thus, delivering billions of cysts to unsuspecting people who inhale the deadly agent."

"I'm sure all of you remember the Godzilla, Saharan Air Layer, dust plumes from a few years ago. It was unusually dense and widespread, causing respiratory havoc and even visibility issues with air flight."

"We could not risk the chance of these balloons reaching any target area within the continental United States, so we neutralized them over Alaska. We cannot be sure of the actual target, but we are sure of the intent of the mission."

"But how did you realize this plan?" asked one of the four-star generals.

"Excellent question."

"Unfortunately, before the doctor, who was serving as a research intern in the Costa Rica research laboratory, could testify to the Senate Subcommittee on Emerging Threats and Capabilities, someone found him dead."

"They ruled it a suicide, but the intensity of our intel left us skeptical. An autopsy is in progress," the Secretary of State continued, a grave look in his eyes.

A phone call suddenly interrupted President Legrand, and his expression darkened as he listened intently.

"Ladies and gentlemen, there's been a significant development."

"We've just received confirmation that Dr. John Roster has died shortly after being admitted to a hospital in Costa Rica. The cause of his death is unknown."

"I've also been informed that the Chinese Ambassador publicly criticized our war games in Alaska across all our media outlets, while neglecting to mention the high-altitude balloons."

"Let's keep it that way for now. This briefing is over."
Friday, June 7, 4:43 P.M.
Watkins & Swindon Medical Diagnostics, LLC (WSMD)
Mandeville, Louisiana

Dr. Watkins scanned the last batch of sequencing results from the 'Nesting Dolls' case, his face reflecting a mix of frustration and confusion. He was confirming the data from the megavirus genome analysis, when he noticed an anomaly flagged on the software program. He could account for all the genes encoded in the virus, and what proteins they would produce in the host. However, this finding was unusual and did not seem to be a part of the megavirus genome.

Dr. Swindon entered the lab, sensing the tension in her colleague's stance.

"What's wrong, Tombak?" She asked, peering over his shoulder at the monitor's genetic map.

"It's this section here," Dr. Watkins said, pointing to the highlighted anomaly on the screen.

"It is neither bacterial nor a fragment from the amoebic genome."

"I'm struggling to identify its origin."

Dr. Swindon leaned closer, squinting at the data. "I've seen nothing like it," she murmured.

Dr. Watkins nodded, his frustration palpable.

"Let's send it over to our NIH research fellow, Dr. Penrith. If she can't find it on that extensive database, no one can."

Dr. Watkins encoded the sequence and, within minutes, emailed it to Dr. Penrith.

"Now we wait," he said, tapping his fingers on the desk, while reviewing another case folder on his desk.

Dr. Swindon settled into a nearby chair, glancing occasionally at the screen. She fell deep in thought about the finding, staring at the approaching dusk over Lake Pontchartrain.

The phone suddenly rang, breaking Dr. Swindon's concentrated silence.

"Dr. Swindon."

"Hi Dr. Swindon, this is Kaaren Penrith. I wanted to call you before sending the results of the genomic search."

"Where on earth did you find the sequence?"

"Dr. Watkins was finishing the case on the 'Nesting Dolls' project and reconciling the sequences from the free-living amoeba, bacterium, and megavirus. This sequence jumped up, and it matched nothing in our databases."

"Since you have the most extensive databases known, we sent it to you."

"Thank you. I am so delighted you sent it to me. You will not believe what I found!"

"What is it, Kaaren?"

"It is a viral sequence, but what's more amazing is that it contains a gene mapping to the Lyssavirus rabies virus. It's not just any gene, it's the dangerous glycoprotein gene of the lethal rabies virus."

"What does that mean for our current theory? Dr. Penrith."

"Foremost, it means you have discovered a virus within a virus. That's rare, but not unknown. What's very intriguing is the insertion of the virulence glycoprotein gene into this smaller virus."

"Dr. Penrith, do you realize the potential implications of this discovery?"

"I do, and I am terrified by the implications. There's a possibility of a new viral mechanism, one that might alter our understanding of viral evolution and pathogenicity."

"Terrified yet fascinated," Dr. Penrith continued,

"This might signify a groundbreaking shift in virology."

"It's a double-edged sword, amazing advances in healthcare on one side or customizing lethal microbial agents for biowarfare on the other."

"Thanks again, Dr. Penrith." as Dr. Swindon hung up the phone as she turned to Dr. Watkins, saying,

"Tombak, we need to secure our findings and contact the CDC immediately."

"I agree." Dr. Watkins replied, tension visible in his furrowed brow.

"We must also reach out to the World Health Organization (WHO)," Tombak said.

"I want to emphasize the global implications of this discovery and the need for handling the information with utmost care and security."

The two doctors watched as the beautiful sunset took shape over Lake Pontchartrain, but could only wonder if it would be their last.

# EPILOGUE

Monday, June 10, 9:11 A.M.
Watkins & Swindon Medical Diagnostics, LLC (WSMD)
Mandeville, Louisiana

The air felt heavy with impending rain. Dr. Watkins furrowed his brow as he adjusted his glasses, glancing at the storm gathering outside. He could see the brilliant flashes of lightning in the distance from Lake Pontchartrain, wondering if the storm could have delayed Dr. Swindon's arrival at the lab.

At that moment, the office door cracked open, and Dr. Watkins turned to see Dr. Swindon standing in the doorway. Dr. Swindon's hair was damp from the rain.

"Sorry I'm late, Tombak," Elise said, brushing a strand of wet hair from her forehead.

"She is beautiful even when she's wet, like the calm drizzle emanating over Lake Pontchartrain before a raging storm." Tombak thought to himself,

"Elise, I was just thinking about you. No worries. "It is always the best policy to be safe rather than sorry."

She sat down and pulled out a bulky manila folder from her bag. She handed it to Dr. Watkins, whose curious gaze settled on the label marked, 'Strictly Confidential'.

"Here it is, one of the most challenging cases we have seen in the history of WSMD," Elise stated, crinkling her wide lips and shaking her head.

"Absolutely, and now we have a 'gag order' on our Senate

testimonies, requiring total silence regarding the pneumonia investigation," said Dr. Watkins, shaking his head in discontent.

"I understand the implications for national security, but it still doesn't sit well with me."

"Tombak. It is what it is. Honestly, I'm excited to work with you in many more cases. What I don't want is the two of us in a prison cell for the next 20 years."

"Elise, I'm just venting my frustration. I always feel that I can share anything with you. You're more than a colleague, you're a dear friend."

Elise hesitated, feeling a mix of warmth and uncertainty. She sighed, then smiled and said, "I appreciate that, Tombak."

"I've been meaning to ask you something. Do you and I…"

Just then, the phone on Dr. Watkins' desk rang, interrupting their conversation.

"Dr. Tombak, Special Agent Lawins, is here for the 10:00 appointment. Can you see him now?"

"Yes, of course."

The special agent walked into the room, his demeanor sharp and professional. He gave a curt nod to Dr. Watkins and Dr. Swindon.

"I understand you have something for me?"

Dr. Watkins reluctantly handed him the manila folder, with a bright red label showing 'Strictly Confidential', and a small SSD hard drive.

"That's it. This is all the evidence from the pneumonia cases. Our IT manager assured us there are no remaining digital files on our system."

"Good. The FBI appreciates your expertise in helping us solve the case. A job well done."

The two good doctors could only stare at Special Agent Lawins in disbelief and shock over his self-acclamation in solving the case. They knew that the credit would always live with the FBI. They also knew that without their molecular expertise, the case may have resulted in dire consequences, on a global scale.

"Now, for an update on the case. Understand, any information shared with you is under the same umbrella of confidentiality document you signed and testified to in the Senate proceedings."

"Yes, we understand," stated both doctors, as they waited in tense silence as Special Agent Lawins thumbed through the file.

"I realize you are aware of our key witness, Dr. Charro Belons, untimely death before his testimony. We now have autopsy evidence of it being a homicide."

"Next, of which you are probably unaware, is the death of Dr. John Roster."

"Someone found him unconscious in his Costa Rica office and transported him to a nearby hospital. He appeared in stable condition upon arrival, but shortly thereafter, the hospital staff found him dead in his hospital bed."

"We suspect that the attending was none other than our CIA alias, Dr. Tod Firehall. The autopsy confirmed the same deadly toxin that served as the signature for CIA Case Officer Art Lifehold."

"Be alert and watch your backs. The whereabouts of Art Lifehold is unknown. He is a seasoned, clever, and elusive CIA agent."

"Now for the fun part."

"This past Friday night, Roster Pharmaceuticals Costa Rica, and all its campus buildings, vanished in a massive explosion. Allegedly because of a major natural gas leak."

"The explosion claimed the lives of a few laboratory personnel and two security guards. Unfortunately, the other executives involved in the design and plans of the biological agent are still at large."

"As for the New Orleans Roster Pharmaceuticals headquarters, government officials raided it shortly after the Costa Rica campus destruction."

"Devon, who was managing the front desk, was the only employee taken into custody. Government officials found all offices vacant, resulting in the inability to locate any of the executives."

"Likewise, we found Roans Medical Supply, LLC vacated."

"Similarly, Jethro Roans, the owner and CEO of Roans Medical Supply, LLC, disappeared and people believe he is living somewhere in the deep jungles of Central or South America."

Special Agent Lawins turned to the doctors, his face grave.

"We are dealing with people who will go to great lengths in order to protect their secrets."

He rose abruptly from his chair with the bulky folder clutched in his hand and marched out of the room, leaving an uneasy silence in his wake.

Tombak and Elise focused intently on each other as they processed the grim reality of the situation.

"Lifehold has skillfully taken care of all the loose ends, except, maybe, for us?" said Tombak with a serious expression on his face.

"Elise. You know what we need at this moment, a quiet dinner out on the town and a night of sheer enjoyment? Just you and I!"

"I'd like that, Tombak. I'd like that very much."

Their eyes met, fixed in emotion, and a loving smile appeared on both their faces.

Monday, June 10, 7:30 P.M.

Mr. B's Bistro

201 Royal St.

New Orleans, LA

In the heart of the French Quarter, Mr. B's Bistro is famous for serving regional specialties in a casual bistro setting since 1979.

Tombak and Elise arrived together at the cozy, busy restaurant, the soft buzz of conversation and clinking of silverware welcoming them. They deliberately chose this restaurant because it was the place where they joined forces in establishing their company, Watkins & Swindon Medical Diagnostics, LLC.

The ambiance, a blend of historic charm and modern warmth, wrapped around them like a familiar embrace. The aroma of Creole cuisine tantalized their senses as they settled into their seats.

"Tombak, do you remember what you ordered on the night we established WSMD?"

"I do, and I can never forget that night. I ordered the Barbecued Shrimp, and you ordered the Gumbo Ya Ya."

They looked at each other lovingly as they placed an order for their favorite local cocktail.

"Waiter, if you please. Two orders of Sazerac."

The ambiance of the dim lighting and candle-lit table created a romantic setting for the couple. They were so intensely focused on each other and sharing their dating stories; they failed to notice the man at the bar, hidden in the shadows, watching their every move.

Art Lifehold, had been following Dr. Watkins ever since he came back from Costa Rica. Now, he finally found them together and plans to finish the job.

## THE END

# ACKNOWLEDGEMENT

I am grateful to my friend and colleague for his valuable time and skills in reviewing this novel.

Dr. Randall T. Hayden, M.D.
Director, Clinical and Molecular Microbiology Medical Director, Clinical Pathology Director, Global Pathology and Laboratory Medicine
St. Jude Children's Research Hospital
Memphis, TN

I am thankful to my family and friends for their invaluable proofing and comments on this novel.

Lanny Terrell
Gail Terrell

# ABOUT THE AUTHOR

## J.p. Banks (Pen Name)

Dr. Matthew J. Bankowski, Ph.D., is a board-certified expert in medical and public health microbiology and clinical and molecular infectious disease diagnostics. His specialized field of medicine lies within a subspecialty of clinical pathology, medical and molecular microbiology.

He has held high-level positions commensurate with his medical and academic training at Purdue University, The University of Michigan at the Medical Center, and Rush University Medical Center, Chicago, IL.

His professional positions include Medical Laboratory Director for hospitals, major medical centers, and a national reference laboratory, professorship at universities and medical schools, and principal investigator (PI) for many clinical trials. His experience in infectious disease diagnostics is vast, and includes work with CDC, public health laboratories and the FDA.

He has an extensive list of publications (i.e., over 185), ranging from abstracts, letters, and journal articles to book chapters. In addition, he has a lengthy list of invited lectures (i.e., over 100) related to medical and molecular microbiology.

Dr. Bankowski has always had a long-term interest and desire to write a novel series based on his knowledge of infectious disease diagnostics. He has experience with novels from his past work with the well-known author, Dr. Robin Cook. He was an invited consultant in two of Dr. Cook's novels; "Terminal" and "Chromosome 6", with an acknowledgment in the books.

"Zoonotic" will mark his debut novel publication, written under the pen name J.P. Banks. Two of the main characters from "Zoonotic", Dr. Tombak Watkins and Dr. Elise Swindon, will continue their adventure in solving mysterious cases involving infectious microbes in a novel series. The idea underlying the series is to introduce a modern day, Sherlock Homes type of medical mystery adventure in this fictional, but plausible, 'deadly agent' novel series.

# GLOSSARY

**Amino Acid**: An amino acid is an organic molecule, composed of carbon, hydrogen, nitrogen, and oxygen. There are 22 main amino acids in the human body. Six are essential, not metabolically produced in the body, and obtained from food sources.

**Blood Cells (Human)**: There are three major types of cells circulating in the human bloodstream: red blood cells (erythrocytes), white blood cells (WBCs or leukocytes), and platelets (thrombocytes). The five subtypes of WBCs are basophils, eosinophils, neutrophils, lymphocytes, and monocytes. WBCs are important in the immune response, the 'innate defense' against infectious disease agents and foreign matter. An increase in neutrophils shows bacterial infection. Likewise, an increase in lymphocytes may show a viral infection.

**CRISPR-Cas 9**: CRISPR is an acronym for "clustered regularly interspaced short palindromic repeats". Cas 9 is one of many enzymes found in bacteria that function as a self-defense mechanism. The enzyme protects the bacterium from viral and other infections. Scientists can use it as a genetic engineering tool for selectively cutting DNA sequences in the human genome, particularly those associated with disease. For example, insertion of cut, 'healthy' DNA into human genomic DNA can then replace the 'unhealthy' DNA and possibly aid in disease treatment.

**Enzyme**: An organic catalyst, mostly protein in composition, synthesized by living cells. Enzyme function is very specific for its target (i.e., substrate). The action of an enzyme reaction is spontaneous and occurs without the aid of an external energy source. Thousands of enzymes exist in the human body, as well as in other living organisms.

**Gene**: The basic unit of heredity in a living organism or virus. A specific gene code sequence in the DNA carries the information for synthesis of a specific protein.
Note: The dispute over a virus being a living or dead organism remains a controversial topic. The debate exists because a virus is non-cellular and requires a host cell for survival. There are both DNA and RNA viruses, which further complicate the viral heredity.

**Genetic Code**: DNA is a blueprint containing the genetic code. DNA comprises four bases, A, T, G, and C. (Refer to Purine and Pyrimidine in this Glossary). The linear arrangement of each base in a DNA strand determines the coding for a specific protein in the final product. The code comprises a triplicate base set. Each triplicate base set will specify the amino acid in that position for the protein molecule. For example, the triplicate, GGA, will code for the amino acid, glycine.

**Genome**: The complete set of the genetic information for an organism. This may include the human genome or a viral genome.

**Gram Stain**: A long-standing, classic differential staining method used for bacterial identification. Depending upon the color of the bacteria at the completion of the staining process, microbiologists may describe it as Gram positive (i.e., purple) or Gram negative (i.e., pink). This Gram stain result with a description of the bacterial morphology (i.e., coccus (sphere) or bacillus (rod) in shape) will further aid in the presumptive identification. Other microbiological testing is necessary for a conclusive identification of the specific bacterial genus and species.

**Gris-gris**: The magical system of New Orleans voodoo. The French definition of "gris-gris" is "gray-gray", between black and white. A powder or a poison associated with New Orleans voodoo. It involves a ritual with an object (e.g., a doll or a small cloth bag filled with magical ingredients). The term could also refer to working a spell or charm. Gris-gris is a form of talismanic magick, an object ascribed with religious or magical powers.

**Innate Immunity**: Innate Immunity (i.e., natural immunity) is an alternate defense strategy used for host defense against infectious agents and foreign matter. In humans, it involves multiple components of the immune system in a complex cascade of events. Simplistically, it may involve such entities as chemical mediators (e.g., cytokines), the complement cascade, specialized white blood cells, and the adaptive immune system.

**MALDI-TOF-MS**: An acronym for "matrix-assisted laser desorption-time of flight-mass spectrometry". The spectrometer functions as a molecular tool and is used to analyze proteins, peptides, carbohydrates, and other molecules. It is linked to a powerful microbial database, enabling precise microbial identification using inactivated microorganisms. Actual testing is much shorter than other diagnostic methods. The targets for this type of identification are most commonly bacteria and fungi.

**Mass Spectrometry (MS)**: A process used to identify an extensive variety of molecules by comparing the molecular composition to an extensive database. The process involves ionization of a molecule followed by assessing the ratio of mass to ionic charge, a measurement of the electric current generated and ends in finding a match on the extensive database.

**Metagenomic Analysis**: A PCR-based process used in determining the genetic sequence for a broad range of genetic nucleotides (i.e., DNA, RNA, and DNA/RNA sequences). Researchers must further characterize the genetic material identified using this method to assign it to specific categories, such as bacterial or viral.

**Microbiome**: Microbes, including viruses, found in a specific body area of an organism or in a specific environmental niche. For example, the human GI tract is a microbiome containing millions of bacteria, comprising thousands of species and often other microbes and even viruses. The terms, microbiota and macrobiota, are typically used to designate microscopic and other organisms seen by the naked eye, respectively.

**Mutation**: An alteration in the genetic material (i.e., genome) of a living organism or virus. The living organism or virus passes on the change to its progeny. The change is in the base(s) of DNA or RNA and can result from many causes. Examples of mutations are point mutations, frameshift mutations, and deletions.

**Nucleic acid**: A large molecule containing nucleotides and harboring a genetic code for production and synthesis of proteins. The two major forms are ribonucleic acid (RNA) and deoxyribonucleic acid (DNA).

**Nucleotide**: The basic chemical building block of nucleic acid. A nucleotide comprises phosphoric acid, a pentose sugar, and a purine or pyrimidine base.

**Polymerase Chain Reaction (PCR)**: An in vitro (i.e., outside a living organism, in a test tube or other vessel) method of replicating DNA by cycling reactions propelled by a specific enzyme.

**Protein**: A large molecule (i.e., macromolecule) composed of nitrogen-containing smaller molecules (i.e., amino acids). The specific arrangement of the amino acid sequence will define the protein. Proteins exhibit many functions, ranging from enzymes and hormones to structural components of the human body (e.g., skin).

**Purine**: The basic compound (i.e., nucleotide) comprising nitrogenous bases found in nucleic acid. Both adenine (A) and guanine (G) are purines found in both DNA and RNA.

**Pyrimidine**: A basic heterocyclic nitrogen compound (i.e., nucleotide) found in nucleic acid. Cytosine (C) and thymine (T) are pyrimidines found in DNA. Cytosine (C) and uracil (U) are pyrimidines found in RNA.

**Vivarium**: A facility, such as an area in a pharmaceutical research building, used for housing living animals for research studies. Researchers often use the animals for drug testing, such as safety testing in pharmaceuticals and even biological agent testing.

**Voodoo**: Voodoo is a spiritual and religious non-standardized practice based on three levels of spirit: God (Bon Dieu or "Good God"), loas (spirits), and ancestors. People revere the ancestors and serve the loas instead of worshiping them. The meaning of the term voodoo is the "Spirit of God". At its core, the practice focuses on healing, often emphasizing matters pertaining to daily life. The loas act as intermediaries between Bon Dieu and a voodoo practitioner.

**Voodoo-hoodoo**: Voodoo-hoodoo is a unique type of New Orleans creole voodoo. It is a blend of religion (e.g., Roman catholic) and magick (juju). New Orleans voodoo-hoodoo is unique and quite diverse. Family lineages pass down voodoo-hoodoo traditions, which are held in the strictest confidence. People commonly refer to Haitian mambos (priestesses) and houngans (male priests) as priests, priestesses, or kings and queens. The voodoo-hoodoo ritual typically involves sorcery and spirit possession.

**Whole Genome Sequencing (WGS)**: Also known as massive parallel sequencing (MPS). The process of sequencing the entire genome of an organism.

www.ingramcontent.com/pod-product-compliance
Lightning Source LLC
Chambersburg PA
CBHW070924260626
47162CB00007B/2780